MW01462361

THE NINE CIRCLES

Adventures across Conflicting Realities

Howard Scott Shuford

CONTENTS

Title Page
Part One: Fault Crossing ... 4
Chapter One: Katherine ... 5
Chapter Two: Billy ... 29
Chapter Three: Katherine ... 54
Chapter Four: Billy ... 76
Chapter Five: Katherine ... 115
Chapter Six: Billy ... 140
Chapter Seven: Katherine ... 159
Part Two: Rule and Consequence ... 163
Chapter Eight: Now is the Place Where the Crossroads Meet ... 164
Chapter Nine: Run On (For a Long Time) ... 171
Chapter Ten: Ceremony ... 233
Chapter Eleven: Endgame ... 236

"Why shouldn't things be largely absurd, futile and transitory-they are so, and we are so, and they and we go very well together."

--George Santayana

PREFACE

The boy sat on a chair in the cold hospital hallway. His feet did not touch the floor (the height of the chair would not allow it) and so his legs swung impatiently back and forth.

The world was very much like that chair. Something was always just out of reach, and if he managed to reach one perch another fell away beneath him, leaving his legs with nothing to do but swing back and forth, back and forth.

Bored, he looked at the precious souvenir he held in his small hands. To adult eyes, it was a tacky trinket that might be found on a scratched coffee table. To Guy the toy was object d'art. His father had bought it for him at the gift shop in the hospital where Momma was first diagnosed; the hospital the Theodoric family rushed to from their hotel when Momma's left side of her body went numb.

"It isn't a stroke," the doctor pronounced a few days later.

Robert Theodoric frowned to himself. Of course it wasn't a goddamned stroke-Julia was too young for that. Cancer, they said. It had started in her right breast some time ago and then spread through her body, sending tendrils into her liver, lungs, and brain. The numbness was from a tumor exerting pressure on her cerebrum.

Guy grasped the base of his gift and turned it upside-down, shaking it gently. He righted it and then stared into the clear dome as a flurry of plastic snowflakes swirled about another hasty likeness: a miniature of the Capitol Building. Mesmerized, Guy watched as the storm quieted, and then he stirred the flakes up again, then again. Playing with the globe was like playing God; he was in total control of the lives of those held captive inside the dome. He imagined he could hear women not unlike his mother telling their Washington husbands not to forget their galoshes...except *his* mother had cancer. Galoshes were hardly an issue this winter.

The door to his mother's room opened quietly. Robert peeked outside, his usually robust face now sullen and dark.

"You can come in now," he said flatly, and then disappeared inside.

Clutching his toy, Guy hopped down from the too-tall chair and shuffled through the door.

Julia was propped up in bed and connected to an array of whirring, bleeping machines. Guy stepped silently over the cords and tubes to her bedside.

Julia mustered a smile and reached out to caress Guy's golden hair. "Hi," she said. "Is Daddy taking good care of you?"

"Yes."

What else could she say? Good-bye?

Her eyes fell to the object Guy held so tightly. "What'cha got there?"

"My toy," he said. He held it up so she could see it, and set the snowflakes in motion—a blizzard, just for her.

"Momma?"

"Yes?"

"You're going to die, aren't you?"

Julia's eyes immediately connected with Robert's. *There was something I could have told after all,* she said silently. *I could have told Guy that the cancer was terminal. Jesus Robert, why didn't we tell him sooner? We shouldn't have waited for him to figure it out on his own.*

She returned her gaze to her son. "Yes, Guy. But I'll never truly die if you remember me. I can live in your heart. I'll always be there for you. Don't forget me Guy. You won't forget me, will you?"

Precious as it was, the toy globe clattered to the tile. Suddenly the world became a much smaller place. The distance between the bed and the floor, between Guy and Julia, contracted. He climbed into Momma's arms, sobbing. "I won't forget you," he said. "I'll never forget you, Momma. Never."

PART ONE: FAULT CROSSING

CHAPTER ONE: KATHERINE

Science is continually judging reality; therefore, it follows that the jury of reality's peers is continually out. There will never be an end to this process, no tidy ten second wrap up like the end of a *Law & Order* episode because no verdict regarding what is real and what is not can ever be reached due to the reality that reality infuriatingly relative.

If a person is psychotic and believes that their weekly grocery receipts bear coded messages from Venus, they have no reason to believe your disbelief. Conversely, if another knows that the receipt shows only that a pound of ground beef was purchased using a debit card, who's to say that *that* person is psychotic and cannot recognize the message from the Queen of the Moon to her paramour Venutian prince?

"There are more things in heaven and earth than dreamt of in your meager philosophy," Hamlet told Horatio, revealing that there may be life on Venus. However, it's dangerous to apply science to dreaming. In dreams, everything imaginable is possible. In science, everything imaginable is merely probable—and there is a wide gap between "possible" and "probable." It's remotely possible a receipt is an alien message, but remotely probable if that. *This* is only logic by which reality can be judged, and when the jury reads the verdict expecting an immediate appeal by claims of insanity.

As for dreams, well, there are common ones, such as falling through space, appearing nude at you high school prom, boogeymen lurking in the closet or monsters under the bed.

One common (and very strange) flight of fancy is a bit more mundane but just delusional. It's called "The American Dream." Like many dreams, The American Dream is recurrent, like the one in which a maniacal clown brandishing a knife burst out of your fifth birthday cake. But the clown dream is always the same. The clown's knife does not become a cleaver, the cleaver does not become a machete, and so forth. The American Dream is recurrent, but it is subject to, in technical terms, recursion iteration in which it repeats itself on the base levels but generates a different set of impressions each time it occurs. The dream of religious freedom becomes immigrant opportunity, immigrant opportunity becomes a chicken in every pot, a chicken in every pot becomes the right to a house in the suburbs, the right to a house in the suburbs becomes the right to a house in the suburbs and a car in the driveway, the right the car in the driveway becomes the right to a SUV in the driveway, *ad infinitum, ad nauseum.*

Now, in the age of technology, dreams are produced not only by our human brain activity but the unavoidable (and perhaps unbearable) technoconsciousness (a euphemism for "media") that saturates and soaks the mind, and it is becoming difficult to tell which is generating what. Marx stated that religion is the opiate of the masses while others have said it is television. However, the delivery devices of an opiate—a pipe or syringe—and the delivery device that television is in and of itself are discreet and can be removed from the environment. On the other hand, the delivery of the media drug is like a permanent I.V., a steady drip directly into the system. There is no place on this earth one can go to avoid it. It will find you just as easily as the dreamer's SUV's GPS system can locate a Starbucks. Moreover, if the dreamer should be carrying an iPhone in his pocket, then all is lost as the electronic age's fancy compass leads to the plunge into the reality media creates. The media opiate of "reality television" depicts a non-reality of realities that simply isn't real, for lack of a better word.

Given this, it's easy to say there's nowhere in the world

where reality is questionable than in the country of Southern California. Make no mistake; Southern California *is* its own country, having seceded from the Union and then broke out as a separate homeland than Northern California. The gulf between the two is wide: Southern California consumes paper at an alarming rate while the Northern Californians hug the trees that supply the pulp. No Cals compost, So Cals recycle. No Cals smoke pot: So Cals can't remember (or deny remembering) what they did the night before.

As the universe expands and the world turns, become *The O. C.*, the media bailing from Beverly Hills and squatting in Newport Beach. (Actually, most of *The O.C.* was filmed in Redondo Beach, which is in Los Angeles County, but a teen TV show called *The L. A. C.* sounds like it was funded by Corporation for Public Broadcasting and not sponsored "by the makers of Sprite.") Still, Newport Beach is a *real* place, and it exists in *real* time.

So that brings us to an office with overstuffed chairs, a tired psychiatrist and housewife.

"I'm crazy," Katherine said.

Dr. Lankly raised his left eyebrow, the one that had the wild, curly, gray hair springing from it. "Oh really?" he said. "Surely you know what they say about people who question their own sanity."

Katherine shifted uncomfortably in her chair. "Yes, I've heard that line before, but something is *definitely* wrong with me." How that eyebrow was annoying! She figured it would be an affront to his masculinity if she asked him to pluck it and tried to ignore it.

"Why don't you tell me about "crazy""

"I don't feel real sometimes," Katherine began. "I mean, there are times when I feel like everything around me is phony, like a movie set. Even worse, there are times when I feel like *I'm* a movie prop."

Langly scribbled a few notes on his pad. Katherine craned her neck to see what he was writing but couldn't.

"Any lapses in memory?"

"What do you mean?"

"Are there any times, for instance, when you "wake up" somewhere and have no idea how you got there, or what you've being doing for the last several hours?"

Katherine thought for a moment. "No, not exactly." She shifted again, bringing her pale hands into her lap, and knitting her fingers together nervously. "I do lose track of time occasionally, but then everybody does, I guess. It's easy just to drift off somewhere else while reading, or listening to music, or just thinking."

"Thinking about what?" Langly asked.

"I'm sorry?"

"What are you thinking about when you "drift off?""

"Well, I guess I daydream a lot. I've always been like that. Dreamy—that's what my mother calls me." Her eyes veered to the floor, away from the eyebrow. A thin smile appeared on her lips. "I know I drove my parents crazy when I was a kid. They still talk about the time they took me to see *Snow White*. I danced around for a month singing "Someday My Prince Will Come" at the top of my lungs. Ha! My mother was always afraid that I was so far off in fantasyland that I'd do something outrageous, like elope with the garbage collector."

Dr. Langly scribbled on his pad again. Katherine wished she could see what he was writing.

"Are you single, Ms. Jameson?"

"No. My husband William and I have been together for almost five years now."

"William Jameson? The doctor, who has a practice here on the Island?"

"Yes, that's him."

Langly smiled. "He's a helluva golfer. Well, it sounds as if your prince showed up after all."

"I guess."

*** *** ***

The secretary looked up from her crossword puzzle,

annoyed at the interruption. "Well?"

"I need to make an appointment for the same time next week," Katherine said timidly.

Smacking on her gum, the secretary handed her a business card with her appointment time and date written on it. "Don't forget to give us twenty-four hours advance notice of you can't come." she snapped. "If you don't, we'll have to charge you for the appointment."

Dr. Langly strode in and pushed a few slips of thin paper into Katherine's hands. "The pink sheet is for your records; we'll take care of billing the insurance for you. The other is a prescription. It should help until we can dig a bit deeper into your little problem. Oh, and for the record, you're not crazy." He turned then and dove back into his office, crazy eyebrow and all.

Katherine mumbled her thanks and stepped out of the office and into the Newport Beach sunlight. So much for making emotional progress. Two hundred dollars down the drain and the good doctor hadn't even said what was wrong with her.

In the parking lot, Katherine easily picked out the Mercedes from the sea of imports. It was a simple task; hers was the one with the personalized license plates that read "WILLIAM."

The Mercedes had been one of the first glories brought on by William's success but sitting behind the wheel of such a powerful talisman couldn't dispel her uneasiness. *So, I'm not crazy,* she thought. *Then what the hell is wrong with me? And just what "little problems" do I have? God, I'm tired of not knowing what's going to happen next.*

A quick check in the rear-view revealed that in the process of being interrogated she had chewed all her lipstick off. She fumbled in her purse for her make-up bag. Inside, the lipstick had turned to blood red goo, insulated from the sea breeze by Italian leather.

Hair black as ebony, skin white as snow...

Katherine frowned in the mirror, replaced her lipstick and started the car. It was time to return to the castle.

*** *** ***

Newport Beach is one of the most fashionable addresses in Southern California-and in the world, as far as Newporters are concerned. Unlike its East Coast counterparts that are steeped in tradition and pride themselves on their stoic nature, Newport Beach is a malleable realm given to snatching up even the vilest fads and then insisting that they had originated within the city limits. Evidence of this cultural plasticity lies everywhere one looks: Nautilus gyms become aerobic dance halls which eventually become Nautilus gyms once more, this time with on-site day-care. "Fusion" bistros give way to vegetarian restaurants and frozen yogurt parlors. Wine coolers give up shelf space for blush wines—not red, not white, but wretchedly pink *vins* of last week's vintage. The old gleefully make way for the new, and vice-versa.

Newport's population turns over just as quickly. Most people living in the city are transient apartment dwellers who are annually forced out of their homes during the summer by skyrocketing rent, only to be replaced by drunken collegiates who saved all their money to spend a few months basking on the beach. These are Newport's second-class citizens, an awful but necessary lot. New blood is essential to the city's morale, and each turn of the seasons brings new gawkers who invariably take harbor cruises and coo at the homes on the waterfront. And if a Newporter is extremely successful, he or she can send a check to the proper post office box and have their home pointed out by the captain of the cruise ship.

The gorgeous Victorian home on the right belongs to Dr. Beachcomber, the credit dentist whose commercials you've surely seen on local television...

The mishmash of architecture that smothers the city and posh Balboa Island (One can almost *taste* the relish with which one says, "I live on the Island!") says just as much about its inhabitants as their New Age interests. House after house is crammed closer and closer together as time passes, each castle looming thinner and taller than its predecessor as divide-and-conquer developers pack as many notable people onto the sand as possible. At night, the houses appear huddled together as if to protect themselves from the Democrat carpetbaggers poised at their thresholds, ready to raise property taxes in the name of education, or some equally outrageous cause.

Such is Newport, the perfect place for Katherine's tale to begin.

*** *** ***

With the drawbridge closed behind her and the deadbolt thrown, the world seemed like a much safer place. William Jr. was sitting at the table in the breakfast nook, eating an endless bowl of cereal. Katherine kissed him lightly on the forehead. Enraptured by a cartoon on the television, the boy hardly noticed.

"Where's Daddy?"

"In the bathroom," Will said, mouth full of Cap'n Crunch. Milk dribbled down his chin.

Katherine hurried down the hall, stopping shortly to straighten a skewed LeRoy Neiman on the wall. God only knew what everyone saw in those paintings; the work was so sloppy that Katherine had to stand at the other end of the hall to allow the brush strokes to resolve themselves into a sailboat.

From the master bedroom came the drone of William's electric razor. Today was the day of his weekly shave.

Katherine slipped into the bedroom and innocently seated herself on the bed. The curtains on the window had been thrown back to reveal the beach and the ocean beyond it. Even after five years the view still awed Katherine, but now that the day was marred by her first visit to a psychiatrist, things were never to be the same.

"I'm home."

The razor ceased operating. William walked out of the bathroom clad in but his boxer shorts, his paunchy belly drooping over the strained waistband. "Where have you been?" he asked. "I don't like to wake up in the morning and find you missing."

Katherine immediately began to wring her hands. "I was at the doctor's office."

"The doctor's office? What's wrong with you that I can't take care of?"

"I'm not sick—not really. I went to see a psychiatrist."

William nearly dropped his razor. "A *psychiatrist*? For crissakes Katherine, there isn't a thing wrong with you." He shook his head and returned to the bathroom. "A psychiatrist? Jesus."

So much for that. Katherine knew full well that William would flip when she told him but seeing Dr. Langly was something she felt she had to do. How did he expect her to raise their son and manage the house if she couldn't manage herself?

Mortified, Katherine turned to check up on Little Will when William's razor again ceased operating, and he exited the bathroom. She often wondered why it took him so long to shave; his beard was so thin it could have been taken off with a butter knife in a matter of seconds.

"Who did you see?" William asked. His voice was calmer, almost concerned.

"Dr. Langly."

"Langly, Langly...oh yeah. I know him. He's a helluva a golfer." He smiled to himself. "What did he say?"

Katherine shrugged her slender shoulders. "He didn't say much of anything. I mean, he didn't say what was wrong with me." She opened her purse and dug for the papers Dr. Langly had given her. She said, "He just gave me an insurance form and a prescription."

"Well, what *is* wrong with you?"

"I don't know. I'm depressed, I guess."

William took the papers from his wife. The insurance from was like that his office issued; it listed services performed, prices and whatnot. In the lower left corner was a line labeled "DIAGNOSIS"; on it was the hasty scribble "DSM-III R . / . ".

Puzzled, Katherine watched as William lingered over the

12

insurance form for a few seconds, and then glanced at the prescription. "Thorazine?" he said. "For *this*? Christ, Langly's a frigging pusher." With that, William left the room with the papers in hand and head shaking in suspicion.

Katherine remained on the bed, a bit numb and not knowing what to do next. A moment later, the sound of a door opening and closing—the door to William's study—and then he was back and rifling through the closet.

"Oh, by the way, Mom and Dad called about a half hour ago. They're coming over for lunch."

"Oh," Katherine replied.

The mental health conference was over, and now it was time to head for the kitchen. This was clearly going to be like any other day that William took off from work. Katherine had no idea how his parents knew in advance when their son was going to play hooky from his doctoral duties; it had to be some sort of mind-meld thing that ran in the family.

The afternoon picnic affairs always started the same way: William's alarm would go off at five-thirty a.m., and instead of getting up, he would reach for the phone. The practice he shared with his medical school chums had a twenty-four-hour answering service, which William would call and leave a ridiculous message about a deathly ill or even dead relative. Then it was off to dreamland for four or five more hours. Katherine often wondered what the other doctors in the office thought of William's absence, but as far as she knew they did the same thing, juggling patients from one to the other with dexterity common only to M.D.s. The whole affair seemed callous; if she scheduled an appointment with her gynecologist only to come face to face with a stranger with lubricated fingers and big grin, she would faint.

*** *** ***

"Yoo-hoo! Katherine? William? It's us. We're here!"

William's parents had finally arrived. Katherine forced a smile and opened the front door.

Elyse rushed past without much of a greeting. Pat,

however, stopped long enough to hand her a six-pack of beer. "Where's my grandson?" he asked greedily.

"He's out on the patio with William. I'll put the beer in the refrigerator."

"Good idea—but maybe I'll take one first." He snatched a can from the plastic holder, nearly yanking the entire bunch from Katherine's hands. Pat popped the top and smiled. "Now I'll go see my grandson."

In the kitchen, Katherine sighed wistfully. Now it was time for the neat little family to romp in the sand—all except for her. There were other duties to perform: sandwiches needed to be arranged neatly on a platter, drinks needed carrying to the patio. It was during times like these that Katherine most wanted to relinquish her title as wife and homemaker. Perhaps she could call Mrs. Brownen, the Jameson's old maid neighbor. The absence of a husband or children in her life made her more than happy to come over and babysit Little Will: perhaps she would enjoy entertaining the in-laws as well.

Katherine found the beach pleasant, but it just wasn't in her blood. Under the proper conditions, the beach was alien to her as the surface of Mars. Those conditions usually arose whenever the Jameson clan chose to congregate. And this was like all others; the unbearable sun forced her to retire under an umbrella and curl up with a juicy romance. Her fair skin burned in an instant, in contrast to the rest of the family, who tanned —except for William, who broke out in freckles as if they were trying to take over his body. And sitting on the patio was out of the question. William would insist that she was not being part of the family and force her into catching a Frisbee as punishment.

Watching little William play offered some amusement. The addition of one tow-headed four-year-old boy to a trio of mature adults was never without surprises: sand kicked in a face; tiny crabs thrown down Grandma's bust line...

In the shade of the umbrella, Katherine leaned back in her chair and closed her eyes.

God, what's wrong with me? I have everything I could ask for: a beautiful home, a successful husband, and a darling son. And yet something is missing. Something...

That was when it happened. Tiny at first, just a small tug somewhere at the underside of her mind, and then the sliding sensation washed over her. Sliding, moving past, out, and away —

"No!"

Her eyes flew open with a start at the sound of her own voice.

No one of the beach took notice of her cry.

Terror set in. Katherine clenched her fists in her lap hard enough for her knuckles to ache under the pressure. Not this time. It wasn't going to happen again. She wasn't going to *let* it happen and that was all there was to it.

Heart pounding, she quieted herself and drew deep breaths. Whatever it was that was going on in her life, she could bear it no longer. Despite herself, Katherine wished as hard as she could that something out of the ordinary would happen to alleviate the numbness and dread she felt clinging to her psyche. And if the captain of the Thought Police had been there (also known as her mother) she would have quickly reminded her daughter of one of her favorite clichés: *Be careful what you wish, for your wish just might come true.*

*** *** ***

Help me...please help me...

Katherine woke to the sound of a voice calling from parts unknown. It was a strange feeling to wake like that; she wasn't entirely sure if the voice had come from her own mouth or from a part of the house other than the master bedroom. Mothering instincts took over; a paranoid part of her mind thought that perhaps Will Jr. was in trouble.

She carefully pushed the comforter off her so as not to disturb William, only to find him missing from his sagging portion of the mattress.

Light poured from the open study into the darkened

hallway. William never felt the urge to get up and work and therefore something had to be dreadfully wrong.

William's pensive shadow played on the wall; he was at his desk thumbing through a book. Curious, Katherine tiptoed to investigate.

"William?"

Startled by her voice, William slammed the book he was reading closed with one hand while stuffing an all-too familiar piece of pink paper into an open drawer. "You startled me," he said. "I thought you were asleep."

Katherine hung in the doorway like a timid preschooler on the brink of her first day-care. "I thought I heard voices."

"Oh?" William said. He arched an eyebrow just like Dr. Langly had done earlier in the day. "What *kind* of voices?"

The tone in his voice sent a chill down her spine. William wasn't always pleasant, but he had never addressed her in the suspicious, almost malignant timbre he did now.

"I must have been dreaming," she mumbled, and hastened back to the safety of the master bedroom neutral zone.

That darn pink paper! There's something that Dr. Langly didn't tell me, and William has somehow figured it out with that book.

William's little universe was a cruel place. Katherine reasoned that if the desk had not been just inside the door, she would have not seen the insurance form and she would have been blissfully ignorant of her husband's mysterious discovery. Now, the blue book and nothing else would surely dominate her thoughts.

The comforter was just as its name suggested. Katherine pulled it over her head, blocking out everything that reminded her of the situation at hand. Now she was free to roam her own little universe; the universe that all dreamy people share.

*** *** ***

At three o'clock Friday morning, Officer Thompson of the Newport Beach Police Department pulled over at the donut shop not far from the A Street pier. For Thompson, tonight's beat was unlike any other: eject a few homeless people here, throw drunken surfers into the tank there.

The night was hot and still but had an undercoat of unease—"earthquake weather," as Southern Californians call it. It was that same unease that caused Thompson to casually glance up at what few stars were visible in the polluted night sky; the same unease that kept his eyes riveted to the heavens as a fiery streak appeared and slashed the dark with an audible hiss. Thompson's eyes followed, followed-

WHUMP!

"Holy shit!"

Whatever the thing was, it had crashed on the beach hardly a quarter of a mile away. Thompson forgot all about the maple bars and glazed old fashioneds. He dashed back to his car and radioed the station as nervous Newporters jumped from their beds, wondering what the hell had happened.

Katherine's wish had been fulfilled.

*** *** ***

Help me, please...

The snow was falling so thickly that Katherine could hardly see where she was walking. Invisible hands pushed her, urging her to come closer, closer.

Steps appeared beneath her feet. She climbed on and on without knowing why, drawn to the voice that beckoned.

Still closer—

The shrill beeping of William's alarm clock tore Katherine from the endless steps, depositing her in her bed. She rolled over onto her side and fell back to sleep.

*** *** ***

"*Wake up, wake up, get out of bed!*
Time to get up, you sleepyhead!"

Completely covered with his blanket, Little Will giggled. He was already awake, but he liked it when his mother sang to him and so he made sure he was back in bed before she got up.

Katherine would never know it, but Will had already been into the Lucky Charms *and* the orange juice.

Katherine pulled the covers from the boy's head. "Ready for breakfast?" she asked, planting a kiss on his cheek.

"Yes," he squealed. At this rate, he was going to be rotund by the time he was six. So much for the starving Armenians.

Will cheered as Daffy Duck got blasted by a trigger-happy Martian while Katherine was busy at the sink trying to clean the frying pan of the eggs. "Are you finished eating?" she asked over her shoulder.

"Yup," Will relied.

"Do you mean, "Yes ma'am?"

The boy turned away from the television. "Aw, Mom! Daddy doesn't even call you that!"

"When you get as big as Daddy you will probably have other names for me, too," Katherine said, not entirely sure that admonition came out the way it was supposed to. "Until then, it's 'yes' or 'no ma'am.' Understand?"

"Yes."

"Yes *what*?"

"Yes, ma'am."

God, how children behaved nowadays! If Katherine had been as disrespectful to her parents as Will was to her, she might not have lived to reach five years old, much less twenty-five.

Will scampered off to the bathroom to brush his teeth. Four-year-olds and toothpaste was a dangerous combination, and today was bath day as well. That meant Chemical Hell was looming just over the horizon, waiting for Katherine to descend anew into the depths of the dread chore of cleaning the lavatory once Will had finished wrecking it.

It was precisely the thought of having to clean the bathroom that brought on the first episode of the new day. How had that queer feeling of phoniness gone unrecognized for over an hour?

Katherine looked up from the sink, trying to dispel her anxiety with deep breathing. The onset of this attack must have occurred while she was sleeping, and for that she was thankful. This time the feeling of slipping away to God only knows where had been avoided.

There had to be something she could do to get her mind off her neuroses. Ah! The patio had not been swept for two days. Only a low wrought iron fence separated it from the beach, and the sand had a way of encroaching onto the brick. Katherine grabbed the broom from its place next to the refrigerator.

The routine was the same. Exit the kitchen. Turn left into the living room-mind that step; it's a split-level house. Take the drapery cord in hand and pull…

Like the auspicious premiere of a new play, the drapes slid open to reveal a throng of people on the beach. Katherine unconsciously dropped the broom and opened the French doors. An invisible force drew her outside; she almost floated across the bricks and onto the sand, entranced by the crowd gathered in what was virtually her backyard.

Fascinated by the drama before them, the crowd took no notice as Katherine elbowed her way toward the source of the excitement. Encircled by the onlookers was a six-foot wide pit in the sand. Its walls were slick and brown where the heat of the impact fused the sand grains into glass. She could not gauge the depth of the pit, but from Katherine's vantage point it appeared as if the hole continued down into the depths of the Earth with no hope of finding bottom.

"A meteorite right here on the beach!" a man behind her exclaimed. "Imagine what the odds of such a thing are!"

Others murmured their agreement. The chances of a meteorite striking Earth were low in of themselves. And the fact that the meteorite had chosen sunny Newport Beach, California, land of blush wines and paper napkins, as its final resting place was astronomical.

A barrier consisting of four wooden stakes with yellow tape strung between them (WARNING: QUARANTINED AREA) had been hastily constructed, thwarting Katherine's inexplicable desire to peer directly over the lip of the crater and into its fantastic, dark maw.

A figure garbed in scientists' whites abruptly stood in the crater, startling Katherine and a few of the onlookers. Shutters clicked and video cameras whirred as layman and reporter alike covered the momentous event of the unveiling of the celestial visitor: Hands clad in asbestos gloves, the man in the pit heaved the iron and nickel lump from its grave.

Katherine was disappointed that the crater was not as deep as she wished it to be, but the dismay was quickly dislodged from her chest. Her heart pounded wildly; muscles in every part of her body tightened with anxiety as her eyes were unwillingly drawn to the terrible object on the sand.

The glow of the fabled California sun could not hide the raw ugliness of the meteorite. It was about six inches in diameter, roughly the size of the red rubber ball Elyse Jameson had given Little Will as a gift last Christmas. Heated by entry into Earth's atmosphere, the meteorite's exterior had melted, shifted, swirled, and cooled into looping ornamentation that seemed carefully designed rather than accidental. In various places the whorls and grooves looked like a phallic symbol, a small, misshapen animal, perhaps a vagina—many things, yet nothing.

"Excuse me, ma'am."

A young, prematurely balding gentleman sporting corduroy, camera and miniature tape recorder was fishing for Katherine's attention. He said, "Are you a resident of this neighborhood?"

Transfixed by the activity, Katherine failed to realize she was still clad in her robe. The oversight was going to cost an interview.

"I live there," she said, nodding toward the house.

"I'd like to ask you a few questions if I may."

Katherine's eyes remained glued to the crater. "I guess that would be OK."

"Great!" the reporter said enthusiastically. He switched on his recorder. "Now let's see. Your name is?"

"Katherine. Katherine Jameson. I live there." She nodded toward the house again.

"Uh-huh. Did the meteorite wake you when it struck? I mean, did you see it happen, or ma'am? Are you OK?"

Blood pounding in her ears, Katherine hardly heard the reporter's words. "I think you'd better interview someone else," she mumbled.

The tape recorder dropped to the reporter's side. Disappointed, he shook his head at his shattered scoop and went in search of other local victims.

That the meteorite produced such a mind-numbing reaction was, to Katherine, an issue too awful to be probed. The meteorite was a bad omen; a harbinger of evil best left alone.

It was time to return to the house.

When Katherine's legs were finally willing to carry her off, her disbelieving eyes found that she and the crater were virtually alone in the beach. The circus had disappeared, rubberneckers, scientists, meteorite and all. Her head whipped from side to side, searching for evidence that the crowd had just dissipated, but there was none. She had been so wrapped up in her fear that the throng's departure had gone unnoticed.

I do lose track of time occasionally, but then who doesn't. It's so easy just to drift off to somewhere else while reading, or listening to music, or just thinking about meteorites.

The lack of spectators caused the desire to approach the crater to blossom anew. Floating again, Katherine crouched under the yellow tape and hovered over the edge.

The crater *was* bottomless. Black churned in the pit not too far below the presumed ledge where the scientist had earlier stood—livid black, ready to swallow anything that carelessly dropped into it, including sunlight and Katherine herself.

What the eyes could not see the ears heard. A voice drifted from the bottom, continually crying out, continually sucked back in by the darkness. Katherine could not make out what the voice was saying.

-help me-

but understood all the same.

"That's a pretty big hole, huh?"

Katherine nearly screamed, convinced that the voice had finally broken through the static. Instead, she looked up to see a tow-headed boy peering into the black from the opposite rim of the crater. Both of his hands were behind his back; one came out occasionally to brush a wisp of golden hair from his forehead.

"Yeah, it's a big hole all right," Katherine replied. The boy's presence made her fear seem foolish, unwarranted. Childish, in a way.

"It doesn't look too deep, though."

"No?"

"Nope," the boy said. "Look there. I can see the bottom,"

Katherine returned her eyes to the crater. The same boiling black remained, as well as the voice.

"Do you...do you hear anything?"

"Only the ocean."

"No, I mean, in *there*."

The boy peered into the crater for a moment, and then his blue eyes rose to meet Katherine's. "I don't hear nuthin. You must be crazy or somethin'. Look, I gotta go, lady. My momma's calling me."

The boy spun in the sand, offering Katherine an impossible glimpse at the object he concealed behind his back as he brought it in front of him. There was little mistaking; the ball was almost identical to the meteorite yet made of gold. The intricate work adorning its surface flashed in the sunlight.

Crazy. You must be crazy-or something. But what?

William's late-night studying came flooding back to her. The answer to questions lay hidden in his chamber.

*** *** ***

"Will? Where are you?"

"In here!" the boy replied. The zings and bleeps coming from the den indicated that he was embroiled in a video game battle with extraterrestrials. Katherine briefly worried that he was as dreamy as she was, for every time she turned around, he was battling Martians in one form or another. Enough of that. There were more pressing matters at hand.

William's study was the only room in the house that escaped a thorough cleaning by her hand. His study was just that, and on moving day he made it clear that his realm was off limits.

Katherine paused with trepidation outside the closed door. To ruminate through his desk was a violation of a sacred vow. Then again, neither she nor William was particularly religious.

The smell of stale cigarettes hit her full force upon entering (Did William smoke?) but nothing would stand in her way. Katherine crossed the room and sat down at the desk, gazing hesitatingly out of the window above it.

Do I really want to do this? Do I really want to know?

The pink slip Dr. Langly had given her was in the top right-hand drawer, right where William sought to hide it. She examined the paper carefully, waiting for it to speak. What had William seen on it that she hadn't?

Perhaps the mysterious blue book would hold the key. Katherine swiveled in the chair to face the bookcase. William had so many books that the hopes of finding the correct seemed slim. Yet right at eye level was a blue-bound volume with the letters "DSM III-R" stamped in gold on the spine. She checked the insurance form once more (DIAGNOSIS: DSM V 300.02/306.6) then pulled the book from the shelf. This was the book; the M.D.'s equivalent to the blasphemous *Necronomicon*. Madness was surely bound within its covers.

The full title of the book made Katherine's heart sink in her chest: *Diagnostic and Statistical Manual of Mental Disorders-Fifth Edition*. This was obviously the book which crazy people like her were judged by. So much for trusting Dr. Langly's opinion of her sanity.

Only a few seconds perusing the book were needed to explain the numbers on her form: The five-digit number was a secret code for what was wrong with the patient. Though the descriptions of the actual disorders were not in numerical order, locating them was not difficult.

300.02 Generalized Anxiety Disorder

What followed under the heading was a list of symptoms (excessive worry, tension, anxiety, and the like), all of which Katherine had experienced at one time or another. Instinctively she knew that the second set of numbers *had* to describe something worse in order to justify William's reaction late last night as well as her more ominous symptoms.

Diagnostic Criteria for 306.6 Depersonalization Disorder:
A. Persistent or recurring experience of
depersonalization as indicated by either
(1) or (2)
(1) An experience of feeling detached
from, and as if one is an outside
observer of, one's mental processes
or body
(2) An experience of feeling like an
automaton or as if in a dream.

There was no need to read further; this aptly described her problem. Still curious, she looked higher on the page at the additional information.

In Schizophrenia, Mood Disorders, Organic Mental Disorders, Anxiety Disorders and epilepsy, depersonalization may be a symptom.

Katherine's mind reeled. *Oh God! Dr. Langly may have only scratched the surface! I could have any one of more of these conditions just waiting to rear their ugly head!*

Katherine slammed the book closed, hoping to contain the demons within it. The book, along with the paper, had to be carefully replaced where she found them so William would not suspect her of snooping. She swiveled in the chair once more in order to replace the book on its shelf.

As she stretched out her arm, book in hand, her grip

suddenly loosened and DSM V fell to the ground, demons, and all. Since when was the desk beneath the window? Just last night it had been just inside the door.

Though instinct begged her to flee, Katherine slowly stood and turned to face the remainder of the room. The entire study had been re-arranged. Bookshelves, desk, paintings—all had been moved from their former positions to new, perhaps more ideal ones. True, William had always wanted the desk under the window, but he was too lazy to move it from where the movers deposited it. Furthermore, he hadn't the time to redo the entire room in the wee hours of the morning.

Katherine closed her eyes, face turned toward the ceiling in desperation. Nowhere in her just-completed investigation had she encountered the mention of hallucinations, and this *wasn't* a hallucination. Even if she felt detached from reality, the room was still real. The desk was real. The bookcase was real. That left only one explanation.

I'm the misplaced object here. I'm the one that's not real. It's as if every time I have that sliding feeling I fall into Wonderland. I just—

"You must be crazy or somethin'."

Suddenly the world seemed too complicated to understand. There was only to wait until this episode subsided and hope that another one did not set in before she saw Dr. Langly again.

Will was still glued to the television set and was about to enter the Kingdom of the Womblaster, where he would meet the ultimate video opponent, the Wizzlebanger. Katherine was not concerned for him; the television could bay-sit until William came home. She returned to the friendly bed and pulled the comforter up over her head.

*** *** ***

When Katherine woke, she was relieved to find that she was back in her body—or that her body was back where it belonged. It was a matter of perspective, she guessed.

The alarm clock read four-thirty. William would be home soon. It was time to get up and put on the face of a normal housewife.

Little Will was still seated in front of the television, as if he had not moved all day. The mess in the kitchen revealed that he had torn himself away from the PlayStation long enough to demolish the kitchen while making a PB&J sandwich. Katherine quickly threw the dishes into the washer and then threw herself into the shower.

Once dressed, other matronly duties loomed. Dinner needed preparing if William was to be kept in check for the evening. At this point, Katherine would have done almost anything to insure a pleasant evening. Controversy was the last thing she needed after the day she had.

William blew in the door at five-fifteen, just as he did every other night. He strolled into the kitchen and kissed his beautiful wife on the cheek. Tonight, however, not even the beauty of the princess-turned-scullery-maid could hide the anxiety that clung to her features.

"You look like hell," William said. His eyes bore into hers, looking for signs of pathology.

"It's been a long day," Katherine said, then pushed past him to the oven. "Dinner's ready. Would you please tell Will to wash his hands?"

William remained for a moment, watching as she removed the chicken from the oven and placed on the table. Katherine imagined that he sighed as he presumably set off on search of his heir.

"William! Wash your hands! It's dinner time!"

One of her mother's old complaints ran through Katherine's mind: *I asked you to find so-and-so because I am busy! I am perfectly capable of shouting but it's not proper.*

William turned back to his wife. "Here. I brought you these."

Katherine finished setting Little Will's place and took the bottle from William. A swarm of brown pills buzzed inside.

"What are they?"

"Medicine. It should help." He sat down at the head of the table and began to carve the chicken.

Katherine was too tired to argue. She retrieved the salad from the refrigerator while trying to think of something to say to fill the strained silence.

"Did you hear about the meteorite?"

William stopped carving. "What meteorite?"

"The one that landed on the beach just a few yards from the house. I guess we're lucky it didn't come crashing through the roof."

Katherine looked up from the salad, the plastic wrap covering still in hand. His eyes weighed so heavily on her that she knew he was staring. She tried to remain calm although the urge to scream was tickling her at the base of her throat. "It left a big hole in the sand," she asserted. "Pull back the curtain and see for yourself."

William had already done so. Twisted around in his chair, he had pulled back the curtains behind him and was peering out onto the beach.

"Can you see the barrier they put up—a couple of stakes with tape between them? Can you see it, William?"

Still facing the window, he shook his head imperceptibly.

Katherine darted from the kitchen, her arm catching the salad and sending it to the floor with a crash. If the French doors in the living room had been locked, she probably would have smashed her way out before charging across the patio and onto the sand.

The night was as dark and confusing as the beach was smooth and unbroken. The crater *had* to be nearby; earlier that day she had stood at the mouth of it and dreamed of casting herself into its yearning maw. But the beach resisted her pleas; there was no crater to be found. Katherine fell to her knees on the sand, sobbing uncontrollably. "I saw it!" she cried. "They must have filled it so no one would fall in and get hurt!"

Behind her, William's voice, but no comforting arm

around the shoulders. "Who filled it, Katherine?"

"The scientists, the lifeguards!" She turned and looked up at him, impossibly tall, making her feel like a child in an adult's oversized world. "It was here, I tell you! Please William, you must believe me."

"Come inside, Katherine."

"But you have to believe me!"

There was no use in arguing the matter further. Katherine allowed herself to be led back into the kitchen, where William fed her a pill and a glass of water to wash it down.

"What's happening to me?" she asked, tears streaking her make-up. The water glass nearly slipped from her fingers as she tried to set it down on the counter. "Oh God, William, what's happening to me?"

William was unmoved. He said, "I think it'd be best if you lie down."

"I don't *want* to lie down. If I spend one more moment in that bed, I'll—I'll go out of my mind!"

There, a reaction: William raised an eyebrow. "Please, Katherine. You'll feel better in the morning."

"Oh yeah, right. I bet that's what you doctors tell your cancer patients: you'll feel better in the morning."

"Katherine, you're becoming irrational."

Irrational? She thought. Irrational? Why shouldn't I be? Life is irrational, this world is irrational—why shouldn't I react irrationally?

William slowly coaxed her past the den and into the bedroom. Again, the comforter made its way over her head, sealing her in black sleep. The plastic blizzard was waiting for her.

*** *** ***

CHAPTER TWO: BILLY

In another time and in another corner of the universe, a young man named Billy Reltin was well on his way to discovering the same truths about the nature of reality that Katherine was. The methods employed were different, and although the answers Katherine would finally formulate are not as elegant as Billy's, they are the same, nevertheless.

*** *** ***

"Is that everything?" Billy asked.

His father closed the trunk of the car and wiped his hands on his trousers. "Yes, that's it," he said.

An awkward moment passed between them; Billy shoved his hands deep into the pockets of his jeans, a sign that he was nervous.

From the passenger seat of the car, Billy's mother called: "Frank, can we go now? I'm tired."

"Just a second."

For a moment Frank moved as if he was going to hug his son, but instead he extended a hand. "Be good, son."

Billy shook his father's hand. "I will," he said.

With that, Frank climbed into the station wagon and started the engine. The car slowly backed down the driveway and into the street, and a few seconds later it turned the corner, vanishing from sight.

That's it? Billy thought. *No lectures about the evils of alcohol or how to use a rubber? I got off easy.* He breathed a sigh of relief and headed back into the brick, ivy-covered dormitory.

Upstairs in his room, Mizzy was sitting among the boxes, perusing a worn copy of *Penthouse*. "You're disgusting," she said to him as he entered the room. "But at least you're not a fag." She tossed the magazine aside.

Billy blushed. Did she have to open *that* box?

"Well kiddo, you're on your own," Mizzy said, heading for the door. Mom and Dad were gone now, so there was no reason for her to pretend she wanted to be around her younger brother. "You know where the apartments are, right?"

"Yeah. They're those buildings on the other side of the campus that look like the bombed-out section of Beirut."

"You got it. Come and get me if you need me. Oh, and try to act normal, will y'a? I don't want everybody saying that my brother's a freak."

Billy frowned and nodded.

With that, Mizzy was gone. He was alone, and at that moment he felt very much like the freak Mizzy hoped he wasn't. He had hoped that being officially enrolled in the university would provide some sort of cathartic experience, but it hadn't yet. Life was like that. He had waited for his sixteenth birthday thinking that things would magically change once the day passed, and they didn't. He now knew that eighteen and twenty-one would be the same. Nothing was ever going to change.

Not knowing where to start the business of unpacking, Billy lifted the *Penthouse* from the floor and flipped through its pages. Now *here* was mystery—not in the subatomic world or in deep space, but in sex and all its secrets. It was far easier for Billy to picture how quarks came together to form other elementary particles than to picture him atop some naked beauty, engaging in intercourse. Too bad the School of Mathematics and Natural Sciences didn't offer a laboratory in the subject.

He tossed the magazine on the bed—the *lower* bed. It was a bunk model, and bunk beds meant he was to have a roommate. What if he turned out to be a Young Republican?

Music. You need to get some tunes going, Billy Boy.

Now where the hell was the stereo? His mother had instructed him to label his moving boxes carefully, but in the end, he wound up just dumping things randomly into open cartons. Billy supposed that for someone who was supposed to be a genius, he could do some stupid things.

Ten minutes later, the stereo was up, and *Dark Side of the Moon* was spinning in the compact disc player. There was nothing like a depressing Pink Floyd album to take his mind off things.

With the chosen album's dreadfully cheerless thoughts in his head, Billy began unpacking in earnest. The stereo and compact discs had been cushioned with the wadded shirts. His mother would have a coronary if she had seen that he hadn't bothered to remove the hangers and fold the shirts for transport, but Mother wasn't here, and *that* was a cheerful thought.

The closet arrangement was the first conundrum brought about by his anonymous roommate's absence. Two closets faced each other on opposite sides of the bedroom. Which was to be his?

A rope of anxiety knotted in Billy's chest. What if his roommate was a psychopath who was infatuated with a particular side of the room? Furthermore, left and right depended on which way one was facing, into the room or out of it. Any choice Billy made could produce a murderous rampage. Which door: the lady, or the tiger?

Stop it. Your imagination is running wild again. Your roommate probably couldn't give a shit if you won the princess' hand or were devoured by a man-eating tiger. Pick your poison.

Billy reached for a closet door, trying not to make a conscious choice. His right hand found the knob of the right door. He pulled it open slowly, deliberately.

Yellow and angry, a tiger leaped from the shelf inside. Billy dropped his shirts and jumped backwards, expecting to feel sharp fangs sink into his flesh.

The ball bounced several times, jingling as if a tiny bell was concealed inside. Some stupid people had left a toy in the closet, which Billy had mistaken for the terrible jaws of death.

Billy angrily kicked the ball, sending it bouncing out of

the bedroom. Clad in sneakers, his feet told him that something was strange about the ball: though it bounced like rubber, the exterior was curiously metallic. Intrigued, his feet carried the rest of him away to investigate.

The ball was heavy in his hands, and the outside was indeed metal, possibly gold. Queer designs had been carved into its surface; designs that meant nothing to Billy's scientific mind. Some other part of his brain, however, felt it recognized the symbols but, not being fluent in their language, couldn't translate them. A bell tingled as Billy turned the orb over in his hands.

Time for a scientific experiment.
Hypothesis: Metal doesn't bounce.
Null hypothesis: Metal bounces
Experiment: Bounce the ball.

Billy dropped the ball. It hit the floor and rebounded—no, it *jumped* back into his hands, as if it felt more comfortable there.

Result: The ball bounces.
Conclusion?

Either metal bounced or the ball wasn't made of metal. Neither made any sense for metal *doesn't* bounce, and yet the ball was metal and bounced defiantly. What the hell was going on?

Billy was smacked from his puzzlement by the sound of someone knocking on the suite door. It was probably his roommate outside—the roommate who had a pathological fear of bouncing metal balls with bells inside of them. Knot tightening in his chest once more, Billy opened the door.

"Hey mister, I was looking for my—*there it is! You found it!*"

The little boy's hands shot out as he greedily snatched the ball from Billy's grasp. The boy's eyes and smile lit up, shining like that impossible gold in his hands.

"Thank you, thank you! I forgot where I left my ball and I've been looking all over the place for it!"

"You're welcome," Billy mumbled, not knowing what else to say.

The boy turned the ball over in his hands, just as Billy had done moments before. Golden light played on the boy's pale face.

"Oops, I think I hear my Momma callin' me. Gotta go!"

The boy dashed into the stairwell, door slamming shut behind him.

*** *** ***

"I've been mad for fucking years..."

With the repeat button in the CD unit depressed, *Dark Side of the Moon* provided ceaseless ruminations on insanity and its causes as Billy continued to settle into his new home.

Bored with and tired of unpacking, he sat on the bed and closed his eyes. His mind wandered up and down the music's guitar chords, in and out of the convoluted lyrics and sound effects. There was an entire universe in there, in his head; it was waiting to be explored and sound waves were the key.

A syncopated pounding noise interrupted his reverie. Someone else was knocking at the door.

It's Dad. He's back to give you that condom lecture.

If it was Dear Old Dad, it was best to get it over with. Billy stepped around the cartons and his trunk and opened the door.

The girl leaned against the doorjamb in what Billy found to be a seductive pose. "Hi," she said with a smile. "I live right above you and I heard your stereo going. You like Pink Floyd?"

The girl's beauty robbed him of his normally articulate speech. "Umm-yeah."

"So do I." She extended a lily-white hand to him. "My name's Rachel."

He looked at her hand for a moment, not knowing whether he should kiss it or shake it.

"I'm Billy." He shook her hand, ever so lightly. "Did you, uh, just get in?"

Rachel corrected her posture and shook her head. "I've been here for fucking hours. I was hoping someone with half a mind would move in soon, and now that I hear Pink Floyd..."

Billy's hands flew back into his pockets. "Yeah, I know how it is. Hey, you wanna come in? I can probably clear someplace off so you can sit down…"

"Don't mind if I do!"

Rachel plowed into the room, deftly sidestepping the jumble. She sat herself down on the lower bunk, noticing the interesting pattern stained into the cover. "Look at these yellow stains!" she exclaimed. "Gross." She held out her tie-dyed T-shirt and compared its pattern to that on the mattress. "Say, you don't think that—nah, it's gotta be a different process. Well Billy, I hope you have a rubber mattress cover."

Billy had begun to unpack out of nerves rather than desire to be finished with it. "As a matter of fact, I do," he responded. "My mother knows that I won't wash anything if I don't have to, so why give me something that would get dirty? With rubber, the shit just slides right off."

Confused, Rachel fell silent. Billy had such a serious demeanor about him that it was hard to tell if he was joking or not. She laughed finally; it *had* to be a joke. "Say, do you want me to help you put things away? I'm pretty good at getting stuff organized."

Billy shrugged. "That would be all right, I guess."

Rachel swept her golden hair from her shoulders and hopped to her feet, ready to dive into the mess that Billy was making trying to clean up.

He handed her the pile of sweaters he was holding and smiled sheepishly. "Here. I really don't care where you put them. The closet, I guess."

"Sounds good to me," Rachel said. "Do you want them hung or folded?"

"Huh?"

"Do you want your sweaters hung or folded? No, wait. Don't tell me. You don't care."

"Right."

"Folded it is then," she said, and worked her way over to the closet. "I know you've probably been asked this a thousand times, but you look kinda young. How old are you?"

Billy gritted his teeth. "Sixteen," he said.

Rachel dumped the sweaters on the shelf and turned in time to see him shove a pile of underwear into a desk drawer. "Sixteen? No shit?"

"No. I'm a little advanced."

"I'll say. I'm not so sure I want to know, but when did you graduate from high school?"

Billy's hands found their way to his pockets again. If there was one thing he hated to talk about, it was his academic achievements. "I didn't—I mean I did—sort of. I took some proficiency test when I was thirteen and I was excused. I've had private tutors since then and was sitting in on some classes at colleges here and there. I held off enrolling in one because I figured they wouldn't take me too seriously until I had a few more years under my belt."

"I bet."

He looked at the ground. This was probably the end of what could have been a beautiful friendship; no one wanted to hang around with a dork that was too smart for his own good.

"Gosh," Rachel said, scratching her head. "I can't imagine being that smart. It's kinda neat. What's your major?"

"Physics."

"Ugh. I can't understand why anyone would want to be a science major."

Unbeknownst to the rest of his body, Billy's left hand found its way out of its hiding place long enough to run its finger through his hair. At this point, he'd say anything to keep the conversation going. "What's your major?" he asked.

"I don't really have one on the books. I guess it's unofficially men."

"Oh."

Men, Billy. Did you hear the way she said that? Men, not boys. Give up now.

"Organizing," as Rachel had called it, turned out to be little more than casually stuffing things wherever they would fit. As the hours wore on more Pink Floyd graced the stereo; it provided ample fodder for small talk. But now the work was done, and the last disc of *The Wall* had ended.

Now what?

"I really appreciate all the help," Billy said.

Rachel made a cartoon gesture that read "no sweat." "Don't worry about it. Besides, there's nothing else to do around here anyway."

Billy shrugged, another nervous habit. "I would have guessed that you would have introduced yourself to everyone in the building." His comment wasn't so much an observation as to the nature of her character as much as it reflected his own lack of self-esteem.

"I did. You and I are it. It looks as if everyone else is going to wait until tomorrow or the weekend to move in. Me, I'm not one for doing things at the last minute. Now I wonder what there is to do around here on a Thursday night besides getting wasted?"

"Not much, I guess."

"Well, I guess we'll just have to get wasted then," Rachel said. She got up from her seat on the stained mattress and stretched. "I'm gonna have dinner with my parents around five, so what do you say we start the party around seven?"

"Great," Billy said, a grand smile breaking out on his face. "I have a meeting with the Department Chair anyhow."

"Seven it is then," Rachel said, and darted out of the room as quickly and as mysteriously she had come in. The last two hours with her seemed strange contrived, just like the little boy's visit. But Billy didn't care; his brain was still hung up in the "party."

Party? he thought. *Am I supposed to supply the booze? No, she asked me, so—oh hell, now what do I do? And what so you do when you party? Sit around and debate the origin of the universe?*

Rachel had skillfully woven his thoughts for him, now leading him by his nose into a realm he would never have explored on his own.

*** *** ***

"Billy?"

The man standing in the doorway had the look of the classic Hollywood mad scientist. Tall and gangly, he sported horn-rimmed glasses and a wild tuft of shock-white hair on his head. Billy did his best to dispel the notion that this gentlemen's countenance foreshadowed what he himself would look like thirty years from now, not realizing that he was already well on his way to becoming Racken's double.

"I'm Doctor Racken."

"Pleased to meet you," Billy said.

Doctor Racken motioned Billy to step into his office. "Shall we?"

Billy felt nerves set in as soon as he stepped into his mentor's inner sanctum. It was the office of yet another victim of harsh toilet training. Dr. Racken was anal-retentive. The technical books in their massive cases were not only freshly dusted but also alphabetized by author. The desk in the center of the room had a grid etched on it that broke it up into spaces reserved for specific items: the phone in the upper right square, the pen holder in the middle top and a note pad in the square below that. Billy figured that if he looked just above the framed diplomas that hung on the wall, he would find that Racken had taken a carpenter's level and had made marks on the wall as guidelines to square the frames by. Racken was a sick man indeed.

"Have a seat, Billy."

Billy sat, silently thanking God that his parents had read Dr. Spock and knew the right way to raise children.

Racken took his place behind hid perniciously neat desk and opened the file before him. Not only did it contain Billy's academic records, but copies of several published papers he had written. Racken said, "I hope you don't mind that I did a little research on your case."

Case? He made it sound like a he had a disease.

Racken folded his hands on the desk. "To be honest with you Billy, we've never some across someone with such advanced knowledge for your tender years. I suppose that what I should do is just pose one question: What can we do for you?"

He cleared his throat. "Well sir, I feel like the best course by which to further my education would be to branch out; to move from the theoretical to the experimental. I have some ideas—I'll submit them to you in writing, of course—and I was hoping to be able to gain access to some research equipment and produce a thesis."

Racken nodded. "That sounds like a fine plan. As you know, we're one of the few undergraduate science departments that require a thesis. It's not completely unheard of, though, and we feel that the thesis process offers valuable experience and makes one more marketable to graduate schools." He smiled. "You, of course, hardly need distinguishing. Perhaps we should draw up a first semester schedule for someone at, say, an undergraduate senior level. From what I've read of your work you might be a tad bored in class, but it will give you a chance to meet some of the other students and become familiar with the faculty. You will also be introduced to experimental techniques and what the university has to offer in the way of facilities."

"Sounds great."

"Fine. Let's review your choices of classes."

Billy listened and nodded for the next half an hour as Dr. Racken explained which courses he would be saddled with for the semester. Nothing was particularly interesting.

"Really, I think the Thesis Methods course is the course you'll get the most out of," Racken explained. It's small—only eight or ten students. That way I can give each one of you plenty of attention. If you want to learn about our facilities, it'll be in this class that you'll do so."

Billy nodded. The Methods course was to be the arena into which he would drop perhaps the greatest scientific bomb of this or any other universe. It didn't matter that Billy had no clue as to what that bomb was specifically, but it would be there when the time came. For as long as he could remember he had been on the verge of an incredible breakthrough. Who knew? Perhaps the knowledge had filtered across the placenta and into his developing brain while his mother watched *Nova,* determined to expose the fetus to science at an early age.

"Well, I guess that just about does it."

Billy took the schedule that had been prepared for him and glanced over it again. He sighed. Schedules were a necessary evil.

Racken stood and opened his door, signaling that the appointment had come to its conclusion. "I look forward to working with you, Billy," he said. "I imagine that this will be a productive semester."

Dr. Racken had begun to lead Billy back to the outer office when a tall young man walked through the door. "Ah, Mike!" Racken exclaimed. "I have someone I want you to meet. Billy Reltin, this is Mike Cohan, one of our standouts."

Mike held out a hand and flashed a condescending smile. Billy shook his hand aggressively ("A firm grip is the sign of good character," his father had said); Mike squeezed back so hard that Billy heard one of his knuckles pop under the pressure. This was not a friendly handshake; it was the type if gesture that said, "I'm the top of the heap and don't forget it."

"Billy is something of a prodigy," Racken continued. "He'll be a senior this semester."

"Oh really?" Mike said. His voice not only betrayed surprise but disdain.

Billy smiled, pleased at Mike's contempt. His opponent was obviously shaken, and if Mike could be judged by his looks, he appeared to spend an awful lot of time surfing. Not only his clothes, but his mane of blond hair also betrayed his avocation. Billy had nothing to worry about.

*** *** ***

As Billy walked along the sidewalk that rimmed the elliptical park that was the centerpiece of the campus, all he could think about was the hum of the electromagnets in the particle accelerator beneath his feet. Soon he would be at the helm of that great machine, and then...

There were more pressing matters at hand. He headed for

Beirut, hoping that he had correctly memorized the number of his sister's suite.

The girl who answered the door was attractive and she knew it. "What do *you* want?" she snapped.

"Um, is Mizzy around?"

The girl retreated into the suite. "Hey Mizzy, it's for you!" she shouted down the hall.

In a moment, Billy's sister emerged from her room. The girl stopped her as she walked by. "Don't tell me that geek is one of your conquests," Billy overheard her say.

Mizzy looked over the girl's shoulder at the open front door. "That geek happens to be my brother," she said.

"Hi," Billy said meekly.

"What's up?"

His eyes darted around the suite for a moment, looking to see if anyone was in earshot.

"What did you say?" Mizzy asked. "You mumble too much. Talk louder! I haven't got all day."

"I said I need your help in getting some booze."

Mizzy raised an eyebrow. "Booze?" she asked. "*You?* Why?"

"Well, there's this girl I met today, and—"

Mizzy suddenly grabbed Billy by the arm and dragged him into the suite. "A girl? Oh my God, you really aren't latent after all!" She pushed him into the den and onto the couch. "First of all, Billy, you can't believe everything you read in the *Forum* section of *Penthouse*."

Billy rolled his eyes. "Oh, give me a break, Mizzy! We just want to have a little party."

"Yeah, right. So, what's she like?"

Billy thought for a moment, searching for the right words to describe his vision of loveliness. "Well, I guess you could say she's a bit retrograde-you know, Birkenstocks, tie-dye and all."

"Yeah, yeah, but what does she *look* like?"

"She's tiny, with blond hair and blue eyes. I guess you could say that she is a typical Aryan-type princess."

The description conjured quite an image in Mizzy's fertile

imagination. She could easily see Billy picturing himself as a gallant prince leaning over his slumbering beauty to wake her with a kiss. What a spaz.

"And you just want booze?" she asked. "What about some coke?"

Billy's eyes widened at the prospect of his sister pushing drugs.

"Mellow out, bro. There's so much snow on this campus you can ski in the summertime."

"I think I'll pass on that."

"Suit yourself. We've got plenty of bottles around here," she boasted. "What do you want-oh hell, why am I asking you? You wouldn't know. I know I'll just give you a bottle of everything I can think of."

*** *** ***

Billy lugged the bag of booze back to his dormitory, thankful that he didn't run into anyone else along the way. How was he, a minor, to explain the booty he was toting?

Because the Earth is thought to be some four and a half billion years old, and that the universe is considerably older than that, Billy knew that the time he had to wait before Rachel returned from dinner was just a tiny grain of sand on the beach of Cosmic Time. That knowledge was little comfort. He paced the floor of his room until he was sure that he had worn a permanent groove into the carpet.

All at once there came a knock at the door. Billy rushed and grabbed the doorknob, then slowly opened the door, not wanting to seem quite so eager-or desperate for company.

"Hey, Billy," Rachel said. She barged her way into the room. Billy saw that she had a couple of CDs in tow; the top one was by Jimi Hendrix and the bottom was undoubtedly The Doors. Rachel wasn't merely retrograde; she was positively enamored with the sixties. But if that was her thing, he would go along with it. It could have been worse—she could have been dwelling in the Seventies and worshipped Abba and the Bay City

Rollers.

"How was dinner?" Billy asked. He closed the door and locked it, silently praying that no adult would chance to stop by.

"Boring as hell," Rachel replied. She had made a beeline for the stereo and was setting Hendrix up. "Boring, but over, thank God."

As she turned to face him in the fading light, Billy felt his head spin on his neck. She had applied make-up (it was heavy enough that it had to have been done so to irk her parents) and the transformation from lady-in-waiting to full-fledged, ravishing princess was stunning.

"Are you OK?" Rachel asked.

"Huh? Oh, yeah," Billy said. "I was contemplating the liquor cabinet." He walked over to his closet and opened the door with a flourish, like a cheap game-show host. Six bottles of liquor had been neatly arranged in a row on the shelf; the sweaters had been relegated to a less important position. Next to the alcohol were several cans of soda retrieved from the machine in the laundry room, soda that had been bought with the quarters Mom had given him to run the washer and dryer with.

Rachel approached the impromptu bar with reverence that is normally reserved for the pilgrimage to Mecca. "Groovy!" she said.

Billy watched as Rachel snatched a can of cola from the shelf and tossed it to him. She then took one for herself and pulled down the Bacardi. "Rum and Coke, or ambrosia. You say to-may-toe, I say to-mah-toe." She sat in the center of the room Indian style; Billy imitated her out of lack of knowing what else to do. She handed him the bottle of rum. "Here. You do the honors."

Go ahead and take it, son. Go ahead and kill a couple of those gray cells. Maybe then you'll relate to people more easily.

He twisted the cap. The crack the seal made was the sound of his growing up, Billy mused.

Rachel opened her Coke and took the bottle from him. "Ladies first," she said with a bat of her eyelashes, and took a large swallow from the bottle, followed by a chug of cola.

The bottle of rum found its way into Billy's hands. It was now or never, do or die. Or do *and* die, however it went.

The rum smelled metallic, caustic. Was this what he *really* wanted to do?

In a word: yes. And you never know if the Forum section of Penthouse is true or not. Why else would they withhold the writer's names and addresses?

He brought the bottle to his lips and took in a mouthful. The gag reflex immediately kicked in, but he managed to force the liquid down without spiting up. His throat, mouth and eyes burned. No wonder Rachel had quickly chased the rum down with the cola.

"Yikes!" Rachel said, admiring the bottle. Between the two of them, almost a quarter of a liter had been consumed, and the party was just getting started. "You didn't tell me you were a pro," she said.

Across from her, Billy was still trying to regain some semblance of order in his digestive tract. It was all he could do to say "Oh."

Rachel chuckled and lay down on her back on the floor. Billy didn't move, lest he experience projectile vomiting.

"Geez Billy, if you're so smart, why'd you come to Darkham U? I mean, why not Harvard or Yale?"

"There are too many people at Harvard and Yale," he replied. "I wanted to find another university with a good reputation and good equipment, and when Darkham opened their supercollider facilities last year, it became the obvious choice."

Rachel shook her head. She said, "God, but you talk like a forty-year-old. What the hell's a supercollider?"

"It's a particle accelerator. Darkham's happens to be a cyclotron. In layman's terms, it's an atom smasher."

"Groovy," Rachel said.

Something was pressing against Billy's back. Confused, he turned his head to the side and found that at some point he too had stretched out on the carpet. *How interesting,* he thought.

The Doors followed Jimi Hendrix as sure as February follows January.

Suddenly Rachel was on her feet and moving in time to the music. As she danced, she produced a small plastic bag from one of the pockets of her faded jeans and held it above her head, waving her prize in the air for the imaginary crowd to see.

Billy looked up from the space on the floor that he had occupied for the past hour. "What's in the bag?" he asked.

"Oblivion," Rachel said, bringing the bag to her lips. She kissed it reverently.

"It looks like bits of paper to me."

"Rice paper," Rachel corrected. "Rice paper stained with pixie dust. Do you want to fly?"

"I don't have a pilot's license."

Rachel stopped moving and sat down on the floor next to him, dangling the bag in front of his nose. "This is your license," she said.

"Yeah, but what is it?"

Rachel giggled-how pretty she looked when she did that! "You really don't know, do you?" she asked.

"No."

"Lysergic acid diethylamide, as you scientists call it," she replied. "Have you ever dropped acid?"

"You're kidding me, right?"

"'S fun; you'll love it."

Before Billy knew what was happening, Rachel reached out and took his hands into hers. Her touch was electric; a shock raced up his arms and along his spine. She led him to the lower bunk and sat him down.

"Now all you have to do is put one of these tabs on your tongue, and away we go!"

As Rachel began to fumble with the knot that sealed the bag of acid, Billy began to fumble for his conscience. Wasn't it enough that he had got drunk on the first night of freedom from his parent's tyranny? Did he have to visit the twelfth dimension, too?

A pounding noise began; for a moment Billy thought it was the sound of his straining heart right before he died of alcohol poisoning.

Rachel's eyes almost bugged out of her head. "Uh-oh! Someone's at the door!" Her eyes darted about the room, looking for a safe hiding place for her heretical Eucharist. She shoved the bag of acid tabs into one of Billy's desk drawers.

Billy sailed through the air with the greatest of ease and casually reached for the door. Rachel dove for the bottles. She too felt Billy wasn't acting very smart for someone who was supposed to be a genius.

Billy opened the door.

"Uh, this is eleven ninety-six, right?" the knocker asked. Even through the rum-fog that clouded his mind, Billy could see the gym bag that his roommate was carrying--the gym bag from which a tennis racket and a baseball bat protruded. Billy was saddled with living with a jock for a year. The Great God of Dormitories was obviously punishing Billy for the sin of under-age drinking.

"Yeah, this is the place. I'm Billy Reltin."

"Dirk Polikaitis."

Oh great, Billy thought. *My roommate has a last name sounds like a disease.*

What followed was another one of those bone-crushing handshakes; this one made Billy feel inferior rather than superior. Knowing his luck, Rachel would probably fall for this dork with muscles, leaving Billy to mourn his lost love and drown his sorrows in the booze his sister had so thoughtfully provided.

Billy realized that he was still blocking entrance to the room; he stepped aside and let Dirk enter. "Uh Dirk, this is Rachel. She lives upstairs."

Rachel waved from her seat on the floor. "Hi y'a," she said. "You want a drink?"

"No thanks," Dirk said. "I'm in training." So, it *was*

alcohol that Dirk smelled, not beer. Didn't these two know what irreparable harm they were doing to their bodies?

Billy found himself fumbling for something to say. "I went ahead and took the top bunk," he said. "If you want it, we can switch—I mean, it doesn't really matter to me all that much."

Dirk put his bag down on his bed. "Whatever," he said. The conversation was stilted as a result of total strangers being forced to sleep in the same room. Both Billy and Dirk were hoping that something would happen to get the ball rolling and ease the awkwardness that had settled in the room.

Eventually, Billy found the right words to say. "Um, do you need any help bringing your stuff in?"

"Yeah. My truck's parked in the fire lane out in front of the building."

*** *** ***

Once Dirk's things were safely inside, he dashed back to his truck to move it before he got a ticket for parking in the fire lane. Rachel took the opportunity to re-open the bar.

"God, what a freak," she said, pushing the bottle of rum back into Billy's hands.

Billy took what he felt was a much-needed slug from the bottle and wiped his mouth with his free arm. "You think so?" he asked.

"Hell yes! He turned down a free drink. He must be total Squaresville, you know what I mean?

Squaresville? Yes, Billy knew what she meant, even if the term was outdated. After all, he was one of Squaresville's prominent citizens, wasn't he?

"I bet Dork's never tried acid, either. You think he'll rat on us?"

Billy's expression grew severe. "Oh shit, I never even thought of that."

Rachel frowned. "We'll have to keep the tabs under wraps," she said.

*** *** ***

Billy had memorized the map of the campus that had been provided in the schedule of classes, but he wound up not needing it. All his classes were in the same building.

On Monday morning he showered and then packed his notebook and books into his backpack. Dirk was already long gone; Billy vaguely remembered his alarm going off at the ungodly hour of six o'clock. Dirk ran every morning for an hour, and the first day of school was to be no exception. He was fanatical about athletics; that much was evident from the amount of time he had spent polishing his trophies. Trophies, he supposed, served the same purpose as grade point average. The former was apparently far more attractive than the latter to mainstream society, but oh well. The affair was summed up best by Albert Camus in his immortal existentialist novel *L'Etranger:* "Ce n'est pas de la juste dans la vie."

A fat girl with a donut in each hand answered the door to Rachel's suite.

"Hi, I'm Billy from downstairs, remember?"

The girl grunted; she at least had manners enough to know not to speak when her mouth was full.

"Is Rachel up yet?"

"Up and at 'em," Rachel called from inside. She came out of her bedroom in her uniform of worn jeans and a tie-dyed T-shirt. The sight of her still winded Billy even though they had spent almost every second of the last thirty-six hours together.

Rachel said not a word to her roommate; she sailed out the door of the suite and closed it behind her. "Don't expect to get much conversation out of Susan," she said. "What a cow. She's usually busy eating. What a pair of geeks we must live with, huh?"

Billy shook his head out of sympathy. "Yeah; they're opposite ends of the spectrum, all right. Ready for breakfast?"

"Yup."

The pair headed out of the dorms and for the commons. Outside the sun was warm and the sky blue. Birds squawked in the trees that dotted the campus.

"You look a little tired," Rachel noted as they reached the commons.

Billy opened the door for her. "Yeah, I didn't sleep well again."

"You think it's the booze?"

"No. I don't know. It's almost as if there's something bubbling just under the surface of my thoughts; something that I can't put my finger on."

Rachel shook her head. "Deep, man," she said.

The cafeteria that occupied the top floor of the commons was dedicated to meeting the nutritional needs of the students whether they wanted them met or not. Billy wrinkled his nose as they moved through the busy line; the prospect of another grapefruit half and wheat toast nauseated him, but it was that or a tofu/egg scramble. Hadn't the chefs ever heard of Cocoa Puffs? After all, Cocoa Puffs are fortified with eight essential vitamins and minerals.

Rachel hadn't paid much attention to what Billy had selected as a meal until they sat at an open table by the window. She frowned at his bacon and hash browns. "Not a very substantial selection," she said. "You should get some of the tofu."

Billy watched her scoop up a fork full of the concoction and eat it without so much as flinching. "Tofu is disgusting."

"It's good for you."

Billy smiled. Ah, here was womanhood in all its glory! Rachel was a bundle of contradictions. "Good for you? This is coming from the girl who drops acid?"

"That's different," she insisted. "Acid is organic."

"The heck it is! It's made in a lab. If you want something organic, go for peyote buttons. Ever read Carlos Castaneda?"

"Who?"

The allusion was wasted.

"Didn't Dirk say he had to be at some sort of tryout or audition tonight?"

Billy stopped chewing his bacon. Rachel's question was a

lead-in sentence if ever he heard one. "Well, yeah…" he said.

"Good. I was thinking maybe…you know."

Yes, Billy knew. In a way it was his fault; he had mentioned the LSD and had thereby brought it to the forefront of her mind. "Gosh, it might not be a good idea. I mean, I must get up early tomorrow for class…"

"Oh cripes, Billy." Rachel said. "Why the hell do you want to go to school five days a week? What are you trying to do? Graduate?"

"That's the idea."

Rachel frowned, reaching for the salt. Billy watched as she again contradicted her healthy impulses by loading her eggs with sodium. She said, "Well, maybe you're right. It would be better to save it for the weekend." And then she sang: "Anticipation! Anticipayyy-yay-shun…" It was the old Carly Simon song that the Heinz Company used to push its mainstay ketchup product. At that moment Billy thought that yes, he was no stranger to anticipation. All his life he had anticipated some great something, but never got close enough to it to know what it was.

Something bubbling just under the surface…something occupying some dim corner of my mind, just waiting to be plucked out when it finally turns ripe.

*** *** ***

The first day of classes was always a dreadful affair. Teachers handed out their course outlines and requirements and felt compelled to go over them line by line, knowing that most students would never bother to look at them on their own. Billy sat yawning for hours; none of his present classes offered anything in a way of a challenge, but they were required and so he would have to stick it out.

However, when the time for Racken's course on lab techniques finally approached, Billy's interest rose considerably. Sure, the material was soporific, but here at last was a chance to get his hands on some of the wondrous machines Darkham had locked up in the bowels of the campus.

The classroom was on the fifth floor of the Physical Sciences building. Billy didn't wait for the elevator; he ran up the stairs, hoping to relieve some of the tension he felt. Racken's classroom was the Holy of Holies, the inner sanctum of undergraduate physics and it made him nervous. Racken had extended him the opportunity to hand in a proposal, but what if Billy found himself at a loss for ideas?

One step at a time, he told himself as he exited the stairwell. *Just take things one-step at a time. When the time is right, the ideas will come.*

The door to room five-fifteen was open. Outside, Billy paused for a moment and took a deep breath before venturing in.

Where to sit? Sit in the front and you're accused of being too eager. Sit in the back and you're not eager enough. Sit in the middle and the teacher will automatically give you a "B." Che imbroglio!

Several seconds passed before Billy realized that in the process of debating the location of his desk, he had strolled into the classroom. Racken had mentioned on Friday that the class was small-about ten students-and so it was. All of them were present, seated and staring. Billy felt warm blood rushed toward his face.

No, I'm not going to blush and look like an idiot. I'm just not going to do it. It's my body; I can control it.

He blushed anyway and sat down at the nearest desk. Out of the corner or his eyes he could see that his classmates were still staring, just as they always did when he walked into a classroom.

"Who the hell is that guy?' he heard someone say.

A deeper male voice replied, it had to be Mike Cohan. "Obviously some genius. I mean, just look at him. He's got it written all over his face."

Someone snickered.

Blood pounded in Billy's ears. Here again was resentment, a tad of jealousy and a ton of contempt. Why didn't American society reward intelligence and academic excellence instead of what Billy saw as unadulterated assholism? Sure, there were places he could go to be among members of his cursed tribe (such as MENSA meetings), but most people shunned such groups and looked upon them as congregations of deviants. A fact is a fact: if you weren't on the first string you were a nerd—or worse, a fag.

At the completion of Billy's thoughts, Racken strode into the room. Even Mike and his buddies quieted down in his presence, for here was an object of respect—or did they behave simply because Racken handed out the grades? Was he regarded as a freak, too?

Racken cleared his throat. "Good afternoon, gentlemen—er, ladies and gentlemen." He nodded at the sole female in the room, a Japanese who sat at the far side of the room. Now there was a culture that appreciated diligence and academics.

Racken blathered his welcome back to the new semester and began to pass out the course outline. Yes, even Racken was going to recite his syllabus, though at this level it seemed hardly necessary to Billy. At least he didn't bother to take roll.

Banter gave way to preaching.

"As physicists, we have committed ourselves to trying to take the physical phenomena we see around us and set it against the backdrop of a handful of laws which we feel govern the universe. It's no easy task, gentlemen—er, ladies and gentlemen, and we must continue to take on the challenge and alter our theories when necessary. Take the atom, for example. For many years we assumed that it was the smallest indivisible particle in the universe until someone cleaved it, revealing neutrons, protons and electrons. Today, we know that even these elementary particles can be further reduced, *ad infinitum*."

From this vantage point at the side of the room, Billy saw the other student's heads bob in agreement. Here again was bias. Was there no one in the room but he that would challenge the old method of splitting subatomic hairs in search of the tiniest fraction of matter? Such endeavors were pointless. Billy firmly believed that if men continued to delve into the confines of inner space, they would continue to find infinity. Infinity was the most confounding of all scientific concepts; it existed no matter what direction one looked. Now if there was only some way to make others realize that they were barking up the wrong theoretical tree! There was a complete forest of theory out there, just waiting to be harvested.

"Well!" Racken exclaimed, clapping his hands together. "I believe that will be all for today. Remember to have your lab coats *et cetera* for Wednesday."

Shocked, Billy looked up at the clock. An hour had passed, and he had missed it due to a mental absenteeism. He had been lost in the infinity contained within his skull.

*** *** ***

just under the surface...

Irritated with life, Billy cut across the park in the center of campus rather than walk along the sidewalk where he might run into a fellow physics major. This was a major university. Why did the students seem cold to scientific inquest? Where was the fire that yearned for the quenching knowledge?

A tight knot of trees stood in the middle of the park. Curious, Billy changed his course slightly, so that his path would take him through the grove. It was a casual decision to do so, but out of such casual choices often comes genius. Isaac Newton was said to have discovered calculus (thereby giving students sufficient warrant to hate him) while watching barrels being assembled from slats and rings. What would have happened if Newton had decided to go down to the corner barber shop and get a shave instead? The world will never know.

Billy was surprised to find a murky pond at the center of the thicket. A gravel path encircled it; benches had been placed at strategic points along the way. Judging from the number of beer cans that peeked out from beneath the shrubbery, this was a popular place to sit and think/drink.

Something bubbling just under the surface...

He stood on the path, transfixed by the play of sunlight on the water. The warm glow seemed oddly concentrated at the center of the pond, drawn there by an object beneath the water.

What the hell?

He kneeled at the pond's edge, squinting into the depths. The murky water would not allow its secrets to be read easily, but Billy could have sworn he spied that infernal golden ball at the bottom of the pool.

As if in a dream, he reached down to the ground and his fingers found a small, round pebble near his right foot. He straightened up and tossed the pebble into the pond. Ripples propagated across the water from where the pebble broke the surface, striking the shore and bouncing back toward the center. The waves crossed, added, canceled in a sublime circular pattern; a true pattern, a pattern of symmetry and uniformity dictated by the pond's circular shore and the impact of the pebble.

Not under the surface, but on the surface. That which was hidden had broken through to the forefront of his consciousness and then—

Billy snapped out of his trance. Whatever it was, he had grasped in that split-second of observation was gone. The ball no longer shone in the depths of the pond.

*** *** ***

CHAPTER THREE: KATHERINE

Help me, please...
The snow was falling so thickly that Katherine could hardly see where she was walking. Invisible hands pushed her, urging her to come closer, closer.
Steps appeared beneath her feet. She climbed on and on without knowing why, drawn to the voice that beckoned.
Still closer...
Snowflakes clung to her hair, face, and body. Katherine held out her hands and caught a few of the delicate crystals. They weren't made of ice at all; instead, they were some strange plastic-like material, permanent snowflakes that were part of a perpetual, defiant blizzard.
The voice continued to plea.
Please! You don't understand how important this is! They can get away from you. I don't know how they do it, but it happens. You've got to come and come now, before it's too late. I know what you're going through, and you just don't understand. They've trapped me, and they'll continue to drain me until there's nothing left. I don't know who you are, but they're coming after you next. I can hear them whisper, feel them plotting. You're in terrible danger.
The steps ended on a vast white plain. Through the clouds of swirling plastic, Katherine caught fleeting glimpses of the prison that towered here: a white, elegant building with a pillared dome crowning its heart. The voice came from inside, penetrating the walls just enough to be heard in her confused dreams.
The scenery abruptly changed. The disembodied voice was

gone, replaced by innumerable points of light sprinkled across the suffocating blackness of space. In the distance a massive object floated toward her, tumbling end over end. The meteor's surface was pitted with craters ready to be molded and reshaped into the mysterious symbols that adorned the fragment that survived entry into Earth's atmosphere and the crash on the beach.

A crack suddenly appeared in the fabric of space itself. Something very small had pierced the black and left it fractured much like a b-b shot or pebble does when it strikes a pane of glass. The interloping electron's wavelength was incredibly large and therefore not very energetic, but its collision with the meteor caused a minute change in the smaller wave's trajectory. The meteor was now on a direct collision course with a massless wave curiously identified as Earth.

Something else was coming through the crack in space. This second wave was out of the range of visual perception but incredibly powerful and getting more so all the time. This was the one that got away; the wave was at one time subordinate to another but now it was free. The Katherine wave recoiled from it, instinctively knowing that this was the mysterious "them" that sought her for its unfathomable, evil purpose.

Terrified, Katherine fled from the dream and back into her body—the body that had a habit of slipping into William's realm enough to give him pause.

*** *** ***

Katherine rolled over in bed, struggling to open her eyes. The medication William had forced on her the night before still clouded her brain, much as the plastic blizzard clouded her dream.

The bed and floor defied her attempts to stand. Both reeled away from her as she rolled out of the bed. She reached out for the nightstand to steady herself on but it too retreated, leaving her to fall to the floor.

Crawling to the bathroom, Katherine resolved not to allow her to be over-medicated again. Madness was preferable to being a total vegetable. And besides, Dr. Langly had asserted that she *wasn't* mad. Maybe the symptoms she was experiencing were trials she had to endure in order to get well again. In any case, last night's was the first and last pill she would swallow.

After several hours, the wooziness brought on by the Thorazine disappeared, allowing Katherine to function normally. She picked up around the house, leaving the draperies on the window that faced the beach closed. Not being able to see the beach allowed her to pretend that the phantom crater neither appeared nor vanished.

About two o'clock Katherine decided to check up on her son. Little Will had been spotted milling about the house a few times, but she hadn't been conscious of what he was doing. Such ignorance was dangerous, especially where Will was concerned.

"William?"

The television in the den was dark and quiet for the first time since Christmas. Perhaps the fascination with the Nintendo was starting to wane, thank God.

Will had to be in his room. Katherine made her way down the hall.

Will had closed the door to his room behind him, a stunt neither Katherine nor William allowed. Katherine rose her fist to knock when suddenly a burst of warm air hit her back and flowed around her body, caressing it, controlling it. The whirlwind begged to twist her face the opposite side of the hall and the door to William's study that was carved into it. When the wind found it could not turn her physically it turned to her mind, and then she was sliding again, dissociating from the hall she was standing in and falling into a new one.

This time the episode would not get the best of her. Katherine gritted her teeth at the sensation that clouded her head and churned her stomach. Soon it would be over, and although she would feel strange for several hours, it would eventually pass.

A moment later, Katherine's knuckles connected with Will's door. "William?" she demanded. "William, you *know* you're not supposed to have this door closed!"

The boy did not answer.

Will was in trouble now! Katherine was in no mood to be toyed with. She angrily grabbed the doorknob and pushed to door open.

William's re-arranged study greeted her.

Katherine yanked the door closed while trying to recover the breath she was robbed of. She turned away from the door in terror, only to come face-to-face with Little Will's *open* door, and his empty room beyond it.

I'm not insane. I'm not, I'm not, I'm not.

"Mommy? Were you calling me?"

Little Will was standing at the end of the hall, hands behind his back and an angelic smile planted on his face.

"Where have you been?" Katherine asked breathlessly.

"Playin' video."

"Oh. Well…never mind. Go and play."

Will took off fast enough to break the sound barrier.

Inside her skull, Katherine's brain was working overtime to come up with a feasible explanation for this terrifying but simple development.

I got turned around. Yes, that's it. It was probably that junk William fed me last night. I'm confused, just confused. Perhaps a bit anxious, too.

Somewhere inside the house a tinny bell was ringing. A tiny bit of terror bubbled up into Katherine's throat at the sound before she realized it was only the doorbell. What could be less threatening than a visit from an Amway salesman or perhaps a Scientologist?

The young woman at the door did a double take when she saw Katherine on the other side of the threshold. "Oh, hello. Is Dr. J. here?"

"Who?" Katherine asked.

Smacking on a wad of gum in defiance, the girl put her hands on her hips. "Dr. Jameson. Dr. *William* Jameson. He lives here."

Katherine's eyes narrowed angrily. The tone this

teenybopper in a tube-top adopted immediately set her on the defensive. "No, Dr. William Jameson is not at home," Katherine snapped. "Why?"

"Hey, look lady, don't snap at me—"

"You can call me *Mrs.* Jameson. I'm William's wife. Who are you?"

It was unclear at first if the girl on the porch had heard Katherine's question, for her laughter had surely drowned the query. "William's *wife?* Jeeeeezus. Tell your 'husband' that Chelsea Brownen dropped by to visit." The girl turned and strutted down the walk, laughing as she went.

Incensed, Katherine slammed the front door closed. Since when did young women drop by the house to visit with William? How long had this been going on?

Chelsea…Chelsea Brownen.

Horror washed away Katherine's ire; terror that she had experienced so many times over the previous day that it seemed mundane and commonplace. Chelsea Brownen was an overweight, homely blob masquerading as a woman, not a nubile, busty blonde.

Anxiety and fear were not the only things that were common now. The study, the meteor, Chelsea Brownen…what was next? Comfortable logic was absent entirely from her life.

Surely you know what they say about people who question their own sanity…

Absence of logic did not imply insanity. By that reasoning, something fantastic was happening around Katherine, something frightening and unfathomable. The time to panic and crawl into bed was past now. The time had come to resist the call of the comforter and try to unravel the mystery she was immersed in.

*** *** ***

At ten minutes after five, Katherine planted herself at the kitchen table and folded her hands before her. In five minutes, William would come waltzing through the door, just like clockwork.

Keys rattled in the door precisely on schedule. William was soon in Katherine's line of sight and moving towards her.

Keeping with the trend of five years, William did not say hello. "What's for dinner?" he asked, loosening his tie.

"I didn't fix dinner," Katherine said sternly. "I don't feel like cooking."

William did not notice her new demeanor as he probed the refrigerator contents for a beer. "Did you take a pill?'

"No, I didn't. And I'm not going to, either."

He straightened up, refrigerator door swinging closed behind him. "Christ, Katherine—"

"Don't "Christ" me. Who's that blond girl that came around this afternoon asking for you?"

William's brow furrowed. "*What* blond girl?"

"The one who claims she's Chelsea Brownen—although she's not the Chelsea Brownen *I* know."

William rolled his eyes. "Shit, Katherine. How many times do you need to be told? You're sick, for crissakes! If you'd just take that damn pill that Dr. Langly prescribed—"

"You want to push this off onto Dr. Langly? Have it your way. But Langly only said I was anxious and had a depersonalization disorder—"

William slammed his beer down onto the kitchen counter. "What did you say?"

"—and that doesn't cover your little Brownen friend."

William ceased to hear her. Instead, he came at her from the kitchen proper, face slowly taking on shades of red.

"You were in my study, weren't you? Goddammit, you were in my fucking study!"

Katherine suddenly realized that she had betrayed her secret research. She didn't care. "Yes, I was in your damn study. So what?"

William grabbed her by her shoulders and shook her twice. "You stay out of that study; do you hear me?" he shouted.

Katherine was past being afraid. "Why? What are you hiding in there?"

William yanked her from her seat, painfully smacking her ribs against the table edge. "Listen to me, you crazy bitch! I'm not going to sit for you drifting in and out of here and fucking with my life! You'll take that pill, by God, or I'll have you committed to a mental ward. Don't think that I can't or won't do it, because I will before I let you ruin things for me and Will!" He shook her violently. *"Do you understand me?"*

Katherine had been prepared for a confrontation, but this was beyond all her careful calculations. *William* was the one who sounded insane; the rage in his voice was not casual displeasure with her accusations, but true fury.

He shoved her into the chair and raised his fist in her face. "I'm going to take you into the bedroom, and you're going to swallow that damn pill and go to sleep. You don't know what you're dealing with. And if you so much as skip one day of that medication, you'll be sorry! I promise that."

William's words sent a chill down Katherine's spine. This wasn't the man she'd married. The man before her was someone else, a monster that had been hiding for five years. A monster that she had inadvertently uncovered. She would have to step lightly until she could formulate a plan.

In the bedroom, William handed her two of the pills he had brought from the office. Katherine looked at them sitting in her palm. If one had knocked her out, two would keep her that way for a least twenty-four hours. And then how many would her force on her? Five? Ten?

He shoved a paper cup of water in her hand. "Swallow them," he ordered.

After downing the water, William grabbed her jaw and squeezed her mouth open. Satisfied that the pills had been washed down, he released her. "Now get into bed."

The covers had ceased to be comforting earlier that day. Katherine pulled them up under her chin, not wanting to blot out the light that seeped through the drawn curtains.

William observed for a moment from the doorway, and then exited, shutting her in. In the darkness Katherine spat out the bitter pills from their hiding place beneath her tongue, relieved that William had not detected her deception. What he would have done if he had discovered that she hadn't ingested the Thorazine was too awful to contemplate.

*** *** ***

William returned to the bedroom about ten o'clock. He leaned over his wife, making sure she was asleep. Satisfied, he undressed and slid into his half of the bed. Over the past two days his worst nightmares had come to fruition in Katherine. What was she going to do next? Would she continue to take the Thorazine like a good little girl, thereby granting him some time in which to determine a more permanent course of action?

The tranquilizer had side effects. If Katherine took the pills long enough and he continued to increase the dosage, she would become dependent on them and all of William's problems would be solved. His great secrets would remain just that. In the meantime, he would have to make sure that her stability was continually undercut. That shouldn't be too hard. Katherine had almost managed to drive herself mad on her own.

I won't let her remain here, William thought as he closed his eyes. *I can't let her remain her, but until her problem is under control, I have no choice. Maybe things will be different with her in the morning.*

This is my world, dammit, and she has no business in it! Our world, the world we share, lies elsewhere. This one is mine, and I'll do anything to see that it stays that way.

*** *** ***

The hours passed slowly for Katherine as she did her best not to fall asleep. The possibility of William being at the bedside ready to cram pills down her throat when she woke was too great. Next time she might not be able to hide the pills. Next time William might not just manhandle her, he might strike her. The time after that he might break a bone, rape her—God, she could extrapolate the current trend all the way down the line to death at her husband's hands.

I can't stay here, she tried to convince herself as she waited for William to drift off. *I don't care if I'm insane. William has worse problems than I do, and to remain under his roof is only to put myself in jeopardy. I must get away!*

There was no time to contemplate where she was going. As soon as William's breathing become low and rhythmic, Katherine carefully slipped out from under the comforter and grabbed her shoes. Thank God he hadn't forced her to remove her clothes before pushing her into bed.

Katherine retrieved an overnight bag from the hall closet and quietly stuffed it with essentials. She crept from the room carefully closed the door behind her. Being away from William's menacing presence was a relief, even if a thin door was the only barrier between them.

As she headed for the door, an image hit her on so hard on her head hard enough to make a crater: In her mind's eye she saw Little Will, asleep in his bed and dreaming of thwarting the Martian's attempts to conquer Earth. William would be furious enough when he discovered that she was gone. How would he react if she abducted their son? Will was, after all, more attached to William than her. William might not settle for commitment to the funny farm if he caught her with the boy; he might opt for more drastic alternative. Still, the thought of leaving Will with that maniac was terrible.

There was no time to debate her actions. William could wake any moment, discover her missing, and charge from the bedroom with the taste of blood in his mouth. Malice was directed entirely toward her, so it seemed. It was best to escape now and make plans for retrieving the boy later.

Katherine tiptoed out the front door, not knowing where she was bound for, or what was to become of her. No matter. Others were happy to write her destiny for her.

*** *** ***

Several blocks down Newport Boulevard sat the Sea Breeze Motel. Katherine checked in, charging the room to one of William's credit cards (Take that, jerk!). There were no hopes of falling asleep. Insomnia was comforting in a way; she wanted to remain alert and vigilant should William somehow discover where she was hiding. The chances of that seemed low; he would probably storm over to her parent's first, assuming she would seek asylum on the other side of the Marina. If he did contact the Marks family, that only went to show how little he knew his wife. Why in God's name would she retreat to her parents' imposing manor? They had always asserted that she was a mite strange and distancing herself from William would only prove it in their minds. Katherine vividly remembered how confused both Mom and Dad had been when she expressed her reluctance to accept William's proposal of a "personal merger." Why would an Orange County Woman hesitate to marry a doctor? Hell, that was better than snagging a lawyer.

Lack of sleep also allowed her to avoid her strange dreams, a subject that she had not begun to deal with yet. Under the current circumstances, the plastic blizzard was easy to ignore, but it would not remain so indefinitely. The ball was set in motion and gaining speed. Sooner or later, she would have to jump out of its path or become caught up in its descent into the blackness of the crater.

*** *** ***

When the alarm sounded, William rolled over and slapped the snooze button with the palm of his hand. Perhaps in another ten minutes he would be ready to get up and face the day.

He pulled the covers up over his torso and rolled over on his side. He did not see the vacancy beside him as much as he sensed it; the familiar sensation of another's presence was absent.

He sat bolt upright in bed. Katherine's flight had achieved what the alarm clock could not, for he was now wide-awake and raging at full intensity. The Thorazine should have completely anesthetized a woman of Katherine's height and build. Her brain should have been incapable of not only sustaining the dissociative episode, but of concocting an escape plan as well.

The bitch tricked me! William thought. He sprang from the bed and yanked a pair of pants from the closet. Katherine had escaped from the house and into the world at large—*his* world—to wreak havoc. Oh yes, she was still here. William could feel her treading on the sacred ground that he had created by sheer will alone, and for that she was going to pay.

*** *** ***

By fortunate coincidence, a travel agent's office was located next door to the Sea Breeze.

The agent was assisting a customer plan an ocean cruise, so Katherine busied herself by perusing the office. Travel posters and cardboard-backed, freestanding photographs spoke of tempting destinations (the Bahamas, Mazatlan, Paris), but all seemed a tad excessive. Katherine hadn't a vacation in mind. For that matter, she wasn't sure *what* she had in mind. She needed some time away from William and the pressures of being the "perfect" wife but as far as how and where that would be, she hadn't a clue.

Against the wall stood a metal rack filled with brochures for the less glamorous destinations. Katherine thumbed through the pamphlets, hoping one of them would speak to her.

What am I doing? she wondered as she replaced the booklet touting the New Age treasures to be found in New Mexico. *Maybe I could just hole up somewhere nearby until William clams down, and then I could ask for a divorce.*

Lost in thought, Katherine unconsciously removed a brochure from the back of the rack. A shock reverberated through her system, a feeling so awesome and terrible that the world around her smeared for a moment, leaving only herself and the glossy picture on which her eyes were transfixed: Capitol Hill in the wintertime. Snowflakes herded in huge drifts at the base of the stairs that led toward the domed cathedral of her dreams; snowflakes that, captured on film, looked agonizingly plastic.

Help me, please.

"Can I help you?"

Katherine snapped out of her trance to discover that she and the agent were now alone.

The agent took an unconcerned drag on the cigarette that dangled from her lips as Katherine seated herself. Katherine said, "I'd like to go here," and tossed the pamphlet on the desk.

The agent crushed her smoke out in a grungy ashtray. "Washington is beautiful this time of year," the agent said. "When would you like to depart?"

"As soon as possible."

The agent's fingers danced across the keyboard, her long mails clicking on the keys in a neat rhythm. The nails made hollow sound; Katherine's Newport instincts were alerted to the fact that these were cheap press-on nails, not the fashionable acrylic type.

"What class would you like to fly?"

"Whatever's available. I just need to get out of here quick."

The agent's brow wrinkled at the tone of Katherine's voice. She paused for a moment as the request information began to fill the screen. "Oh, there's plenty of flights," she said, running her finger down one column. "The cheapest fare will run you three hundred-fifty, even."

"Three-fifty?" Katherine exclaimed.

"If you waited 'til later summer the fares might be a lot lower."

Katherine thought for a moment. Perhaps if she chose a city a bit less distant.

No. I must go to Washington. I may be crazy after all, but I still must go.

"Well?" the agent asked. She obviously had better things to do than make money for the company.

Katherine dug into her purse and removed a credit card from her wallet. "I'll take the first flight out—the cheapest one, please.

The agent sighed. So much for taking an early lunch; this broad wanted to fly. She took the credit card and slid it through the machine. "Damn, the woman said, glancing at the small screen. She picked up the phone and rang the authorization service. A few seconds later one of the crayon-black eyebrows arched out of curiosity. She handed the phone to Katherine. "Here. They want to talk to you."

"Hello?"

"Mrs. Jameson?" a frigid voice asked.

"Yes?"

"I'm sorry Mrs. Jameson, but the account for the card you're using was closed as of this morning."

"*What?*" Katherine exclaimed. "I didn't close any accounts."

"That may very well be, but the primary cardholder did." the voice replied.

The bastard struck again.

"Can he do that?" Katherine asked.

"Absolutely. The credit card is in his name; you're only an authorized buyer."

Amidst the horror of the situation, Katherine could hear her mother's voice ringing in her ears: *I told you should have started establishing your credit as soon as you were married, but noooooo! Didn't you read the newspaper article I sent you about women who suddenly find themselves widowed and with no credit? But thank God you have your savings account—William can't touch that. You do have your savings, don't you?*

"Yes," Katherine muttered, and returned the phone to the agent. "I guess I won't be needing that plane ticket," she said.

*** *** ***

"*What?*" Katherine exclaimed. "What do you mean I only have a thousand dollars in the account?" She pushed the open passbook across the counter, pointing at the total typed at the bottom of the page. "Your own computer computed this balance, and it says there's over five thousand in there."

The teller shook his head. "You don't understand," he said, pushing his glasses up his oily nose. "Yes, our computer printed that total, but look at the date. That was almost a year ago. You've been using the automated teller since then to make withdrawals but haven't brought the passbook in to be updated."

The clerk took the passbook from Katherine and placed it faced down in a machine on the counter. The printer clicked for what seemed like an eternity before spitting the book back out. He handed the still warm pages to Katherine. "One thousand two dollars and thirty-four cents, Mrs. Jameson," he said. "How do you want it?"

"Fifties, I guess. Maybe a few twenties."

The teller began counting bills as Katherine's spirits hit bottom. If someone had asked her to enumerate the things that could have hampered her escape, the top two would be already crossed off as becoming realities. William must have found her missing quite early in the morning and canceled the only credit card he allowed her to carry. He controlled the checking account as well. It was almost as if he had foreseen her flight years ago. The whole situation was unimaginable, surreal, and yet it was happening around her.

*** *** ***

The Greyhound station was nothing more than a storefront in one of those wretched mini malls. It was a fact of life in Southern California that where there's over watering a frozen yogurt/dry cleaners/one-hour photo combo sprung up.

Katherine purchased a one-way ticket to Washington and sat outside on the bench that had been thoughtfully provided by Greyhound. She shortly entertained the thought of calling her parents for financial help, but they would surely want to know where she was headed, and it was too dangerous to tell them. William was a charmer; all it would take was a simple phone call to worm her secret from them.

Now let's see. I'm going to have to find a place to live first, and then a job—or vice versa—and then...

Katherine sighed. She had hoped that making plans for her new life would be quite involved and occupy her mind the length of the trip-so much for that. She supposed that she could pick up a nice juicy romance somewhere along the way (preferably one involving lusty pirates or virile Indian braves) but in the long run, it was a waste of scarce money. She could always daydream.

After a while, two servicemen pulled into the shopping center in a black Trans Am (the official car of the United States Marine Corps.) A husky private with one continuous eyebrow got out and ventured into the station, eyeing Katherine as he passed.

Ugh, she thought. *It would be just my luck if he was going my way. God, but these buses attract some weird people.*

The bus pulled up just then, relieving Katherine of the toil of a potential conversation with the jarhead, who was evidently going her way.

The driver lazily trundled down to the asphalt, belching, and scratching his ass. Katherine handed him her ticket. He counted her bag and tagged it, returning the baggage claim stubs with the receipt for her passage. "No lose teeket," the driver said. "No get bag then, comprende?"

Katherine nodded.

The driver then opened a compartment on the side of the bus and motioned her to put her bags on board. Katherine frowned and lugged her bag off the curb. Wasn't it in the driver's contract to help with luggage, or did he have some sort of union code that forbade heavy lifting on the job?

She had only been struggling with the bag for a few seconds before she felt a gentle tap on her shoulder. Startled, she dropped the bag and looked over her shoulder. The Marine with the one eyebrow smiled, exposing a two tooth-wide gap in his mouth. "Can I help you with that?" he asked in a soft midwestern accent.

"Please," Katherine replied.

The Marine hoisted her bag into the luggage compartment, along with his own. What a nice man! He had been sorely misjudged.

On board, Katherine found several sets of empty seats among the sea of faceless passengers who couldn't afford to fly. She took the window seat of an empty pair, and her spine immediately began to ache. There was something about the angle at which the backrest was reclined and how it connected to the seat that was totally uncomfortable. That was bad enough, but the tinted green windows were almost too much. The tinting rendered the landscape a most distasteful shade; it was like peering through a huge bowl of lime gelatin. She figured tinting had something to do with ultraviolet rays and skin cancer.

The jarhead sat down next to Katherine. His choice of a seat only confirmed that the morning's travesties had not been isolated occurrences.

"You heading for Vegas?" the Marine asked.

Katherine turned to him, trying not to breathe deeply lest the Old Spice asphyxiate her. "Who, me?" she asked. "No, I'm heading back east."

"Oh."

The Marine farted, coughed, and tugged at his pants, which had a habit of creeping down his butt. "Yeah, I got myself a coupl'a day's leave and figgered that Vegas was a better place to get drunk than L.A."

"Oh. Have you been in the Corps long?" she asked, figuring that feeble conversation was better than silence.

"Five years," he said, wiping his fist-flattened nose with the back of his hand. "It sucks, but what the hell. It's beats goin' to jail. Back in Clarkesville, see—that's in Iowa—I had this girlfriend. Wanna see a picture?"

Without waiting for an answer, the Marine shoved a meaty hand into the back pocket of his jeans and removed a leather wallet. Katherine had to squint through the yellowed plastic to make out the face on the picture he cradled so fondly in his hands.

"She's beautiful," Katherine said, swallowing the truth.

"Ain't she?" he asked with a gaping grin and replaced the wallet in his trousers. "Anyhow, Bess—that's my girl—she kind'a had a rovin' eye. I mean, she's right pretty, ain't she?

She had lotsa boyfriends before me. Well, one night when she was supposed to be at choir practice, I caught her at the drive-in with this squinty-eyed Wop. Boy, did I kick his ass good!" He ran his tongue along his upper gums. "He got a few of my teeth, though."

"Then what happened?"

"Oh, they didn't call it murder, it was mankillin' or something like that..."

"Manslaughter."

The Marine's face brightened. "Yeah, that's it!" he exclaimed. By the expression on his face, the exact term for his crime eluded him for some time. "Manslaughter! He wasn't much of a man though, what, ballin' my girl behind my back. Anyhow, I got off easy, 'cause the judge hated Wops too. He sent me to the Corps instead of jail."

A chill ran down Katherine's spine. This was the sort of person responsible for keeping democracy safe? Then again, if he was a natural killer, he would be even more effective in time of war. Still, serving in the Corps instead of going to jail was a peculiar sentence.

*** *** ***

Las Vegas is but eight hours by car from Los Angeles, but the bus's progress was far from rapid. The driver pulled over to pick someone up or let someone off every five minutes or so, and at that rate, Katherine figured she would reach Washington by the year   or later.

At long last, the bus pulled onto the Strip. It wasn't dark yet, but as Katherine peered through her window, she saw the lights that adorned the casinos were perpetually lit.

So, this is Las Vegas, Katherine thought. *Big deal. It all looks so very tacky.*

The driver swung the bus into the depot and headed for an open parking space. As the vehicle began to slow it was clear that the driver wasn't going to stop in time; Katherine braced herself for the collision with the concrete curb. Baggage flew out of the overheads and passengers were thrown forward in the seats as the bus came to a jarring halt, but none of her fellow passengers complained. Stunt driving, it appeared, was typical of Greyhound.

"Forty Minot meel brayk!" the driver hollered. "Every bodeee off!" He dove out of the bus.

After the nauseating journey, the prospect of eating hardly appealed to Katherine, and neither did spending her time in one of the grotesque casinos. Perhaps the depot was outfitted to waste forty minutes of her time.

The Marine insisted on letting everyone pass before he ventured into the aisle. He turned to Katherine. "Se y'a later," he said.

Katherine smiled feebly. "Have a good time."

Inside the depot, Katherine noticed a small group of people huddled against the far wall of the room. Curious, she approached them to see that they were crowded about three slot machines that were set into the wall. *Gambling!* she thought. *How ridiculous! I've never gambled in my life, and I'm not about to start now.* Katherine shook her head and headed for the rest room.

All the stall doors inside the seedy bathroom were closed. Could they all possibly be in use? Faced with that most vexing of predicaments, Katherine kneeled to see which of the toilets were occupied. To her surprise, they were all empty, and so she chose the center stall out of habit.

She previously had no idea that women had the same propensity for vandalism as she presumed men had. The walls of the stall were covered with graffiti, making for very interesting reading (I HATE DIESELS AND ALL OTHER SLOW, OVERPRICED PIECES OF SHIT to which someone had scrawled the witty reply OH, YOU'RE JUST JEALOUS. I DRIVE A GAS-GUZZLING CADDIE AND LOVE IT!).

After she finished, Katherine chuckled at the poetry one last time, pulled up her pants and opened the stall door. The nice young Marine was standing in front of the stall, brandishing a wickedly curved knife.

"I thought I'd help y'a with one last bag," he said.

Katherine's heart was sucked out of her chest and into a vortex of terror and rage. What in God's name had the country come to when innocent women were robbed in broad daylight? So what that the sun didn't shine in the bathroom—it was daylight somewhere.

Dizzy with fear, Katherine solemnly let her purse strap drop from her shoulder. The purse clattered to the floor.

"Now get back inside that goddamn stall and stay in there for ten minutes or I'll hack your tits off," the Marine snarled, bending to pick up his plunder. He spied the gold wristwatch on Katherine's wrist. "Oh yeah—and give me that watch, too."

"How will I know when ten minutes is up if you take my watch?"

"SHUT UP!" the Marine shouted. *"Now get in that fuckin' stall!"*

Katherine obeyed.

Sitting on the toilet and trembling like a six-year-old at her dread piano recital, Katherine contemplated what to do. She could always go to the police, even if the stall scrawls recommended against it (PIGS DIE! ANARCHY RULES! Or even better HERE I SIT ON THE POOPER/JUST GAVE BIRTH TO ANOTHER STATE TROOPER).

The anarchists were probably right. What could the police do? The chances of nabbing the suspect before he blew her life savings on blackjack were slim. Thank God she had the foresight to stuff two fifty-dollar bills into her bra for security's sake.

Horror dawned in the quiet stall. Katherine shoved her hands into the pockets of her jeans, searching for her bus ticket and baggage claim receipts. All she came up with were a few pills of lint and thirty-nine cents. Surely the bus driver would recognize her. Maybe that way she could put off doing the unthinkable until she arrived at her destination.

Fifteen minutes later (it was better to wait longer in the stall than to risk a dual radical mastectomy) a new gaggle of passengers were lined up at the bus. With hopes running high, Katherine took her place at the end of the queue.

"Ticket please," the driver asked. Where was the Hispanic? This new guy was so Aryan that he probably had relatives who served in the SS.

"Oh, the last driver took my ticket," Katherine said.

The Nazi's brow creased. "No, the last driver only took the first page of your ticket *booklet*," he informed her. "Booklet" was punctuated with a fine spray of spittle.

"No, the driver took the whole thing," Katherine insisted. She was stretching the truth, but maybe the driver would fall for it.

"If the driver took your whole ticket, then you've gone as far as you've paid us to take you," he said, nodded to her and then clicked the heels of his shoes together. "Next."

Other passengers began to push past Katherine. "But my bag is on board!" she protested.

The driver frowned. "Give me your claim ticket."

"Uh—he didn't give me one."

"Then you didn't give him a bag. Good day, *fraulein*."

Alarms began to sound in Katherine's brain as the other passengers continued to shove past her. The week had begun with craters and magical studies, but quickly moved into a string of implausible events that left her high and dry in beautiful Las Vegas. The same part that spurred her on to Washington was vocal once more, telling her that a plot was afoot. It was almost as if the world entered a conspiracy with William; a conspiracy designed to slow her down so he could catch up to her. Falling into William's clutches was the last thing she would allow to happen. She had not yet explored other avenues. The time for the unthinkable was now.

*** *** ***

Katherine chose a telephone that was well in sight of as many passengers as possible lest the Marine return and try to rob her out of her last hundred dollars.

"Operator."

"I'd like to make a collect call please."

"Name please."

"Katherine."

"Number?"

"Seven-one-four, five-five-five-six-seven-zero."

"One moment."

The phone rang twice, three times. Four rings, five. Mom and Dad had sure as hell better not be out on the golf course. Their daughter's fate was dangling by a fiber-optic cable.

The operator would soon tell her to try again later, in fact, Katherine heard the women take in a breath—and then a male voice answered.

"Hello?"

Was that her father? His voice was strained, almost peculiar.

"This is a collect call from Katherine," the operator said. "Will you accept the charges?"

Silence for a moment, and then "Yes."

She didn't wait for a greeting. "Thank God your home, Dad! You won't believe the terrible thing that just happened to me—"

"I knew you'd call here sooner or later."

Katherine cringed at the sound of William's voice. Penetrating cold swept over her entire body, freezing her brain and blood and vocal cords. The frosty phone clung to her ear though she desperately wanted to hang up and run away screaming.

"I was going to give you another chance—I *offered* you another fucking chance—but this disease is the last straw! You can try to wipe out everyone around me, but you can't touch their master! You've crossed me on every level imaginable, and now you're going to pay. Go ahead and keep running, bitch. I'll find you sooner or later. There's no hiding in here. It would have been so much easier for you to accept what's happening to you as insanity, but now it's too late. I should have known what you were capable of, but I didn't. *When I get my hands on you, you'll*

HOWARD SCOTT SHUFORD

wish you'd never stumbled across this place!"
*** *** ***

CHAPTER FOUR: BILLY

"Is that you, Billy?" Dirk called from the bedroom.

"Yeah, it's me."

In a moment Dirk appeared in the doorway, clad in nothing but boxers shorts. The sight of Dirk's iron-pumped physique made Billy painfully aware of his own perceived shortcomings.

"Some chick came by looking for you," Dirk said. "It wasn't that Rachel girl, some older gal." He disappeared back into the room to dress.

That Rachel girl. It was a derogatory phrase. Dirk obviously hadn't taken a shine to Rachel the way Billy had. Good.

"What's her problem, anyway?"

Billy set his backpack down and leaned against the bedroom doorjamb. "What do you mean?" he asked.

Dirk pulled his jeans up. "Rachel's a druggie, right?"

"Give me a break," Billy retorted. "She just likes to party."

Dirk shrugged. "Anyone who likes to party that much has to be runnin' from something."

Now there was a thought. Billy knew all about running away from oneself. Maybe he should meter his substance intake. "So...what'd this girl look like?"

"A lot like Rachel, but older, like I said."

After Dirk left for points unknown, Billy sat at his desk, wondering what to do. The phone wouldn't be up and working until Wednesday, and the prospect of making the hike to Beirut only for Mizzy to say something stupid did not appeal to him. If it were important, she'd come back.

A lit like Rachel, but older. A druggie.

Now what the hell could it be that Mizzy was running from? Mizzy was the one of the few people that Billy thought had it all together. She always knew where she was going and what she wanted.

Maybe I'm not such a freak after all, Billy thought. *Maybe everyone has something they're running from, but we all do it in different ways. Rachel and my sister drink and do who knows what else. Dirk is a compulsive athlete. Susan overeats. And me? I crawl into a corner of my mind and think about things that I can't prove exist yet know are real. What's the difference?*

Maybe everyone on the face of the Earth feels just as empty as I do.

He sighed and peered out the window in front of him. There had to be answers to life's questions somewhere. Maybe God had a monopoly on them. Maybe there wasn't a God at all. And yet Billy couldn't help but feel that someone somewhere was pulling the strings.

Ten minutes later, someone knocked at the door. It had to be Mizzy or Rachel—Billy didn't know anyone else besides Dirk, and he had a key. He rose from the desk and opened the door.

Mizzy sailed into the suite and deposited herself on the couch that was built to order for the university by the kindly inmates of San Quentin. "Hi y'a," she said.

Billy closed the door. He couldn't help but look at his sister in a sudden new light due to Dirk's comments.

"What's the matter, Billy? You look sorta down."

Not brave enough to sit on the couch beside her, he leaned against the wall. "I was thinking."

"You think too much." She glanced around the suite. Things had changed since she had been there last. Dirk had hung posters of half-naked, oiled women reclining on the hoods of sport cars. "Don't tell me your roommate's undersexed, too," she said.

"No, he's a jock," Billy replied, as if Dirk's penchant for sports was the core of his psyche.

"Yeah, I saw him. What a stud!"

Silence passed between them.

"So how are you getting on with this Rachel?"

"Fine, I guess."

"You guess? I would have guessed that you never guessed at anything, Mr. Know-It-All. Anyhow, I came over here to help you out."

"Oh?"

"Yeah. Nice of me, huh? Some of the Greeks are throwing a big bash on Friday and you and your girl are invited."

"Really?" he asked.

"Well, technically. I mean, you'll be riding the tails of my invitation to the gig but who cares? There'll be so many people there that no one would notice if you slipped in. It's the Kappa house. Eight o'clock."

"Well, I don't know..."

Mizzy rolled her brown eyes. Billy could see a blob of eyeliner that floated on the white of her left eye. "What do you mean, you don't know?" she asked. "Come on, Billy! This will be your first college party! You'll never forget it."

Billy sighed. Something told him that his sister was right.

*** *** ***

Billy told Rachel that he would come upstairs and get her when he was ready to head over to the party, but she didn't wait. She pounded on his door a little after eight PM.

"You're early," he said. Rachel had obviously come down for a cocktail.

She stood in the doorway, shaking her head. "I thought we were going to a party," she said.

Billy turned from the closet, confused. "Aren't we?" he asked.

"From the looks of you, we're going to a funeral." The need for a drink was suddenly overridden; Rachel headed for Dirk's side of the room and opened his closet.

"What are you doing?" Billy asked.

"I'm trying to find something to wear."

"What's wrong with what I've got on?" he asked.

"You look like a pall bearer! Here. Put this on."

Without turning from Dirk's clothes, she handed him a pale blue, oversized shirt.

"It's too big!" Billy protested.

"It's made that way. Oh, and put these on, too."

Billy took the white pair of Levi's and the pair of sneakers from her and shrugged. If this was what Rachel wanted him to wear, he'd wear it. In fact, if Rachel had told him to jump off the proverbial cliff, he probably would have done that too.

"Do you think Dirk will mind that I'm borrowing his clothes?"

"That moron?" Rachel asked. "He'll be so worn out when he gets back from his silly little camp-out that he won't notice a thing. Besides, we'll slip them into his closet before he comes back. Now get dressed."

Billy looked around the room for an embarrassed moment. "Do you mind stepping into the living room?"

Rachel rolled her eyes. "For crying out loud! Last night you took ol off almost all your clothes in front of me, and now you want me to leave? Whatever." She exited.

He blushed once she left the room, finally having learned how to hold that rush of blood off until he was alone. Yes, he had disrobed last night, but had forgotten it.

"Are you done yet?" Rachel called.

"Yeah." Billy said, saddened even more by the fit of muscular Dirk's clothes.

"Then let's get going. We don't want the kegs to be empty by the time we get there."

Rachel stopped just before the door and placed her hands on her hips. *What's wrong now?* Billy wondered.

"For God's sake, Billy! Don't you read *GQ*? Take your socks off!"

"Oh, all right, I'll do it. But if I catch athlete's foot, it'll be your fault."

When Billy was finished, Rachel stepped back and admired her handiwork. "I'd say the whole ensemble looks pretty damn good."

"It would probably look better on Dirk," Billy said out of the corner of his mouth.

He had hardly uttered his self-defeatism before Rachel was upon him, planting a wet, teasing kiss on his cheek. She pressed herself against him in a way that made Billy's world spin for a moment, as if he had just downed a cup of   proof rum.

"You look terrific," she said. "Now let's go."

*** *** ***

Mike wound his way through the crowd that already had jammed the lower level of the frat house. It wasn't long before a partying co-ed grabbed his rear. He turned to see Mizzy don a fetching smile. She threw her arms around his neck and kissed on his lips.

"Hi Mizzy," he said.

Mizzy broke the embrace and frowned. "God, but you're cold as a cucumber," she yelled over the pounding music.

Mike smiled indifferently and continued his way, leaving Mizzy standing alone.

"Forget him, sweetheart," a voice said behind her. Mizzy turned; she did not know the girl offering the advice, but the girl obviously knew Mike.

"You can forget him if you want, but I'll keep trying," Mizzy said coldly.

The girl smiled knowingly and took a swig form her beer. "Good luck, then," she said. "I fished for six weeks last semester without so much as a nibble. And I'm not the first, either. It's almost as if he's waiting for something—or someone."

The crowd closed in around the girl; the brief conversation was over. Mizzy watched as Mike headed into the kitchen. Despite the unknown coed thought, Mizzy knew that there was more than one way to skin a cat.

*** *** ***

He knew that if he waited long enough that she would come. Mike had no idea what she looked like, but he could feel her radiant presence calling out to him, reaching for him. How many nights had he lain awake in bed, listening for her whispers? More nights that he could remember, he mused. Yes, he would wait. He could wait forever if that was what it took. He had the time.

*** *** ***

The closer Billy drew to the frat house, the more he wished that he had not only given Rachel a welcoming cocktail, but that he had made one for himself as well. He felt like an absolute clod. And Rachel? She was walking alongside if him holding his hand as if he were a baby just learning how to walk.

The party was audible long before it was visible. This was it. There was no turning back now.

Rachel squeezed his hand. "There it is, buddy boy," she said, alluding to the frat house, which had just come into view. "I can smell the puke already."

Great. Billy hadn't had the pleasure of alcohol induced vomiting yet and wasn't looking forward to it. Rachel obviously had and liked it.

Other couples began to join the sidewalk trek to the festivities. To Billy they all looked so comfortable, so *with it*. This was not his element.

"Aren't we going to need to show an invitation to get in the door?" he suddenly asked/hoped.

Rachel shook her head. "Hell no! What do you think this is a tea party? The object of this sort of thing is to get as many people blasted before the cops show up. Relax!"

In the daytime, the simple frat house would not look as threatening as it did now. As far as Billy could surmise, the structure had started out as a modest, two-story colonial-type dwelling, but over the years negligent architects had made bizarre additions, creating a scaled down model of the Winchester Mystery House.

Frat rats had taken the time to hang streamers in the house; this was obvious from the outside because every inch of bunting had been pulled down and trampled into the lawn, along with bottles, cans, and Styrofoam cups. So many people were about that Billy imagined the walls of the house bulging outward to accommodate everyone. The music was so loud that it was nothing but cacophony with a beat.

The interior of the house was worse. Rachel hadn't stopped on the lawn to visit with anyone; she pushed her way through the front door, Billy in tow. Just inside a pile of broken wood and upholstery did its best to trip up the dancers. Had the chair been intentionally trashed, or had it been an accident? Billy could almost hear the inmates of San Quentin lamenting the demise of their handiwork.

"Keep an eye out for the bar!" Rachel shouted in his ear. She had nothing to fear; Billy's liquor radar had been on since the moment they entered.

They continued across the dance floor (which, incidentally, was not limited to the floor, but to the chairs, couches, and tables) in search of drink. Every now and then someone bumped into or stepped on Billy; some offenders muttered slurred apologies, others gave him a dirty look, as if it was his fault for being in the wrong place at the wrong time. There was no way that he was going to enjoy himself.

Someone was fumbling with his hand. He tore his eyes away from the thong to see Rachel trying to get him to grab a soggy paper cup. When had she let go of him?

"Where'd you get this?" Billy asked.

"From the bar, silly," she replied. Billy looked over her shoulder, but people obstructed the view. He shrugged and sniffed at his drink. "Vodka and Coke?"

Rachel said something to him, but it was hard to hear. "What?" he asked.

"I said that I'm going to look for the bathroom, and then we can dance, OK?"

"Oh."

She drifted away into the sea of students and was swallowed by a wave of dancers. Billy was alone in a roomful of strangers, wondering what to do.

Gee, the Christmas lights sure look nice tacked up around the ceiling. What a tasteful decor.

What a load of shit. I've seen Rachel for the last time this evening, I bet. I don't blame her for dumping me. Just look at these people! They look like they know how to have a good time. Me? All I can do is stew in my juices. I don't fit in here and I don't fit in class. Why me? Why do I have to be so goddamned different?

As his eyes roved about the room horror set in, for leaning against the far wall was Mike Cohan. Not only was Billy's displeasure with the party complete, but his whole day was ruined as well. Mike was at home in the classroom and the party as well; this was obviously *his* element. Shit, this might be also his party, for all he knew.

Mike looked so cool and smooth as he talked to other guests. Girls walked by him tossing him an appreciative glance. Billy had to face it: Mike was perfect. He obviously had enough brains to rise above his fellow students, and he had looks and attitude to boot. Mike made Billy feel like an afterthought, a freak.

Distracted by Mike's presence, Billy did not see the couple whose dance put them on a collision course with him. Before Billy knew what was happening there was a three-way collision that knocked Billy's drink from his hand.

The dancing girl laughed, but her partner was not as amused. "Watch where you're going, you stupid asshole." he bellowed.

For a moment Billy had no idea as to what happened, and then he saw the empty cup on the floor and the wet spot on the dancing dude's clothes. And when Billy's presence finally registered on the Greek's mind, the flames of anger were only fanned. "You fuckin' geek! You think that's funny? Why I ought to—" He grabbed Billy by the collar, pulling him toward his doom. The Greek's breath was foul with whatever concoction it was that the hosts were dishing out, and the presence of alcohol in the frat rat's system only made the situation worse.

"Oh, leave him alone," the girl said, giggling. "Can't you see he's just some freshmen dork?"

The Greek could see that, all right. His eyes narrowed,

and as he spoke, spraying Billy with spittle. "Listen you faggot, you don't belong here, got that? Get your fucking ass out of here before I kick it!" He pushed Billy away and into another couple, who screeched and pushed him back. In that moment Billy saw the room transform into a pit in Hell reserved for freaks like himself; the transformation was an expression of what the larger world outside would surely be like should he venture outside of academia. Everyone was watching and laughing (they weren't, for amidst the chaos of the party no one noticed the accident) and Billy had to get out before he went down for the third time and drowned in his contempt for his own self.

And so, before anyone had the chance to hit him, Billy headed for the door. Getting out was no easy feat, especially if he wasn't planning on bumping into anyone else and causing another altercation. Collegemates were dancing with no regard for their neighbor, but after a minute or two of effort outside cool air began to reach Billy's nostrils.

Meanwhile, Mike was canvassing the chaotic fête from the other side of the room. By now the revelers were switching into high gear and began to drift upstairs to the pharmacy. Selling cocaine was the best fund-raising activity the fraternity had yet devised. It sure beat the pants off a car wash.

The music paused for a moment as the current album ended and the DJ fumbled for a replacement. A tiny sound reached Mike's ears; it was the sound of a little bell that perhaps belonged at the end of tassel on a child's Christmas stocking. Curious, Mike sought out the source of the sound.

The bell tinkled in his brain even after the deafening music resumed, like an itch that refused to be quieted by even the most diligent scratching. Could the sound be coming from the kitchen?

Mesmerized, Mike floated toward the sound. It was coming from the kitchen, but when he pushed his way past an entwined couple blocking its entrance, he found the kitchen empty. His eyes scanned the room with his ears not too far behind, but the divine music had ceased playing. Perhaps it had been a hallucination brought on by the coke and whiskey. Something told him differently. Mystified, Mike leaned against the refrigerator to wait out the disturbance.

Mike looked up from the floor at the door, his eyes drawn there apparently for no reason. Barely a second later a young woman floated into the room, her deep eyes searching for an unknown quarry. So strong was her presence that for a moment Mike thought he had lost contact with reality all together; his brain spun in his skull, coming to rest slightly askew of its former position. The waiting was over.

"Do you know where the hell the bathroom is in this dump?" Rachel asked.

Mike folded his brown arms in front of him and flashed a sly smile. "Maybe," he replied. "What's your name?"

"John Brown. Ask me again and I'll knock you down,"

"I tell you what, Miss Brown: if you dance with me, I'll tell you where the can is."

Rachel shrugged. "It's a deal, but if I pee on your shoes, it's your own fault." She sashayed into the living room *cum* dance floor, her eyes giving Mike the once over as she passed. Mike had received the same more-than-casual glance many times before, but the weight of Rachel's gaze was heavy enough to push him back against the refrigerator door before he was yanked from his shoes, caught in her force field.

*** *** ***

In the meantime, Billy Reltin had made his way out of the house and past the littered lawn. He paused at the edge of the sidewalk, toes hanging dangerously over the curb, ready to leap into the depths of the gutter. His already low self-esteem, confidence and entire countenance had been shrunk so small by the business inside the frat house that the tiny distance between the curb and the street was space enough to drown in. One small step and then the torrential trickle of water would carry him down through the storm drain and into the sewer where he could mingle with the socially unacceptable filth he had vainly aspired to escape from.

At the exact instance before Billy jumped, his mind flashed on one of his mother's favorite songs:
*"You better look before you leap,
'Cause there's water running deep,
And there won't always be someone there to pull you
Out...
...I beg your pardon,
I never promised you a rose garden..."*

Oh God, it was that horrible Lynn Anderson song. It was easy for her to say, "smile for a while and let's be jolly," because as far as Billy knew, no frat rat had threatened to kick her ass.

Then again, what had he expected? Carte blanche in a new, more popular world? Hardly. Mizzy *hadn't* promised him a rose garden, just an invitation. Ah, but there was a rose inside after all, a single, solitary flower: Rachel.

"Fuck it," Billy said to the leaf that floated past his toes. He hastily calculated the probability of bumping into the same Greek Joe, and, finding it low, decided that the risk involved was worth endangering himself.

With the initial shock of the party's size and volume dissipated, the house was less threatening. Billy scanned the room for the ever-elusive bar, where Rachel was undoubtedly waiting for him.

Perhaps the bar was located near the stereo system. This was logical, because in that corner of the room was the only space not occupied by revelers. Billy slid against the wall toward the far side of the room, careful not to contact anyone who wasn't too drunk to notice. This was perhaps the most dangerous stunt he could perform, for the closer her drew to the booming speakers, the harder the beat thudded against his chest. By the time he reached the system, his teeth were painfully chattering with the percussion track. Billy feared that if Rachel *was* nearby, her brain was probably so damaged by the sonic bombardment that she wouldn't recognize him.

Where the hell was Rachel? There was a slim chance that she was still in the bathroom. Living under the same roof with

Mizzy for sixteen years taught Billy that women took more than twice the time to relive them as men did. Perhaps if he moved to a quieter, less painful spot he could spy her blond locks as she returned from the can.

The air inside the house was redolent of tobacco, alcohol, and marijuana and so Billy chose to wait for Rachel near the front door. There, not only would he catch a few wisps of fresh air, but also an escape route was readily available should his assailant return.

The music faded momentarily, then roared back to life with renewed ferocity. Billy waited and waited, his head growing light as the alcohol seeped into his brain, accompanied by the THC suspended in the second-hand pot smoke. Before him a sea of bodies gyrated, faces turned to ceiling and eyes rolled back in their heads as they danced in ecstasy, led closer to the infinite by chemicals and rhythm.

Moses drifted by arms lifted toward heavens. On his command the waves of the sea parted, and there in the dry basin Billy saw Mike and Rachel. Rachel gyrated, teased, and mocked with her hips, making love to the music. She was tantalizingly close to Mike, within his grasp one moment, then backing away, casually stepping around the fish at her feet, fish that longed for the ocean to swallow and drown them again. And the sea did just that. In a moment Moses moved on and the wave of dancers filled the void, drowning whatever forces Pharaoh Billy I could muster. In the face of defeat, Billy retreated into the night.

*** *** ***

As Billy made the agonizing pilgrimage back to the dormitory, such was his anguish that not even throwing himself into the storm drain to take his chances with piss and shit and Pennywise the Dancing Clown would end the torment he felt in his soul. Knowing his luck, someone somewhere wouldn't rule out the stunt a suicide, and he would be cast into the circle of purgatory where the rest of the envious dwell. And when he eventually managed to work off his sin, he would surely rise no further than earthly paradise.

"Look kid, I can take you only so far," Virgil would say to him. "You've come this far on brains, but *that* ticket booklet is empty. I can't give you the coupon that gets you into the Higher Realms."

Above, the heavenly Rachel gazes down from the Premium Mobile with Beatrice and Mike at her side, all chuckling at the fact that poor Billy Reltin is unable to escape from human wisdom and reason into the perfectly ordered world of the sublime nine circles of heaven. Those circles were reserved for the celestial bodies and their creator, not the nerdy scum.

And then the shit would *really* hit the fan. Disgusted, Billy casts his lowly eyes to the ground and says "Goddammit, but this really *sucks*."

Click --WHOOOOOSH!

Below him a trap door falls open, and before Billy knows what is happening, he is falling past the sewers and Pennywise and purgatory, straight for the *other* nine circles: Hell. God certainly didn't have a spot in his heart for punks who went around telling him what to damn and what not to.

Landing flat on his ass, Billy would open his eyes to the circle that will be his home for the rest of eternity. Misshapen creatures with extended keyboard teeth, modem genitals, and pustulant CPU brains exposed by trepanned video displays shamble forward with new hardware for Billy to try out.

"One of us. One of us. One of us..."

*** *** ***

Billy sat down at his desk and desperately fought back tears. He wouldn't allow himself to cry. No, he *couldn't* cry. It didn't matter if this was 2020 and men were supposed to be sensitive; crying would only add another cup of lemon juice to the already sour cake of shame he was so masterfully baking.

"Fuck Rachel," he said to himself to console himself. Maybe God would be merciful and deem her a traitor. That way, she would spend eternity being chewed like a cud in one of Satan's dark maws with Judas and Brutus. *Et tu, Rachel.*

Depressed, Billy sat down at his desk in a moment that fed

his agony. For as long as he could remember he had stood outside of the mainstream, watching happy people drift down the river of life while he was trapped in his miserable little eddy. He had watched from the edge of the elementary school playground as other boys played frenzied, chaotic versions of soccer or softball, knowing full well that he would only make a fool of himself if the others agreed to let him play.

The same scenario repeated itself in junior high school, only then the Phys Ed teacher *forced* Billy into the group where, yes, he *did* humiliate himself. There was no sense in dredging up exactly what happened or what was said, the thinnest of associations brought the fullness of the pain back, hitting him harder than any of the playground bullies ever could.

And then eighth grade hit, and he was given an aptitude test—and another, and then another. Mr. And Ms. Reltin, your son's a fucking genius!

Genius. The word has a distasteful ring, like "penis"—something one never said outside of an anatomy lecture. In such cases, "cock" or "dick" was more appropriate, and as for euphemisms for "genius," there were none. Genius had no place outside of academia. A label had finally been attached to Billy's "problem" which, in his eyes, was not a gift but a curse. Every man has a penis, but very few have genius. Billy was, therefore, a freak.

He sighed and reached for his well-worn paperback of Ciardi's translation of *Inferno* that sat in the slim bookcase next to the desk. The book automatically fell open to a special page: the page on which Dante crossed the fault line between earth he lived upon and the realms beyond. Inscribed above that most terrible gate are words that Billy was sure he would never forget:

> *Sacred justice moved my Architect.*
> *I was raised here by divine omnipotence,*
> *Primordial live and ultimate intellect.*
>
> *Only these elements time cannot wear*

Were made before me, and beyond time I stand.
Abandon all hope ye who enter here.

The entrance to Darkham University might as well bear the same inscription as the gates of Hell.

Enough, his mind cried. *Enough of this self-pity. What happened tonight was nothing new, so get off your ass and do something to take your mind off it. Lose yourself in your genius. That always seems to help.*

Indeed, there were plenty of things to do. What about his thesis? He could doodle, maybe think up a few wild concepts worthy of testing...

With a plan firmly in mind, Billy opened the desk drawer to retrieve some paper—paper that rested beneath the plastic bag and its magic contents. A thought so alien grazed his consciousness that he wondered where it came from: Dirk was gone for the weekend and Rachel had abandoned him, so why not perform an experiment in the confines of his room? Sure, it was Rachel's LSD, and she had saved in hopes of their dropping acid together. He'd show her!

Billy carefully removed a slip of rice paper from the bag and held it up to the light. It looked innocent enough, but every scientist knows that looks are deceiving.

Fuck looks. He opened his mouth.

-What are you doing? his brain screamed. *For God's sake man, think! You might be on the verge of destroying a part of your precious mind. Don't do it! Don't—*

Too late. Billy closed his mouth and stretched out on the floor.

For a few minutes, he felt no new sensations other than a bitter taste in his mouth. And then slowly the ceiling was replaced by stars of a drug-induced nighttime, and he was swept away on the tide of neurotransmitters the LSD pumped into the synapses of his brain. That which was below the surface did not raise to the top. Instead, Billy plunged beneath the waters and met the theory at the bottom of the boundless sea. It was done in a dangerous, illicit way, but the surface if the thought pond had been breached all the same.

From the void, a voice. Hushed at first, then growing louder. The world was trembling, shaking. His name rang out in the darkness, echoing inside his skull.

Billy slowly opened his eyes. Rachel was squatting over him; hands on his shoulders as she shook him awake.

"Jesus Billy, I thought you were dead!"

Billy slowly sat up, his stomach churning with nausea. Sunlight streamed in through the window above the desk; outside, the ivy-covered buildings of Darkham U. were shaking of the ill effects of last night's various fêtes.

"Billy...? Are you OK?"

"I'm fine," he growled, trying to stand. His legs were wobbly beneath him; they sought refuge in the chair at his desk.

Rachel watched him keenly, apparently puzzled by his sharp reaction to her concern. "You don't sound fine," she said.

Billy stared out of the window. "Wow, you're really observant," he said sarcastically.

Rachel brushed his callousness off. "What happened to you last night? I looked all over the place for you, but I couldn't find you."

"I was there," Billy spat. "Oh, and by the way, you and Mike Cohan make a great couple."

"Oh, fer cryin' out loud! One dance! *One*."

"One's all it takes. You looked like you were going to blow him right there on the living room carpet." Those were not his words, no, they were right out of the pages of *Penthouse*. Perhaps he had learned something useful from those magazines after all.

Behind him, Rachel shook her head. "You're jealous, aren't you?"

Billy turned to her with rare anger in his eyes. "Another brilliant deduction, Ms. Holmes."

Rachel ran her slender fingers through her hair, hair that Billy wanted so desperately to run *his* fingers through, hair that Mike Cohan had probably spoiled with his vile touch. "You men are all the same," she said wistfully. "You see what you want and that somehow makes it yours. You want me to lay things on the line for you, just like I did with Mike?"

"Please. I'm hanging on your every word."

"I bet you are. It's like this: no one takes me unless I give myself away. Yeah, Mike's cute, but that only goes so far. And you, you're smart, and a nice guy, but that only goes so far, too. None of you guys get much further than that. You all think you can build a bridge between yourselves and us women with your dicks, but I've never met anyone hung low enough to do that. So, what's the answer? I dunno. It's a sort of game, and may the best man win. Know what I mean?"

Billy knew what she meant, all right. She was teasing him, giving him false hopes when Mike had already won. He turned back to the window, drumming his fingers on the desk. Rachel waited for his next move, watching his pinky hit the desktop, his index finger, middle finger, and then that fourth, useless digit landed on the open plastic bag. She smiled to herself. Perhaps Billy was going to play the game after all.

"So, you stormed back here and dropped acid, huh?"

Shocked at her revelation, Billy unconsciously looked down at the bag beneath his finger.

"God, you've got balls. What if you'd had a bad trip?"

He was silent for a moment, not able to think of a snappy retort. "It wasn't that big of a deal."

Rachel leaned over him, putting both of her hands on his shoulders, melting his defenses. Devil Woman! Rachel was surely an incarnation of Helen of Troy, ready to start a war at a moment's notice.

"Not that big of a deal?" Helen cooed. "You're not stupid, so you must be a lunatic. What's that you're working on?"

"What?"

"Those papers?"

"*What* papers?"

"Right there in front of you, silly."

A neat stack of graph paper had been piled conspicuously

on the desk before him. Billy examined the first page. It was undoubtedly written in his script, even if the letters had a queer, almost forged quality. "I must have written this junk last night," Billy mumbled. "Yeah, I think I remember now."

Rachel leaned closer; against his back Billy could feel the gentle rise and fall of her breasts, but he was too perplexed with his writings to become aroused.

"You wrote this stuff while on acid?" Rachel asked. "Cool."

Billy absently picked up the second page, which was dominated by a diagram meticulously drawn with a compass and pen: three circles intersected by three rays, each with the common origin of point "Z."

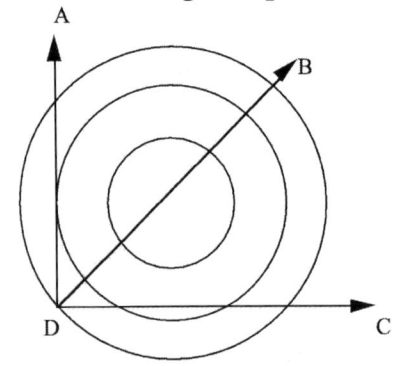

"What does that picture mean?" Rachel asked.

Billy's reply had a ghostly tone, as if it came from a part of him other than his mouth. "I was trying to think of a pathway through the inner circles and out the other side, to the higher ones."

"Oh. Did you find one?"

"I guess not."

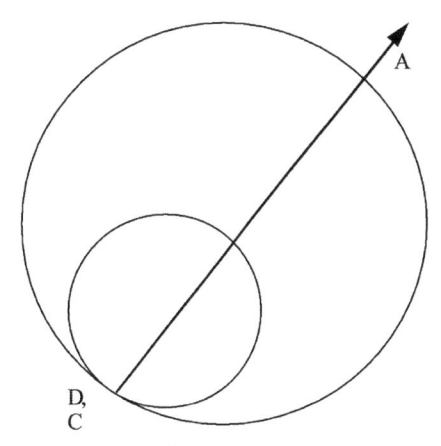

On the next page was another diagram corralled in a box. There was no angle here, only a ray that started at point "D" (Or was that supposed to be "C?") that passed through point "A."

"Where's the line that starts with point D?" Rachel asked.

"What?"

"You have the same point labeled "C" and "D." That doesn't make any sense. Even I've had enough geometry to know you're not supposed to do that."

"It's not a line. Lines go on forever in both directions. It's a ray. And you can't see it."

"Oh yeah, an invisible ray," Rachel said jokingly.

"No, it's not invisible, I just don't know where it is." He chuckled. "Maybe it's in the alternate universe." He thought for a moment. "I can't put my finger on it, but I feel like I'm missing some critical piece to the puzzle. And I'm not so sure I want to find out what it is."

Just what the puzzle or its missing piece was, Rachel didn't ask.

*** *** ***

For the rest of the weekend, Billy was consumed by his mysterious work. Rachel hovered over him, intensely interested in the project, although Billy knew she couldn't possibly understand the project's implications.

Monday saw boredom swim back and slap Billy in the face. True, the weekend had been productive, but that did not outweigh the burden of daily classed. Just when it seemed that life was unbearable (that was by Wednesday), things picked up. Billy was walking past the Physics office on his way back to the dorm when he heard a voice behind him.

"Billy?"

It was Dr. Racken. He was leaning out of the office and was obviously pleased to see his pupil.

"Yes?"

"If you're not on your way to class, I'd like to speak with you."

Racken closed the door to his office, motioning to a chair. "Sit down, son," he said.

As Billy sat, he immediately recognized the packet of papers on the doctor's desk: the same parcel he had dropped in Racken's box on Monday afternoon.

Racken lowered his glasses onto his beak and cleared his throat. "Frankly Billy, I was a bit surprised when I saw that you had turned in a proposal for thesis work so quickly, but I must say that I'm quite impressed. I—well, I'm at a loss for words. What you propose is radical, but conceivable. I cannot communicate to you my feelings as I read the report. It's some of the most bizarre theoretical work I've ever read but everything follows. I'd be inclined to say you're crazy if it wasn't so well thought out. The work does seem, however, to lack a conclusion. What do you expect to find?"

"You wouldn't believe me if I told you. You'd *definitely* tell me I'm crazy."

Racken grinned and rocked back in his chair. "Well? Are you crazy?"

"Not that I know of."

"Then try me."

Billy drew in a deep breath. "Well sir, I think I've discovered a chink in what we assume is the true structure of the universe. A quantum loophole, so to speak. Theoreticians can talk all they want about parallel universes and glitches in space-time, but no one can demonstrate that any of it is true beyond computer simulations and equations. Ultimately, I hope to either find what others have proposed, or discover where they went wrong and provide an alternate theory."

Racken laughed. "That sounds like the work of a lifetime, not a three-unit course. If we let you hurl atoms at each other as you propose, what do you expect will happen?"

"I don't have any expectations at all."

"Ah, but that's not sound science. The eyes see what the mind anticipates."

Billy nodded. "And there," he said, "is the rub. Any physicist can design an experiment to prove that light behaves like a stream of particles, and he can similarly demonstrate that light behaves like a wave of energy. We say light is both; that it is dualistic in nature. In that sense, the anticipation of the result *dictates* the result. Instead of being precise, why can't we be imprecise? Why not approach a new experiment with no expectations whatsoever? The experiment is then free to run its true course."

Racken's face went slack with contemplation. Billy was sure that at any moment the good doctor would shake his head and reject the entire project, but that didn't happen.

"Give me a day or two to think about it," Racken said finally. "If I decide to back the project, we'll do it without submitting a formal proposal for funds. The department would never dole out money without something more concrete than what you have here. In the meantime, I think you should look for something more concrete to write your thesis on. Just in case."

Just in case. Oh, sure. Just in case meant that Racken already anticipated the outcome of his deliberation and that Billy's proposal would ultimately be rejected.

After Billy left, Racken flipped through the proposal once more, drawn to the more philosophical portions of the document:

"Modern physics is a hodgepodge of vexing theories that assert that the universe we live in is not the only one, that is linked to others by infinitesimal gaps in the fabric of space-time to parallel

universes which may or may not be governed by the laws which are evident in our own. Even within our own cosmos there is more than meets the eye: hypersymmetry over multiple dimensions, a unified force that eluded even Einstein, links between consciousness and matter that may never be fully understood. Instead of searching for an answer that links these complications to the body of knowledge we already hold, perhaps we should discard what we have learned and start with a clean slate, a tabula rasa..."

Racken swiveled in his chair and gazed out of the window at the park that was the centerpiece of Darkham University. Billy's words were not those of a seasoned researcher. They were the words of young man who had read *The Tao of Physics* and *Synchronicity* too many times for his own good.

On the lawn, a small, golden-haired boy was playing an unfathomable game with an imaginary friend. The boy flung his gold ball into the air, watching as it returned to Earth in a path dictated by the forces of nature, not the laws men write to describe them. The ball bounced, came to a stop; the boy retrieved it the game began anew.

Watching the boy at play, Racken decided that Billy's proposal research was absurd and pointless. Yet there was something attractive about the idea of the illogic the budding genius had scrawled in the throes of an acid trip.

There *was* another force additional to those physicists were comfortable with, and that force lay behind Billy's words. It was a force that conceived empires, built them, brought them to their knees; a force that molded the cosmos as well as brought it meaning; a force that caused unwary housewives to slip from their husbands' world and into one of their own.

At Darkham University, the force was too strong for Racken to overcome. He decided to allow Billy a few precious days with the cyclotron in order to amass hard data for a grant proposal. Billy's—and Katherine's—fates were sealed.

*** *** ***

When Mike entered Racken's class on Friday, he immediately noted that the class was buzzing with some urgent news. The group of desks where he and his buddies always sat was a knot of discussion that failed to unravel as Mike sat down. "What's up?" he asked.

Max, a hawk-nosed Kappa brother, turned to Mike in disbelief. "You mean you haven't heard about that Reltin kid?"

"You mean that dork genius? What he'd do, blow himself up in the lab?"

Max shook his head. "Worse. He turned some weird proposal into Racken, and he snorted the whole thing up his nose like it was a kilo of the best coke you've ever had. Now we have to "observe" Reltin's bullshit experiments."

Mike had to clench his teeth to keep from frowning. Billy's quick popularity with the faculty wasn't a good sign. There was room enough for only one star pupil. Perhaps it was time to start thinking of ways to bring Billy Reltin down a few notches—better yet, to grind him into the dirt.

*** *** ***

The brain and nervous system of Darkham's particle accelerator was housed in a small underground chamber, while the guts of the system ran along narrow corridors beneath the campus' central park.

The Senior Thesis Methods class packed themselves into the tiny space that was made unbearably hot by computers and other electronic equipment. Billy was seated at a computer terminal in one corner; Dr. Racken stood watching over his shoulder.

Max tapped Mike on the shoulder as Billy prepared for the experiment. "What the heck is he trying to do?" he asked.

Mike shook his head. "Who knows and who cares? He's full of shit."

"If Billy's full of shit, why won't Racken tell us what he's doing? They must be onto something big."

Mike whipped his head around to face Max, anger straining his blue eyes. "I told you: Billy's full of shit. There's nothing special about him. *Nothing.*"

Mike was too blind to see it, but the look in Max's eyes

revealed that the other Kappa was not convinced. Furthermore, there was not merely distaste for Billy in Mike's voice, but something that approached absolute hatred. History spoke for itself, for no one that Mike disliked lasted for long in the department.

Billy hit the master computer's entry key one final time and then turned to the other students. "For this preliminary experiment, I am merely seeking to play subatomic billiards, if you will," he began. "A single electron will be accelerated to a random velocity and then strike a neutron target at a random angle. Several runs will be processed, and the angular relationships of the collision results will be studied as a sort of calibration for further collision experiments."

Mike rolled his eyes. What was the point of such elementary nonsense? It just went to show that Billy had somehow duped Racken and was merely spinning his wheels.

The accelerator's powerful electromagnets began to hum with life. In a moment an electron was isolated from its source and began to careen through the track piping, propelled by the oscillating magnetic fields. Faster and faster it sped around the track, topping out at a velocity a fraction under the speed of light. As the electron circled the park one last time, a new magnetic field was created near the control chamber, diverting the projectile toward its target.

The experiment was completed in just under a couple of seconds. The terminal's screen went blank as the computer and its sensors began to trace the path of the electron and the result of the collision. Billy cast a glance over his shoulder at Dr. Racken, who scratched his chin in anticipation of the results.

The waiting was the hardest part. One of the obstacles the nuclear scientist must face is that he cannot see the reactants or the products. Subatomic particles are so infinitesimally small that not even the most powerful of microscopes can magnify them to a visual level. The scientist is forced to find other methods of examination. In this case, Darkham's fantastic computer was connected to sensors in the accelerator and collision chamber by which a given number of particles' progress could be charted. Sensors fed the information to the mainframe, which then created a line drawing and equations that described the nearly invisible events. All of this took time, and though it was but a few minutes, it was an eternity to Billy.

What if someone told you that everything you held in mind as truth was a lie? What if—

The terminal's screen blinked, and data appeared, Billy squinted at the picture.

No. It can't be. Something had to have gone wrong. I knew it had; I didn't feel anything when the electron struck the neutron.

Racken was soon peering over Billy's shoulder. He too did not understand what had happened. Billy turned his head' his eyes met with those of his instructor.

"Try it again," Racken said.

*** *** ***

It was two hours later when Billy finally turned the system off. The other students were long gone; only he and Racken remained in the dungeon of a laboratory.

"The composite is coming up in a moment," Billy said. "It should be an average of all of the electron's paths."

Racken rubbed his eyes and replaced his glasses; the mound of paper in his lap tumbled to the floor with the rest of the wadded trash.

When the printer finished its work, Billy tore the printout free and looked it over briefly. He then handed it to Dr. Racken.

"What does this mean?" Racken asked. "What's happened?"

Billy sighed and leaned back in his chair. "I wish I knew," he said. "We've been over it twenty times, and it always comes out the same. The electrons vanish-*poof*."

Dr. Racken traced the trail left by the electron with his finger. The electron entered the chamber from the left-hand corner, struck the neutron and then rebounded into a crazy, spinning jig that ended abruptly without a trace. "Vanished?" Racken asked. "Couldn't it have been annihilated?"

Billy shook his head. "See for yourself. There are no readings in the data that indicate any event of that kind. The electron simply entered the chamber, struck the target, and then disappeared."

Racken too began to shake his head. The data was right in front of him, and the numbers were irrefutable. "Where did it go, Billy?" he asked.

"I wish I knew. But I have a feeling that we really don't want to know the answer." Billy said. Happiness that had been generated by the act of performing his experiment had turned to horror born of the results.

There must be some other explanation. There must! But what if...?
Something bubbling just under the surface. Something so close yet so far away...

Earlier, a bewildered Mike stepped out of the accelerator's bunker and into the sunlight, lightheaded and with his thoughts tangled. He wondered if his brain had been fried by a massive dose of radiation from some of the equipment downstairs, although no one else seemed affected by the experiment, not even Billy.

What was it I saw downstairs? What happened? Billy started the cyclotron and then—

There were no precise words for what happened. It was as if his mind had sensed that the veil between this reality and the next had been momentarily pulled aside to let the electron out.

The electron's gone. I don't know how I know that, but I do. That's why they didn't say anything about the results. That's why they shooed us out so quickly. Billy's on to something all right, but neither he, nor Racken saw what I saw. I turned and there they were, staring at the computer but I was somewhere else. I followed the fucking electron! I followed it into space where it became something huge. No, it collided with something huge, an asteroid, or—fuck, I must be going out of my mind!

Maybe I'm special in some way. Billy is consequential. He's a consequence of...what?

The answer to that question was still out of reach. One thing was clear, though: Billy had to be stopped. If anyone should have uncovered the secret Billy had, it should have been Mike himself. Billy was ordinary, a consequence of life that had no claim to fame or glory. If Mike could solve the problem, if he could answer the unanswerable question as to where the electron went, then who knew what power or glory was waiting for him?

I'll take the wind from his sails. I'll complete the experiment. But first, I've got to figure out just what the hell they're doing.

He continued to walk aimlessly; some part of him that was not wrapped up in the Billy problem was guiding his feet toward a run-in with *her*. She was heading across the park too, heading for the freshman dorms.

Oh my God, there she is! I saw her at the party a few weeks ago. The girl with the golden hair and the fair skin.

Drawn to her, Mike's pace quickened as he sought to catch up with his prize. "Well, if it isn't John Brown," he said as he came alongside of her.

Rachel turned her head to see him walking beside her and smiled. "Well, if it isn't the frat rat." she retorted.

Mike watched as her eyes fell to his feet, then up his legs. They lingered for a moment on his muscular chest and torso, and then boldly met his eyes. Mike needn't be told that she was interested.

"You never told me your name," he said. Their pace slowed to a stroll meant to prolong their rendezvous.

"I like to be mysterious," Rachel replied.

"I like a mysterious woman. You're new on campus, right?"

"How did you know?"

"I would have remembered your face from last semester if you weren't. Can we get together sometime? I'd like to get to know you better." Mike's smiled widened as he poured on the charm. How could she resist?

"Maybe. I might stop by your next party."

"I meant before then."

"Let's leave it "sometime." It wouldn't be mysterious if I told you when and where, now would it?"

Teasing bitch! Very few of the women who hung around the Kappa house had as many scruples as this one, making her pursuit more irresistible.

Rachel said nothing more. Her gate quickened and soon she was fading from sight.

"Hey! You never told me your real name!"

"John Brown!" Rachel yelled over her shoulder. "Ask me again and I'll knock you down!"

Tantalizing, infuriating! This was The Game as Mike had never played it before, but he was not to be undone. He followed Rachel's retreating figure at a distance to determine where she was headed. Ah! The freshmen dormitories!

A freshman living on campus. There must be someone around who knows who she is.

Noise. A ball bouncing, feet treading on the pavement. In front of the dorms was a basketball court where some Joe was out shooting hoops. This was going to be easier than Mike thought.

"Hey dude. You wanna play Horse? Loser buys the beer?"

Dirk stopped dribbling the ball and grinned. "You're on," he said, "but I don't drink."

"You will, I bet."

Mike "let" Dirk win the basketball game—at least, that was how Mike's ego saw it. He hadn't a prayer of winning, seeing as Dirk was a member of the Darkham Knights, the university's basketball team. Besides, a six-pack of beer was a small price to pay for important information and a bruised ego.

"Oh, you're talking about Rachel Carter," Dirk said. "If you ask me, she's a flake, not the type of girl I'd go out with. Hey, did you see the Celtics game last night?"

Dirk behaved as if he did not want to talk about the girl, so be it. Mike smiled to himself. John Brown was really Rachel Carter. Now he was one up on her, for he had learned her secret name, the talisman whose power she hoarded for herself.

There was little time for partying over the next few weeks. Billy spent most of his spare time at his desk or in the laboratory, and what time he did have for Rachel seemed less than quality.

"What's going on, Billy?" she asked, pouring him a drink of straight rum into a paper cup.

"What do you mean?"

Rachel handed him the cup and sat on the floor in front of him, obviously preparing for a long, serious discussion. "Is something wrong?"

Billy gulped the rum graciously. "I'm very busy."

"Yeah, I know, but is something wrong? We hardly get a chance to be together anymore, and when we do it seems like all you want to do is get drunk."

"I would have thought that getting drunk was fine by you," he snapped.

"See what's happened? Your mood's changed. You seem, I don't know, upset, like."

There was nothing there to argue about. Rachel was right; Billy was upset, and he desperately wanted to tell someone about it other than Dr. Racken. Racken didn't see where the experiments were going, almost as if he had blind spots that didn't allow him to see the entire scientific picture unless someone like Billy spelled it out for him. And yet there was no confiding in Rachel either. How could she grasp the darkest secrets the Creator (whoever the hell he/she was) had woven into the fabric of the universe?

"You wouldn't understand," he said. "Don't press me on the issue, OK?"

"OK, OK! I'm not trying to piss you off. It's just that I'm a little worried about you, and your sister is too."

"My sister? When did you talk to Mizzy?"

Rachel shrugged, trying to downplay her cards. "Oh, she came around a few days ago when I was waiting here for you. She just wanted to know if something was up. You hadn't been around to see her, and it bugged her, I guess."

What? Mizzy cares? Surprise, surprise!

"We both think you're working too hard," Rachel continued. "There's a party on Friday night and—"

"I can't go."

"Aw, c'mon, Billy! Can't you tear yourself away from that damn computer for a couple of hours so we can have some fun? Please, Billy? All work and no play makes Billy a sourpuss."

He cast his eyes toward the ceiling and God. Why couldn't people understand that he didn't feel like being social? Hell, he didn't even feel like being Billy these days. He was unraveling a secret in the laboratory that was in turn unraveling himself as well, peeling away the layers of personality to find what sat at the very core of his being. And what did he anticipate finding there? Nothing. There were no expectations, only dread that his theories might be right.

"OK, I'll go."

"Great!" Rachel suddenly leaned forward and planted a kiss on his forehead. "You'll have fun, Billy. And you'll see what you've been missing."

*** *** ***

Mike spied the black notebook as soon as he reached the bottom of the stairs. Billy had left it next to the computer terminal, and there was no one around...

He dashed over to the desk and began to flip through the pages. Equations here, notes there... What the hell was all this shit? It might as well have been written in some bizarre code for he could make no sense out of it.

Dammit! There must be something here to go on. Billy can't be so far advanced in his knowledge that I wouldn't be able to understand his work. It's just possible for a consequence to—

Now here was something strange. Toward the back of the book were pages that had nothing but circles on them, circles drawn in almost every conceivable configuration. The corner of the last page was marked with a hot pink highlighter pen.

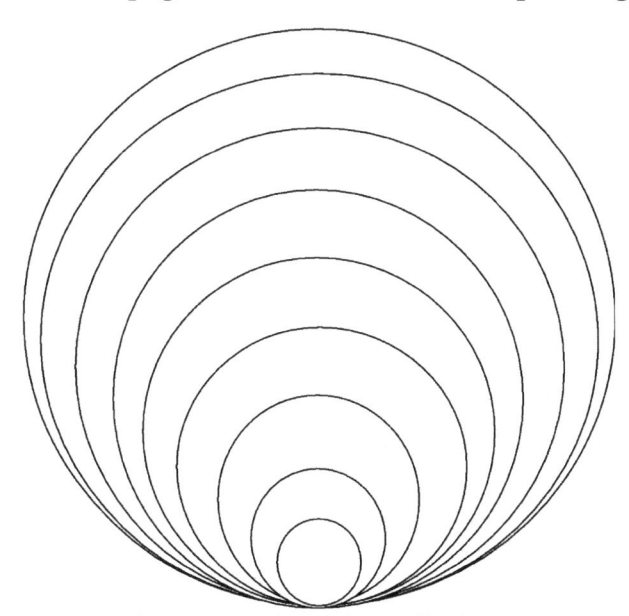

Nine nested circles, all sharing a common point. There were no notes on the page, no equations, nothing. What did the diagram mean?

Footsteps on the stairs. Someone was coming! Mike

hastily closed the book and repositioned it on the desk. He then turned and waited for the interloper to appear.

It was Billy. His clothes and hair were a mess; it looked as if he had just crawled out of bed. "Sorry I'm late," he said quietly.

"Hey, no prob," Mike replied.

Billy stood at the base of the stairs for a moment, trying to get a fix on his helper's intentions. *Why had Mike pleaded with Racken for permission to work with me?* he wondered. *I know he doesn't like men but now he's kissing my ass. What does he hope to gain? Does he want to ride on my coattails to success? That hardly seems like his way of doing things.*

Whatever the reason, Racken had asked Billy to take Mike (the former star pupil) under his wing in what Billy saw as an ironic turn of events.

"Let's get started."

Billy sat in front of the terminal and switched the computer on. "Turn the rest of the equipment on so it has a chance to warm up," he said over his shoulder.

"Gotcha.

Why is he here? I feel uneasy with him leaning over my shoulder asking so many questions and grinning with all of those perfect teeth. Why me, Lord? Why me?

No sooner did Billy begin to enter commands into the computer did the ever-curious Mike saunter up behind him and peer over his shoulder.

Give him something to do, for God's sake. Anything would be better than his hovering.

"Is there enough Cesium in the chamber to supply the electrons?" Billy asked. It was the only thing he could think of.

"Yeah, I checked it when I came in. Why are we using electrons? Why aren't we splitting atoms?"

"We're using electrons because we don't *want* to split atoms."

"Wait! What's that equation you're entering there?"

"That's the trajectory of the electron once it enters the collision chamber. It sets the motion at the proper angle."

"And what angle is that?"

Billy sighed. "The angle really doesn't matter. In fact, the computer chooses one at random. The electron's kinetic energy holds the key, as far as I can guess. Is the door locked upstairs? Racken wants us to keep it locked just so we won't forget to do it when we leave."

"Oh," Mike said. "I dunno. I'll go check it."

Mike dashed up the stairs. He certainly was interested in the experiment, just like Racken said— too interested, for Billy's taste. Good natured as he was, Billy could find no pleasant motives for Mike's involvement with the project. He obviously planned on getting something out of it.

"It's locked. Now what?"

Was he back already? "You must run up and down stairs for fun, just like my roommate, Dirk," he thought aloud.

Mike's brain froze for a split-second. Billy and Dirk were roommates? What a fortunate coincidence! Now there was a new front for the assault on Billy.

Billy started the accelerator and leaned back in his chair. "Now we watch and wait."

Time after time Billy ran the experiment, trying to find the threshold value of kinetic energy that caused the electron to light out of existence. The value he found experimentally was strange. Kinetic energy describes the amount of energy possessed by an object by virtue of its motion and is a function of the object's mass and its velocity. With an extremely low mass (.   kilograms), an electron must be accelerated to extremely high speeds before it attains any significant energy. Still, the speed was attainable by Darkham's equipment, which certainly wasn't the most powerful in the world. Why hadn't anyone noticed vanishing electrons before? Or vanishing atoms, for that matter?

Something's wrong here, Billy thought. *None of this should be happening, and yet it is! It's almost as if God has made some sort of weird mistake or that He's asleep at the switch or that He doesn't know diddlysquat about modern physics.*

What if the laws of nature that fill our textbooks don't apply at Darkham? What if my theories are correct here and only here, and those in our books are not?

Now I know what was beneath the surface. It's the waves, like that on the pond. By giving the electron increased velocity, I've changed its wavelength! It didn't disappear; the computer can't see it! It still exists, it just—

This is insane! It shouldn't work and yet...

What else can't we see? I don't operate in eight out of nine circles, just in four-

"Is something wrong?"

"Huh?"

Mike regarded Billy curiously. "You looked lost there for a moment."

"It's not just me that's lost," Billy said quietly. "It's *us*. Mike, I've just discovered something *dreadful*."

*** *** ***

Rachel came down the stairs slowly, her footsteps sending unpleasant tremors to her hungover brain. Breakfast was out of the question, but Billy always liked to eat after a night of drinking and acid.

The door to his room was open. She stuck her head in and peeked around the corner into the bedroom. "Billy? Are you in there?"

He stepped out of the bedroom, clad in the sweats and T-shirt that he usually slept in. His eyes were dark; blue circles hung beneath them. His hair was matted into a knot on top of his head.

"What's the deal?" Rachel asked in shock. "Are you going to class?"

"Screw class," Billy said, and yawned. "And Dirk won't be back 'till late this afternoon. It's Friday. Let's party."

"Cool. Let's party."

As Billy retrieved the last bottle of booze from the closet (Ah! Finally, a good reason to visit his sister!) Rachel started the stereo. "How's your work going?" she asked innocently.

"Better than I thought. It's just that it bugs me, you know? Things get crazy in the lab, but I guess I can handle it. I'll just finish the experiments, and then..."

Then *what?* If Rachel had bothered to ask, he wouldn't have been able to tell her. What was there for any of them to do but wait and see what happened next?

"Do you want to talk about it?"

"What? No, I don't want to talk about it," he snapped. "Besides, you wouldn't understand or believe me, for that matter. Now do you want to party or not?"

Rachel shrugged. "Let's party."

*** *** ***

The pair made every effort to be out of the room when Dirk returned. Billy had suddenly acquired a new sense of daring and insisted that they go for a walk in the park while drunk off their asses. The walk turned into an inebriated dinner at the commons and then another walk, and suddenly it was well after nightfall. The day had slipped down their gullets with the rum and vodka.

Seated next to Billy on a bench beside the pond, Rachel yawned. "What's next?"

"More partying," Billy replied.

"There's supposed to be a real bash down at the Kappa house tonight," Rachel casually suggested.

"The Kappa House!" Billy exclaimed. "I'm not going back to that hellhole."

"Aw come on, Billy!" she pleaded, her voice smooth, bewitching. "Where else can we go? We emptied the last of your sister's stash, remember?"

Billy angrily glared at her. "Do you think I'm stupid? I'm not going back to that dump just to stand around while you dance with that fucking Mike Cohan."

"I already explained that to you: I didn't know where you were, and he asked me to dance. Jesus Billy, I was drunk! It's not like I'm screwing him."

"Are you?"

Rachel slipped her arms around Billy's thin shoulders. "Not unless you give me a reason to."

Yes, Billy was not stupid, but he *was* under the influence of booze and Rachel. It was almost as if she was manipulating both Billy and Mike, forcing them to play a game whose spoils were unknown. Both men let themselves be led along a path to parts unknown.

Yes, say yes! Billy's inebriated brain urged. Or were those Rachel's thoughts, craftily planted in his head?

"Well...OK."

Rachel squealed with happiness, jumping to her feet. "Let's go back to the dorms and change."

*** *** ***

The scene at the Kappa house was much the same as it was the first time Billy attended a party there, but he was, for the most part, oblivious to it. And if the Greek who had almost creamed him was there, Billy took no notice of him.

An hour rolled by without incident. Billy and Rachel danced, drank some more, and then danced and drank again. It was still early, and the floor wasn't as crowded as it could be (and no furniture had been busted up yet).

Billy had no idea what time it was when he heard a female voice call his name. Confused, he glanced about the crowded room. It hadn't been Rachel who had called him; she was busy grooving away to the music, her eyes closed, her face turned to the ceiling and hands waving in the air like a crazed Hari Krishna.

"Billy! Billy! *There* you are-ohmigod, you look *awful!*"

It was Mizzy. She was closing in on him fast, wearing an atypical, concerned look on her face and a typical drink in hand. He hardly recognized her under her heavy make-up; she would never have worn that much in the presence of her parents. "Where y'a been, Billy? I've been worried to death about you. You look sick."

Billy stopped dancing to speak with his sister; Rachel continued to gyrate, bumping other dancers right and left. "I've been busy," he said. He teetered momentarily before regaining his balance.

Mizzy regarded him with suspicion. "For cryin' out loud, Billy. Are you drunk?"

"The pot can't call the kettle black," he said, echoing one of their mother's favorite sentiments. It was a cliché totally alien to Billy's normal patter. He *had* to be intoxicated.

On any other occasion, Mizzy would be prone to think his drunkenness was a good sign, but tonight it was different. The look in his eyes distressed her. She took him by the arm and began to lead him away. "Maybe we ought to have a little talk. Mom and Dad were upset that they hadn't heard from you."

Billy resisted, wanting only to return to the dance and the bar. "I don't want to talk. I want to dance."

"Dance later. This isn't like you, Billy. Maybe I shouldn't have given you all that shit to begin with."

"Too late!" he exclaimed and swerved back toward the spot where he and Rachel had been dancing. But where *was* Rachel? The crowd had consumed her; not even her waving hands were to be seen under the Christmas lights and the mirrored disco ball.

"See what you made me do!" Billy cried to his sister. "You made me lose my girlfriend!"

Mizzy was long gone too. She had done her duty; her concern was expressed, and he had spurned it. Let the little fucker drown in his own Bacardi.

As Billy searched for Rachel, another person in the room was also searching for that special someone. And if she brought a boyfriend? No problem. He could be dealt with.

OK. So, where is she? Mike thought. Playing hard to get was one thing, while total rejection was quite an unacceptable other. He stubbornly made his rounds through the house once more, searching for that head of golden hair and that pale face.

Maybe she isn't coming. What if she really does have a boyfriend and they're screwing right this minute as I search for her?

No! She's mine, dammit! It was meant to be. I can feel it.

It's a feeling like that time I was in the lab when Billy ran his first experiment. There's something just out of reach, a body of knowledge that's mine but I can't freely access.

Where is she, dammit?

The party had begun to boil by now. The tinkle of shattered glass reached his ears, and even though replacing the window would cost the frat a good deal of money (money tagged for beer or coke) Mike continued undaunted. The world could have ended in that moment, and he would have continued searching for *her*.

What if...nah. But then again, maybe she isn't—Yes! There she was, spinning like a top to the music. She was dancing alone in the corner, and there was nowhere for her to run

. Mike swam across the floor like a shark with the scent of blood in its nostrils. He held his prey firmly in the crosshairs of his sight. This was going to be a bull's eye. This was the night.

As if sensing his approach, Rachel stopped whirling. "Oh, it's you," she said.

"What's going on?" Mike shouted, as cool and smooth as can be.

"Not much," Rachel said with a frown.

He flashed his teeth in a huge smile (row after row of teeth, he imagined). "Hey, I'm glad to see you here! Things are lookin' up!"

Rachel looked at the crotch of his jeans to see as if to see whether Mike was referring to his penis.

"Are you alone?" he asked.

"No. I brought a friend with me."

Mike chuckled and looked to either side of her. "Oh yeah? Looks like your friend deserted you."

Just then, Billy spied Rachel. He called to her, making his way to her side. "Hey Rachel! Where the hell y'a been? I've been looking all over for you."

Rachel winked as he approached, confusing Billy for a moment until Mike came into view. Rachel had *winked!* She was planning a prank. Tee-hee!

"Hey Billy, I want you to meet someone. This is—what did you say your name was?"

"I didn't," Mike growled.

"Mike!" Billy said jovially. "How it goin'?" And then to Rachel: "Are we gonna stand around all night, or are we here to dance?"

"Let's dance!" she said, and then the two drifted away into the tide.

Even if Mike had managed to speak, there was nothing to say. Not only had Billy proved himself to be smarter than he and had stolen the spotlight in the Physics department, but this intruder had stolen the girl that was meant for him as well. *The girl that was meant for him!* Billy probably put Rachel up to leading him on as a joke, a demonstration that Billy really *was* smarter than he was.

I can't believe it! I won't allow it! Something must be done about Billy—something drastic. The tables must be turned. This is war! I'll show him who's the best. I'll show him and he'll be sorry...

*** *** ***

CHAPTER FIVE: KATHERINE

After paying the bill at the Excelsior Motel, Katherine had a little over eighty dollars. It was time for breakfast.

McDonald's wasn't exactly the cheapest place to eat (four dollars for leathery pancakes, greasy cubed/formed/pressed/oil-bathed hash browns and coffee) but at least she was assured that she wouldn't catch beriberi or whatever it was that Mom-and-Pop cafés were notorious for spreading.

In the cold dining room, she jotted down her thoughts on her situation with the pad and pen the Excelsior management had so thoughtfully provided.

Possibilities:

. I am insane and none of this is happening to me.

. William is insane, and all of this is really happening to me.

. Both of us are insane and who knows what's really happening?

She sipped at her coffee, cringing at its metallic aftertaste. None of the theories she had come up with were easily tested, but none of them lacked supporting evidence either. Her behavior and perceptions certainly seemed crazy, as well as William's outrage and threats. And what was the malarkey about a disease and killing everyone?

The third possibility seemed the most likely, but Katherine didn't want to consider it in more than a passing manner, for it was the most disturbing.

Katherine chewed on the end of the pen for a moment, and then took to the paper once more:

. Neither of us are insane, and all of this is really happening.

Now *that* was the most frightening possibility of all. Dr. Langly asserted that she wasn't crazy, and William had no history of even temporary insanity—in fact, he was the most cool, reserved human being Katherine knew. As for her strange experiences, they seemed too real to be hallucinations. If number four was the case, then she had no choice other than continuing her present course of action, making her way to Washington as best she could. Perhaps the mystery would resolve itself somewhere along the way.

Katherine looked out of the window onto the Strip. There was no turning back now. William would no longer settle for a truce, and so the point of sanity was moot. Her mind embraced possibility number four, shutting the door on the others.

*** *** ***

Pick and Pay Thrift was undoubtedly the cheapest and seediest outlet in the cosmos. Katherine moved from rack to rack in the store, hoping to find the least profane fashion items as possible. Second-hand was normally unthinkable (especially because people who ate at the infected cafés probably sold their likewise infected clothes to thrift outlets) but extraordinary times called for extraordinary measures. Two pairs of jeans, two somewhat acceptable blouses and a ratty gym bag to carry everything in. Hmm. Not a bad haul for twenty dollars. Katherine wondered if the Salvation Army made such deals of the junk that she and William donated back in Newport to cast out the demons of conspicuous consumption.

Second-hand underwear was out of the question, and she still had to buy make-up. The drugstore took care of that; Katherine found a clearance basket at the end of one of the paint aisles, which was right next to the economical lingerie aisle. The basket contained everything she could possibly need, though it was not exactly high quality.

"Beggars can't be choosers," Katherine said as she dropped her marked-down booty into her shopping basket. A fat woman who had also been sifting through the make-up looked at her with a wary pair of eyes and shook her head. Katherine chuckled to herself; the other shopper had obviously mistaken her for a lunatic.

With the shopping done, Katherine sat herself down on a bench in front of the drugstore and counted the money. It was hard to believe, but after spending the night in a motel, eating a reasonable breakfast, and outfitting herself for frugal travel, she still had forty dollars left. Maybe it was some sort of a miraculous thing, like that biblical story about the magic urn that never runs out of oil. It didn't matter.

A co-op of local farmers had set up a tarpaper produce stand right at one juncture of a Strip-side street and the highway. The stand was attracting plenty of business, and Katherine figured that the Interstate entrance closest to it was the most likely place to catch a ride.

The stand was like any other that she and William had stopped at on the way to Lake Tahoe: a one-room shack that housed bins of neatly arranged fruits and vegetables kept moist by a misting spray of water. But as Katherine stepped into the gravel lot a sense of uneasiness descended upon her. For the past twenty-four hours the feeling of phoniness had buzzed in her head, and she had hardly recognized it. She may not have done so at all if had not been heightened as she neared the stand, but the old feelings of anxiety were now replaced intrigue. Katherine felt sure that the phoniness was directly connected to what she was experiencing.

Curious, Katherine inspected the stand. Nothing was amiss here; fragrant fruits and vegetables were neatly piled in their bins, over which passers-by picked and bargained. She reached out for a particularly enticing cantaloupe and brought it to her nose, smelling the stem end in a test of ripeness that had been handed down from mother to daughter. The melon smelled *too* perfect, nauseating her with its sweetness.

Unsettled, she replaced it on the pile.

The melon sat behind the one she had originally chosen. It had been in the pile too long; liquid oozed from its gray, moldering skin. The sight of the rotten fruit was enough to repel her, but it was how the mold had chosen to attack the melon that worried her the most. The curves and loops of the fuzz were ominously like those that had been melted into the surface of the meteor that had left the transient crater on Newport Beach.

The meteor/melon was enough to roust the last slice of anxiety that Katherine had managed to bottle up, but the sight that greeted her as she hastily backed away from the stand was worse. She rubbed her eyes and squinted against the morning glare as the black Mercedes pulled into the impromptu market's dirt lot. Could it be...?

The door on the driver's side of the car opened, and out stepped William.

William!

Terrified, Katherine froze in her steps. There wasn't any place to hide other than behind the shack, and the distance between her and it seemed too great to safely cross. What was William doing in Las Vegas? Had the operator somehow traced her phone call to the depot? Had William driven to Vegas in a murderous frenzy in order to kill her in her sleep? He might have called every cheap hotel in a hundred-mile radius of L. A. to locate her!

Katherine ducked behind the cantaloupe bin. Thick juice from rotting melons deep in the pile had accumulated at the base, causing her to clamp her hand over her mouth to avoid retching. Tiny fruit flies buzzed about her head, presumably sniffing her hair spray to see if it was edible. William's voice reached her ears.

"...looking for a woman...about so tall...pale skin, jet black hair. Haven't seen her? ...know she's been through here..."

How does William know where I've been? Katherine wondered. *How does he know I didn't fly out of Vegas on the first plane bound for anywhere? It's like he's reading my mind!*

William had said on the phone that there was no hiding from him, and apparently, he was telling the truth. His monologue had been so confused that she hadn't taken stock in it, nor could Katherine remember exactly what he said. She would have to be very careful if she were to keep from falling into his clutches.

In the distance a car door slammed, and an engine came to life. Katherine recognized the purr of the Mercedes, and as the sound began to fade, she slowly stood, peering over the melons to make sure the threat had passed. William's car was indeed receding into the distance, but it was not so far away that her eyes could not discern the head and shoulders of a small boy sitting in the rear seat, peering out of the windows in vigilant search for his mother.

The sight of Little William filled Katherine with a mixture of rage and sorrow. William had dragged their son into what she perceived as a private war. By now had surely begun brainwashing the boy into believing that uncaring Mommy had fled because she didn't love either of them. In that moment Katherine's maternal instincts almost boiled over. She promised herself that if William harmed her son in any way that she would divorce him by planting a bullet in his head faster than he could ask for custody of their son.

Katherine tore her angry gaze from the retreating Mercedes and stomped into the sunlight. Tears stung her eyes. William was playing dirty, and she didn't have the wherewithal to combat it. She closed her eyes, shutting out the pain and impossibility of the world.

A great rushing sound filled her head, and for a second Katherine thought that she was finally going out of her mind, and quite noisily at that.

The hot wind on her back told her differently. Katherine's brain did a quick check of her body, revealing that at some point she had extended her arm, holding her thumb out in the universal gesture of hitchhiker ship. When had that happened? She wasn't even aware she had walked to the side of the road!

A huge eighteen-wheeler pulled to a stop alongside the gravel lot. The driver moved across the seat and opened the passenger door.

This is insane, Katherine! Hitchhiking is a dangerous and foolish thing to do in the Nineties. Sure, it used to be safe, but you have no way of knowing if this guy is one of that robber-Marine's buddies or a relative of Charles Manson or—

There was no time to debate the driver's integrity. It was imperative that she got away from William more than ever, especially if he should decide to double back along the highway and spy her alongside of the road waiting for a pickup.

The space between Katherine and the truck magically began to close; her feet had taken steps without the rest of her body's knowledge. The cab door's red metallic paint gleamed in the sunlight like an impossible jewel. Information about the owner was stenciled upon it in blue, looping script:

AUSSIE MUTT
PRIVATE SHIPPING
WASH., D.C. U.S.
SYDNEY, AUSTRALIA
(704) 813-5717

*** *** ***

Katherine had never been in the cab of a semi before, so figuring out how to get up to where the door was posed a problem. Just when she thought the driver was beginning to have second thoughts about giving a moron like her a ride, she saw the little footsteps on the diesel tank and the handle by the door. So that was how they did it.

"I really appreciate the ride," Katherine said as she climbed through the door. "I don't normally—"

Her words lodged in her throat. Katherine had come face-to-face with the most drop-dead gorgeous man she had ever met.

"I don't normally pick up hitchhikers," he said with a blinding smile.

He had might as well stepped right out of a Jackie Collins novel: six-foot three, athletic build, nice tan, blue eyes, brown hair, good teeth, and if Katherine had a dirty mind in her head, she would have instinctively known that he was hung like a brontosaurus—except that there is no such thing as a brontosaurus; "brontosaurus" bones really belong to a beast called *apatosaurus*. In this case, such trivialities hardly mattered.

Katherine was so smitten with the man behind the wheel that she was unaware that she had closed the door behind her and that the journey was underway until he spoke again.

"What's your name?"

"Katherine," she said.

"Katherine what?"

She shook her head. "No "what"; just Katherine."

The driver smiled as the truck pulled away from the produce shack. "Well then, as long as we're being informal, you can call me Mutt," he said.

"Mutt?"

Was this guy serious? What the kind of a nickname was that? It certainly didn't apply.

"Oh, I get it," she said a moment later. ""Mutt" is your radio nickname."

"Handle," Mutt corrected. "Mutt is my radio *handle*."

"OK, Mutt it is, then," she said with an unthinking smile. His speech was not at all like that which she expected to come from a truck driver; he was far too articulate.

As the truck entered the flow of traffic on the Interstate, a pause drifted into the conversation inside the cab. Katherine found herself wondering what to say to someone so attractive.

Mutt solved the problem for her. "So, where are you headed?' he asked.

She looked out the windshield to avoid staring at his biceps. "East," she said. "Washington D.C., to be exact."

He grinned again; he was clearly the genial, smiling type. "D. C.'s a nice city," he said. "I got an office there. Got one in Australia, too."

Aha! Here was something to fill the silence with. "I saw that on the door when I got in," Katherine said. "I used to live just outside of Sydney."

"Oh really? When did you move Stateside?"

Katherine curled a leg under herself, a sign that she was at ease with this total stranger. "Oh, it was a long time ago. I was only three or four, I guess. My father was working as a legal advisor for a multinational; he transferred Down Under before I was born. My mother made him move back first chance he got; it was too dry and hot down there for her."

He glanced at her quickly, concern flashing in his eyes. "Say, are you OK?"

Katherine gave the polite, expected answer: "I'm fine, thank you. Why?"

Mutt shrugged, not letting go of the wheel. He was a careful driver, a quality that would lessen the hysteria that Katherine's mother would undoubtedly go into if she knew her daughter was hitchhiking.

"Well, you looked a bit worried back there."

"Oh," Katherine sighed. "I thought I saw my ex-husband back there at that fruit stand."

"Your *ex*-husband?"

Uh oh. Hadn't she told him that she was getting out of a rotten marriage? It might burst his bubble, so to speak.

Katherine's face flushed; she turned her head back toward her window in hopes that Mutt wouldn't notice. "Yes, my ex-husband. I left him because he's a lunatic and I think he might want to hurt me. He might have been cheating on me, too. I don't know. I guess you could say that I'm pretty confused right now."

Mutt looked at her incredulously. "Now why would a man cheat on a good-looking woman such as yourself? Is he a fag or something?"

Katherine nodded. "He's something, but not gay. To tell the truth, I'm not sure why he was unfaithful, or even if he was. Things have been so strange lately! From the way William talked —William is my husband—I thought he wanted to kill me, or worse. I took off before he had the chance, and there's no way he knew where I was going." She shook her head pensively. "And then to see him at a fruit stand outside of Vegas…"

"Maybe it was a coincidence," Mutt theorized. "He might have just been passing through."

"Passing through? You don't know William. He was looking for me."

"Hey..." Mutt gave her a pat on the knee intended to comfort. "That might not have been your husband back there, you know. It could have been some Joe who just *looked* like him. I remember reading someplace that everyone is supposed to have a double somewhere in the world."

"Yeah. I think I read that, too."

*** *** ***

Katherine shifted in her seat; her rear end was beginning to ache from all the sitting around she had been doing for the past two days. How did truck drivers do it?

She filled the next few hours with a censored account of the events leading up to her departure, leaving out the loopier elements, such as the crater or the fact that she might be psychotic.

"So anyway, I decided just to head for Washington and forget everything that happened in Newport," she said. "I can't really tell you why I chose Washington, I mean, I don't understand it myself. I have reasons."

"Like what?" Mutt asked.

"Well, it sounds kind of weird, but I keep having these dreams about D.C., I mean I *guess* the dreams take place in Washington, though I can't be sure. You know how dreams are. Anyhow, in the dream someone is in trouble and is calling me for help. I know that sounds crazy, but I just can't shake the feeling."

She turned her head away from him and looked out her window over the desert landscape. Her voice grew distant. "When I was a little girl, I would try to frighten myself as I fell asleep so I could have a good nightmare and my dream prince could come and save me. I loved to dream back then, but now that I've grown up and have learned what dreams really are, they're nothing but a nuisance."

Mutt said, "What are dreams, anyway?"

"Dreams are garbage. It has to do something with how your brain decides what goes into your long-term memory and what doesn't. But you'd be surprised what some people think dreams represent. Folks used to believe that the soul wanders at night and dreams are recollections of adventure in other worlds. Isn't that ridiculous?"

Mutt smiled. "Is it?" he asked. "I mean, how do we know what we know about this world we live in? Everyone seems to think everything is so damn simple nowadays; that every one of life's mysteries can be explained in simple terms. What if we're wrong? What if *you're* wrong?"

His words knocked the psychology book out of Katherine's hands; it fell to the floor of the dark library of her fears and became lost in the shadows.

What if we're wrong? Sure, some dreams may be caused by the brain processing memories, but what if some of them aren't?

These were unwelcome thoughts. Katherine hurriedly left the library for the safety of the logical, rational left side of her brain. Mutt was quick to make use of the silence her retreat caused.

"Hey, we drove through lunch, but how about stopping in Salt Lake for a bite to eat? I need to fuel up the truck, too."

"Sounds good to me."

*** *** ***

Katherine would never have gone to a Denny's out of her own free will, but seeing as Mutt was providing the transportation, she wasn't going to argue.

Not much of a date, she mused as she waited for Mutt to open the cab door for her.

The Denny's was of the late fifties type that made Katherine anxious. The roof was perched on top of the building at a peculiar angle and the interior color scheme included only multiple shades of brown and orange.

"We should have found one that served beer," Mutt said as he slid into the first available booth. "They have them all over the place, but not in Utah. I just can't figure it out."

Katherine leaned across the table and whispered in his ear: "Mormons," she said.

"Oh."

A dumpy waitress clomped her way over to the table. "Y'a ready to order?" she asked between chomps on a wad of purple bubble gum.

Mutt motioned to Katherine. What a gentleman!

Katherine had hardly enough time to peruse the menu, but then Denny's wasn't known for its diversity in fare. "I'll have a hamburger and a cup of coffee," she said, seeing no sense in pushing her luck with the cook by ordering liver and onions.

The waitress turned her full attention to Mutt, which was far more that she had given Katherine. "I'll have the same," he said.

The waitress blew a big bubble and popped it, leaving a film of gum on her nose. She picked it off her skin and returned it to her mouth.

Katherine put her napkin in her lap, and watched as Mutt did the same, as if he hadn't known what the napkin was for. He said, "You know, I just can't help but think you look familiar, like we've met before."

Katherine shrugged. "I can't imagine where," she said. Her comment wasn't meant as an insult, but as an observation that the odds were low, seeing as that she didn't hang out at truck stops. "I have a pretty good memory for faces, but all the same..."

All the same what?

"Anyhow..." Katherine glanced about the restaurant, hoping that he wouldn't ask her to finish the sentence. Mutt was staring at her, something he did more and more of with each passing hour.

The waitress brought the coffee. Mutt proceeded to load his with sugar (at least six packets full, by Katherine's count.) "It's pretty dangerous for a woman like you to be hitchhiking, you know," he said.

Katherine almost pointed out that he said "you know"

repeatedly but bit her tongue. "What do you mean, "a woman like me?"" She sipped at her coffee and then began to load it with sugar, too, realizing that Mutt had done so to kill its awful taste.

"It's a safe bet that you don't know karate," he said. "I just mean that you're lucky that you haven't got into trouble, you know."

"Getting robbed by a Marine and being chased by an angry ex counts as trouble in my book."

"I mean *worse* trouble."

"Such as?"

"You know; like winding up in a ditch with your throat cut."

The cup of coffee nearly fell out of Katherine's grip. The comment about being murdered was something her mother would have said to her. "Thanks," she said. "That makes me feel really secure."

"But it's the truth," Mutt insisted. "It happens all the time. If you don't believe me, just turn on the television or look at the newspaper."

"Here y'a go!" The waitress was back, and with a vengeance. Laden with gristly burgers, their plates slid across the thin film of grease on the tabletop, coming to rest in front of them like beer mugs slid across the bar of a Hollywood saloon. Mutt curtailed his morbid diatribe until the waitress left.

He then continued, saying, "I think I read somewhere that good-looking women suffer from a higher rate of violent deaths than ugly ones do."

"Don't believe everything you read," Katherine warned while trying to find some delicate way to grasp her unruly burger. "I've been OK this far. I can be tough if I have to, I guess. I'll make it."

"Yeah, you probably will," Mutt said. "But I have a proposition for you."

Katherine set her burger down in anticipation of what he was going to say.

"You need to conserve funds," he began. "Hitching is no

good at night, you know, and believe me, motels can take a big bite out of your wallet. Why don't you just ride with me? The load I'm carrying is Washington-bound anyway."

Not wanting to meet him eye-to-eye, Katherine looked down at the table. "It's very sweet of you to offer, but I'm not able to repay you and I'd feel like a leech."

Mutt laughed. "What's the difference if you leech off one driver instead of ten or twenty? And I'm not asking you to pay me back. Giving you a ride seems like the Good Samaritan thing to do. You know; a damsel in distress and all that."

Yes, Katherine knew. She had daydreamed it a thousand times as a child, but never figured on it happening.

"Well, I—OK, thanks."

A split-second later, Katherine realized what she had said and couldn't believe she had said it. What the hell was she thinking? Yes, she felt safe in Mutt's company, and her first impression of him was favorable. Still, there was a feeling of dread circulating below the surface of the entire affair; something was amiss, and Katherine couldn't help but feel that she and Mutt had somehow been sucked into something bigger than either of them could guess.

*** *** ***

Katherine's father had visited Washington D.C. back when she was but a child. He always returned from his business trips bearing gifts, for it lifted some of the guilt of not being with his family from his conscience.

He gingerly handed the little girl a plastic bubble that was filled with liquid. Inside was a small model of the Capitol Building. Katherine immediately knew what to do with the toy; she shook it, setting into motion a patriotic blizzard of plastic stars and stripes.

In the dream it was the night that the meteorite landed on the beach. Katherine found herself at the foot of the stairs that led to the crest of Capitol Hill. The edifice was no longer of marble, but of tacky plastic; a mawkish, child-like replica.

She could not see his face; in fact, the disembodied voice seemed to come from deep within the Capitol Building itself. His voice had a cold, hollow ring brought on by the empty halls of his prison.

"I'm sorry it had to be this way," he said. "I didn't mean for this to happen. There's always a consequence to what you create, but how was I supposed to know what mine would be?

"Don't lose control. When we were kids, we knew it was wrong to play all the way out, but we didn't know the reasons why. I've figured it out. It's happened to me. If you play it out too far, if you give them enough rope, then they'll try to get away from you. And that's exactly what they've done. Now they hold me prisoner. I know they'll try to stop you and that it might get ugly, but won't you help me?

"I can feel you getting closer every minute, every hour. Please help me before something else happens! Who knows what they're capable of—

Katherine woke to a darkened cab. Mutt was asleep beside her; his head was back against the headrest of the seat.

When did he pull over? she thought.

Outside, the rest area was teeming with bugs that swarmed about the gray-white lights that illuminated the parking area.

Where are we? How long have I been asleep?

That was the last conscious thought she would have before daylight. Katherine drifted back to sleep, her head against the passenger window of the cab.

*** *** ***

Katherine had fallen into the crater.

As she fell deeper and deeper into the pit, she saw the glint of metal at the very bottom, an impossible sight, considering that the base of the crater was miles and miles away. Yes, there was something at the bottom. Soon they began to resolve themselves into long, thick blades of cold steel. Someone had set a trap and there was no way to keep from falling into it-

The terror of the impending impaling shook Katherine from her sleep.

"Good morning," Mutt said.

Katherine rubbed the sleep from her eyes. From somewhere in the cab came a strange hissing noise, like that of air escaping from a punctured tire. "Where are we?" she asked.

"Just west of East Bum-Fuck," Mutt said. "You hungry?"

Katherine had to think about that one. A tight knot of fear still lingered in the pit of her stomach; fear of the death trap at the bottom of the crater had followed her into the early morning sunlight. "No, I'm not hungry. Well, yes, I guess I am."

Mutt chuckled at her indecision. "*I'm* hungry. I know a place where we can get breakfast not ten minutes from here." He reached over to the dashboard and turned the tuning knob on the radio, the source of the hissing sound. "Damn. Not a thing but static."

"Maybe there isn't a station nearby," she suggested.

"Nah, I've been through here a hundred times. We're no more than two or three hours from Omaha. We should be getting some local-yokel country bullshit." He fiddled with the radio for a few seconds more before turning it off in disgust. "The damn thing must be busted."

A small town came into view a few miles down the road, just as Mutt had predicted.

The black and yellow facade of the twenty-four-hour Waffle House stirred the same feelings in Katherine that the ghastly Denny's had. But Mutt was paying, and so she would grin and bear it.

The parking lot was deserted save for two cars that had presumably carried the waitress and the cook to work.

"Say, we got lucky," Mutt said, switching off the truck's engine. "Looks like we beat the six o'clock rush."

It was hard for Katherine to imagine that such eatery as this could produce much in the way of a rush hour, but then again, she didn't know much about highway eateries.

Mutt chose a booth next to a window and a waitress, a Waffle House psychic, immediately swooped down on the table with two cups of coffee.

"I'll have four eggs with toast-oh yeah and some hash

browns, too." Mutt said. If William had been there, he would have warned the truck driver about his cholesterol count.

Ordering the restaurant's namesake was probably the safest bet, she reasoned. Katherine said, "Just waffles for me, please."

Yet another strained hush washed over the table; not knowing what to say, Katherine let her eyes wander about the dining area.

Sitting atop the hot chocolate machine was a portable television that was turned to a local morning newscast. The sound was off, but at least it was something to focus attention on.

Bodies.

A slow panning shot of empty streets littered with corpses and men in white coveralls.

Katherine frowned in disgust. Carnage seemed to be a newscaster's middle name no matter where one went. Why, she could remember a Southern California broadcast that showed the aftermath of a terrible traffic accident, complete with a stray Mutt munching on one of the mangled victims.

As if on cue, the waitress darted behind the counter and turned up the volume on the set.

"—ifornia city of Newport Beach," a reporter said in a voice over. "Researchers are baffled by the strange nature of the disease that seems to leave no survivors in its wake. There has been some speculation that the disease is of extraterrestrial origin; scientists point to a suspicious crater—"

The scene on the television changed, and Katherine spat a mouthful of coffee back into her cup.

"What's wrong?" Mutt asked. He had been staring aimlessly out of the window, not paying the TV any mind.

"That's my house!" Katherine exclaimed, pointing to the television set. "My God, that's footage of my house and the crater in the back yard!"

Mutt squinted. "Plague? What the hell are they talking about?"

"People are dying," Katherine said, still riveted to the screen. "People are dying all over the place and it sounds like they think some virus came from that crater—or the thing made the crater. But that crater wasn't there just a day ago! I mean, it *was* there, but then they filled it up, or it vanished, or—oh heck, I'm so confused!"

Mutt shrugged. "Now don't get your panties in a bunch. So, people are dying? People die every day, but you're obviously not sick."

Katherine whipped her head around to face him; the look on her face was one of sheer panic. "I stood on the rim of that not a week ago. Oh my God, what if I've got that disease? I might have just a few days to live!"

The newscaster continued while scenes of capacity-filled hospitals and clinics graced the screen. "The disease has an incredibly short incubation period, and is fatal within twelve hours of first exposure—"

"See?" Mutt said. "You can't have it; you'd be dead by now." He dumped salt on his eggs, which had materialized as if from nowhere. In her panic, Katherine was totally unaware that the waitress had been back. "Just be glad you're on your way East."

This was no time to be eating or even thinking about food; Katherine leaned out of the booth so she could hear the rest of the newscast.

A female newscaster appeared on the screen; she was out of doors and standing in what appeared to be a large park.

"I tell you Jerry, most of the people out here at the University are laughing at this alien disease bit that the Californians have come up with. I'm standing right now in the middle of Darkham University, which is where most researchers believe the epidemic really started." The camera panned across the campus. "As you can see, there's no activity here. Those students who didn't succumb to the initial wave have long since headed for home. I believe we have some footage from two days ago—Bill?"

Mutt moved methodically from the eggs to the hash

browns, dousing the potatoes with ketchup before eating them.

The scene on the television changed as the network rolled the tape form its files. It was the same area of the campus, but now students with suitcases were marching across the park, some were bundles against hopeless feverish chills, while still others congregated around the news camera, looking for their fifteen minutes of fame.

Katherine watched transfixed as the camera settled on a young man near the front of the pack. His blond hair, tan and surfer garb betrayed a California origin that unsettled her. No, his eyes were the problem; they were so deep, so blue, so penetrating.

Katherine glanced at Mutt, who was continuing to eat, unaffected by the newscast. Was food all he ever thought about? Didn't the plague worry him?

Mutt looked up from his plate. "Are you OK?"

"Huh?"

"You look a little green," Mutt said.

"I'm not very hungry after all, I guess."

*** *** ***

"Where are we?" Katherine asked.

Mutt glanced away from the road a moment. "You startled me," he said. "I didn't know you were awake."

"The scenery put me asleep. That, and the drone of the engine. It happens all the time when William and I go—I mean when we *used* to go on vacation." She looked out at the rolling hills along the highway. There was nothing but row after row of grain: sometimes wheat, sometimes rye, sometimes corn. It was exactly what she expected to see in the Midwest.

"So where are we?"

"In the middle of a corn field." He smiled again, that same enigmatic smile that matched the surfer's, but Mutt's was more...more what? More sincere, perhaps.

Katherine frowned. "Yes, I see it's a corn field, but what state are we in?"

"Illinois."

"Illinois? Do they grow corn in Illinois?"

"Apparently."

So be it. For someone who was supposed to be on a tight schedule, Mutt certainly was taking a roundabout route to Washington.

So maybe he doesn't want to get there at all. Maybe he's taking me to meet my doom at the hands of that damn punk surfer. Or maybe he doesn't know much about geography. Maybe he doesn't know much about truck driving, either. Maybe he isn't who he says he is. Maybe—

Katherine realized that she was staring at Mutt's flawless profile and forced her eyes back to the corn.

*** *** ***

Mutt yawned, and a split-second later Katherine did the same out of sympathy. The day was stifling, drawn-out and boring. The road was almost hypnotic in its effect.

Katherine said, "You're not too tired to drive, are you?"

"Huh?"

"I said you looked tired. I just don't want you to wreck your rig."

Mutt smiled at her. "Yeah, I guess I am a little beat. Look, don't get me wrong, but if I try to drive much longer without a good eight hours of sleep, we'll probably wind up in that accident you're thinking about. What do you say we pull over in the next town and get us, uh, two rooms?"

"Sounds like a plan," Katherine said.

That was too much for the gremlin that lived in Katherine's skull. Its voice piped up almost immediately:

Katherine twisted at the spigot that controlled the internal dialogue as hard as she could. It wasn't as if Mutt were coming on to her. He did say two rooms, didn't he? She could hardly imagine him trying to take advantage of her, for he was so—

So what?

Familiar. Yes, that's it: Mutt's presence felt familiar. Being with him was like being with an old friend.

*** *** ***

"I'll see if I can get the rooms on the second floor," Mutt said. "That way we won't have people stomping on the roof all night. You comin' in, or you wanna wait out here?"

Katherine peered out the window at the green monstrosity of a motel that Mutt had chosen. The man behind the desk in the tiny office looked like a *jihad* terrorist. "I think I'll wait in here if you don't mind," she said.

"I don't mind at all. I'll only be a few minutes."

Katherine folded her arms in her lap, trying to weather another period of heightened anxiety. The motel's parking lot was completely devoid of cars, making her uneasy. They hadn't seen a soul since pulling off the Interstate; in fact, they hadn't seen a soul *on* the Interstate, either. Perhaps the population had evacuated in the face of the senseless plague she had heard of on the television; the plague that William mentioned on the phone and blamed on her. It seemed that as the distance between herself and Newport Beach grew, so did the number of outlandish twists of fate. A part of her buried deep in her psyche wondered how fantastic things would get before she finally faced what was obvious to her unconscious mind.

*** *** ***

Mutt opened the door that separated the two rooms and stuck his head in. "Are you decent?" he asked.

"So far," Katherine said. She looked up from her seat on the bed. The television was on, and she had been flipping channels to see what the local stations had to offer.

Mutt hesitatingly came into the room. "I saw a Chinese restaurant on the way into town. Why don't I pick us up some dinner? You can stay here if you want; if you feel anything like I do, you probably want to stand under a hot shower for an hour or so."

She switched off the TV "That sounds great."

Mutt nodded, and for a moment he acted as if he was going to say something else. He headed back into his room.

"Mutt?"

With one foot out into the dark parking lot, he stopped and turned to face Katherine, as if hanging on her every word.

"I can't thank you enough for what you're doing for me," she said. "I mean I'm not sure that I would have made it this far without you."

Mutt smiled. It wasn't just the casual smile that he sported so much of the time, it was the aw-shucks smile of a lovesick boy who had just given his pretty teacher an apple. "You're welcome," he said. He crammed his hands into the pockets of his black jeans in an expression of his embarrassment. "I just follow the Golden Rule, I guess." He looked at her for a moment-a long moment-and then picked up his keys and left.

Whew.

Now that Mutt was gone, Katherine let her disgust with the room register on her porcelain features. The bed was spread with a tacky comforter that was embellished with a jagged, brown, and silver design of awful metallic thread. Worse still there was matching wallpaper; it was that heinous foil type that belonged on a tissue box rather than on the walls of any room.

At least the shower stall looked clean. Katherine turned on the hot water and undressed, silently thanking her Creator for the privilege of a hot bath.

The shower felt wonderful, but it wasn't long before the tiny bathroom filled with steam and the pleasure turned to disgust. Opening her eyes after rinsing her hair clean of shampoo, Katherine found her gaze fixed on the little yellow droplets that were raining down from the steam-coated ceiling. The speculation of what those droplets were composed of and how they got all the way up on the ceiling was enough to drive her screaming from the room.

She hadn't anything in the way of a robe, so she dressed in the next day's selection of clothing and sat down to watch the television again. Where there had been game shows and sitcom reruns just minutes before, there was now nothing but news flashes about the mysterious plague. Katherine sighed; she didn't feel like contemplating anything of greater magnitude than brushing her hair, but just sitting in silence didn't appeal to her either. She sat down on the bed with her brush and watched the newscast anyway.

More street scenes of bodies.

Wasn't that the same Denny's that she and Mutt had eaten at back in Salt Lake? She squinted at the grainy picture the remote cameras were sending to the newsroom.

The plague was closing in on her with remarkable speed; in a matter of time, it would catch up to the two of them. And then what would happen?

The picture on the set suddenly turned to snow. Irritated, Katherine stood and reached for the fine-tuning knob. The television responded by lurching crazily toward her, its cabinet boiling and shifting grotesquely, trying to take on a form other than the one Zenith intended.

Terrified, Katherine jumped on the bed and backed against the wall. The television continued to close the gap between them as the seething audio track resolved into an impossible broadcast: *"I'LL FIND YOU!"* William bellowed. *"YOU'RE GOING TO BE SORRY WHEN I GET THERE, YOU STUPID BITCH! I'LL—"*

With that, the set overextended its cord, yanking the plug from the wall. The television instantaneously reverted to its normal, transistorized self, but now stood a full five feet from where it had initially been.

Katherine jumped off the bed and ran into Mutt's room, closing and locking the dividing door behind her.

*** *** ***

Mutt came in not ten seconds later. He was carrying a bag of Chinese food in one hand and a six-pack of beer in the other.

"The heat is off in the other room," Katherine blurted. It was a lame excuse for why she was in his room; it wasn't even cold outside.

Mutt looked at her for a second, trying to read her

thoughts. He set the beer down on the rickety table that had been so thoughtfully provided by the motel. "I hope you like Moo Goo Gai Pan," he said.

"I love it," Katherine replied. Actually, she hated Moo Goo Gai pan. It was full of nasty mushrooms.

It occurred to Katherine that she was very uncomfortable, but it was hard to pin her restlessness on either the mushrooms, the television or Mutt's presence. There had to be something else to fix her mind on. What about the take-out cartons? How was it that every Chinese restaurant in the United States gave out the same little waxed cartons with a picture of a pagoda stamped in red on the side and "Thank You" on the lids?

"Do you want me to open that for you?"

"Please," Katherine said, and handed him the beer she had been fumbling with. God, she hoped she hadn't chipped a nail; there was no hope of getting a manicure.

Mutt handed her the opened beer. Being quite thirsty, Katherine took a big swig from the can. The taste wasn't as bad as she remembered. Perhaps the company she was keeping changed the flavor of the brew. Whatever the reason, before she realized what she had done, Katherine split the six-pack evenly with Mutt. It seemed to please him in a sexist sort of way.

Katherine pushed the empty carton away from her. "Odoo, I'm stuffed. You know, I'm surprised the restaurant was still open. This whole area looks deserted."

"Business owners are always the last to go," Mutt said. "Remember when they had that big hurricane back east? The National Guard had to practically shove some of 'em out of their shops so they could be boarded up. Here. Have a fortune cookie." He held out two cookies, urging her to try her luck.

Katherine reached for the cookie on the left, and then changed her mind, taking the one on the right. Picking your fortune was a big deal. If you choose the wrong one, who knew what kind of future you'd wind up with?

Katherine crushed her cookie and removed the slip inside. It read: "I'LL EAT YOU FOR DINNER, YOU IGNORANT

SNATCH."

"What does it say?" Mutt asked.

Katherine crumpled the slip and casually tossed it into the bag. "Nothing. It was blank."

Mutt gave her a curious look and shrugged. "Scary," he said. "No fortune at all? That can't be a good omen."

"And yours?"

He looked at his fortune. "Uh, "You will get very lucky tonight.""

Now what the hell was that supposed to mean? Katherine cleared her throat and looked away from the table. Those damn fortune cookies. There had to be some horny old Chinese man sitting around writing those insidious proverbs, trying to think of things that would send patrons into a frenzy.

Again, the air was dead, like that of a radio station whose playlist was temporarily disrupted by a snoozing disc jockey. Katherine figured that now was the proper time to thank Mutt for dinner and retire to her room. Yet some force held her in place, forcing her to remain in her chair. Suddenly she was aware that the air wasn't dead after all; it was *alive*, charged with a mysterious force she'd never experienced before.

The energy in the room flowed about her limbs and torso, forcing her conscious brain from her body. Completely dissociated, she watched as her body stood. Mutt stood too, moving toward her with enough intent to cause alarm in Katherine's floating brain.

With the first touch of Mutt's lips to her neck, Katherine suddenly rejoined her body. In her absence she had thrown her arms around his neck; her fingers had found their way into his thick brown hair.

"You're so beautiful," Mutt whispered into her ear, speaking the magic words her prince had whispered thousands of times through the pages of historical romances tempered by children's fairy tales. The spell that had been cast upon her by marriage to William was finally broken; the sleeping princess was awake and ready to claim her prince.

But this was no ordinary prince. As Katherine's hands slid down his neck and to his pack, they did not find the flaccid flesh of an idle nobleman, but the sinew of a knight who had driven his horse over countless miles of asphalt, struggling with all his might to keep his mighty steed on the path that would lead him to the fair damsel whose touch would make him king.

The bed somehow materialized beneath Katherine, and as Mutt pressed the heat and size of his arousal against her, she mused that home was *never* like this.

*** *** ***

CHAPTER SIX: BILLY

Monday.

By now, Mike knew Dirk's schedule, and Billy's as well. Monday afternoon meant extra hours in the lab, hours that Dirk occupied shooting baskets and attending his freshman English class. It was pitiful the way those clods stuck to their routines so religiously.

Mike smirked as he headed for the dorms, knowing his plan would not fail. Something in the air guaranteed it.

He casually entered the building and waited in the stairwell. Dirk was undoubtedly showering off as he always did after basketball, and all Mike had to do was hang around and wait.

The bathroom door opened. Out strode Dirk in a fresh pair of sweatpants and a T-shirt. Mike stepped out into the hall. "Hey bud, what's up?"

Dirk smiled at his cool new friend. "Not much," he said.

"You headin' to class already?" Mike asked.

Dirk opened the door to his suite and motioned Mike to follow him in. "Yeah, I got an in-class essay to do. It really sucks, you know?"

"I hear y'a man, I hear y'a."

Look quickly. There! The desk with the computer on it must be Billy's. God, this is too easy!

"Bummer," Mike said, watching Dirk don his shoes. "I was hoping to get a game going."

Dirk shrugged. "Class only lasts an hour. I'll take you on then, OK?"

Mike feigned a smile. "Great."

Time for class. Mike and Dirk headed for the door; Mike (always the gentlemen) motioned Dirk to go through first. "Hey, could you check to see that it's locked?" Dirk asked. "Billy'd be ticked off if he came back and found it open. Valuables, you know."

"Sure." Mike reached around the door to the inner knob. It was locked, so he purposely *un*-locked it.

*** *** ***

Alone in the university's basement nuclear laboratory, Billy sat staring at the quiet terminal.

Why should I bother? he wondered. *Now that I've proved the unprovable, why bother trying to disprove it? The truth can be hard to face sometimes. Racken won't believe it, I know he won't. I hardly believe it myself.*

Pounding on the door at the top of the stairs interrupted his thoughts.

Oh shit, its Mike. He's come to see what I'm doing. Maybe he'll go away if I ignore him.

The pounding continued.

"Billy? I know you're in there. I want to talk to you."

It was Rachel. Billy dragged himself out of his chair and up the stairs. "What?" he asked, opening the door.

Framed by the bright light of the sun, Rachel looked more impossibly beautiful than ever. A part of Billy hurt when he looked at her. Billy knew he was totally undeserving of such a perfect prize. He often thought that she had been made for someone else, and that he had got to her and staked his claim first.

"Do you have to close yourself off from the rest of the world every day?" she asked. "C'mon. Let's take a walk."

*** *** ***

Mike slipped into the suite. His heart began to race; at last, that asshole Billy's secrets would be his. The entire affair was Billy's fault; if he hadn't been so secretive, he might not have aroused so much suspicion.

Mike quickly moved over to the desk he had earlier

identified as Billy's and opened the top drawer. The contents were for the most part uninteresting (pencils, pens, paper clips and other supplies) but as Mike began to close it, the glint of metal caught his eye.

In the jumble of junk sat an ornate letter opener that Billy's father had given him as a gift. The letter opener was a miniature of samurai sword plated with gold. A purple band of silk had been wrapped around the handle, from which a tiny bell hung. The blade was thick and sharp; it drew a small line of blood when Mike slid it across his open palm. The glint of the cold metal was curious in the afternoon sun that filtered through the window; the light was so bright that Mike imagined he could hear its flash calling to him from that thin world beneath its surface.

"I keep telling you that you won't understand that you'll think I'm crazy."

Billy's voice! He was returning from the lab early!

Mike quickly shut the desk drawer and jumped to his feet. Keys rattled in the lock; in a moment Billy and whomever he was with would be inside.

If he finds me, he'll know what I'm up to. He could report me to the Dean. I could get expelled!

Mike dove for Dirk's closet in a panic. As he closed the door behind him, he realized that he still held the letter opener; he only hoped that Billy would not find it missing and decide to search the place.

"Don't tell me what I'll think," Rachel said in her usual sarcastic manner. "I'm curious, and besides, whatever you're working on is really eating at you. I care, Billy. I just want to know what's caused that black cloud that's been hanging over your head, that's all."

Billy stopped inside the door and looked up, as if he really thought a cloud was above him. "A low-pressure system off the coast," he said.

"What?"

He shoved his hands into his pockets. "Never mind. It

142

wasn't much of a joke anyway. You wanna sit down?"

Inside the closet, Mike had an eye pressed to the crack between the door and the wall. He watched as Rachel moved over to the bunk. Billy, who had begun to sift through the notes in the folder on the desk, was out of sight.

"I don't suppose you've had any physics, have you?" he asked over his shoulder.

"Nope," Rachel said. "You know me: a humanities major 'til the end."

Billy's frown went unseen. "Right." He straightened up and carried the folder over to the bunk and sat down next to her.

"What'cha got there?" Rachel asked, trying to see the diagram Billy was concealing.

"Not so fast! I've got a little background to give you first." He cleared his throat. "Science is great. I mean, we've learned so much in so little time on this planet—well, in this universe. But science has its shortcomings. It isn't science that has the problem; it's *us*, the men and women who practice it. Sometimes we can't see past the end of our noses, and someone must come along and point out that there's something besides our schnoz out there."

Rachel nodded her head. "You mean like how people thought the world was flat until Columbus came along, huh?"

Billy smiled. "Right, even though Columbus wasn't the first to prove the Earth was round. The Greeks figured it out first. Anyway, as I see it, science is currently at another one of those sticking points. Today's theories about the universe point to so many contradictions and so many unexplainables that we really need to stop, go back to the beginning, and redefine the cosmos and everything in new terms. That's what I've tried to do, but my work is a failure *and* a success, in a weird way."

Rachel blinked. Billy hoped that was a sign that she was still with him.

"Now suppose, Rachel. Suppose for just one moment that everything you have ever learned about the world and life and you was totally wrong, that it was a lie. How would you feel?"

"Like shit."

"Thank you. That's exactly how I feel."

He paused for a moment, trying to think of the simplest terms to put his discovery in. There was no way around it; he had to explain to her some basic physical problems.

"In physics there is a quirky quality that all matter possesses called wave-particle duality. Sometimes physical objects act like objects, other times they behave like waves, which are nothing but movements of energy. Waves have no mass. A simple example is that of light. It has no mass—it obviously isn't made of matter—and yet it comes in little packets called photons that can be easily detected. Understand?"

Rachel grinned. "Piece of cake," she said. "So, when do we get to the freaky stuff?"

Billy chuckled once; it wasn't a sound of glee as much as one of resignation. "The freaky stuff is coming, believe me. Now to continue the lecture: Light is a bad example of wave particle duality because it's composed completely of energy, which can be deflected by its own right. But what about physical objects that sometimes behave like waves? Electrons are like that. They don't weigh much; in fact, their mass is so negligible that they might as well not have it at all. Although the electron is incredibly light, it still has mass, and that fact is undeniable. How is it then that an electron can behave like a wave?"

Billy flipped to a page in his notebook and began to sketch, lecturing as he drew.

Addition of Waves in Phase

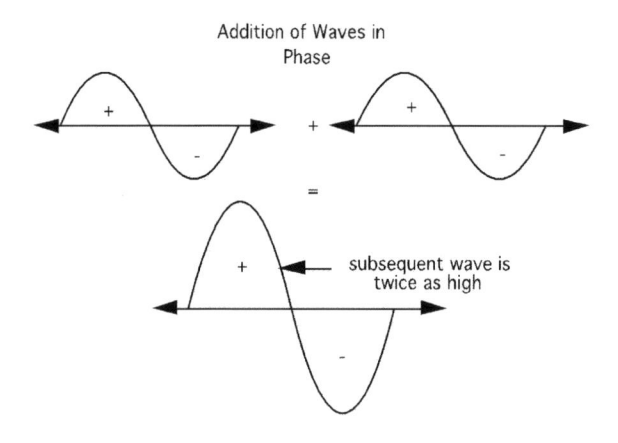

subsequent wave is twice as high

"Here is a diagram of two waves. Both are said to be in phase; that is, their troughs and the peaks are in the same position and, in this case, of the same height and depth. If these waves collide under the right conditions, they will add to create the third wave, the sum of the two. The magnitude of the two addend waves determines the resultant's amplitude, wavelength, and energy value.

"But what about waves that are out of phase? In the second example you see what happens: The waves cancel, and nothing is left! You can prove this to yourself in the bathtub while washing or at the sink while doing dishes.

"Under certain conditions electrons behave like waves too; it's been observed time and again. Sometimes they add to form bonds between atoms, but if they're "out of phase" they don't, and nobody seems to be able to come up with a satisfactory explanation that doesn't raise a hundred new questions."

Addition of Waves Out of Phase

=

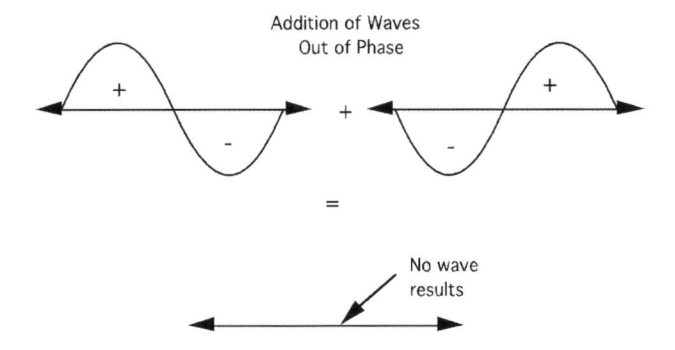

No wave results

Rachel sighed. "OK, I believe you. But what has this got to do with your discovery?"

"Be patient! In nineteen twenty-four, a physicist by the name of Louis De Broglie proposed that all matter had wave properties and that the more mass and energy the object, the smaller the wavelength. For example: by the De Broglie equation, the wavelength of an off-speed baseball pitch is so small that it is out of the range of our senses, and we perceive nothing but a conglomeration of particles—mass. This is all fine and dandy, except De Broglie made a mistake. He assumed that it was matter that had wave properties and that matter was the basic building block of the physical universe when it's the other way around. It is the waves themselves that form the universe; matter is but a consequence of different waves adding and subtracting from each other to form new waves."

The blank look on Rachel's pale face persisted. "So, what are you trying to say, Billy? That matter is a joke, that it's not real?"

"No. No matter is real, but it just isn't the basic building block that the universe is made of. Our eyes aren't designed to see the waves, just matter. Our eyes only see in three dimensions, too, while these waves can and do spread themselves over many dimensions. We see only a very small portion of the cosmos.

"But what about those waves, you ask? Where do they

come from? What causes energy to flow? I had this idea that some sort of massive consciousness was the key, and that it gave rise to the waves, and eventually to matter. I knew that it would be relatively simple to prove: if I could tap into that consciousness, the answers would be waiting there for me."

Rachel sighed. "You gotta stop doin' the acid, man," she said. "*Please* stop doing the acid! I don't think I can take much more of this weird shit."

The judgment of his work as weird flew right by Billy. "LSD has nothing to do with it," he maintained. "All I needed to do was let go of my inhibitions and look inside and find what was waiting there. Who needs drugs when we can bend reality at our will? Reality isn't based upon anything but that which our consciousness tells us, and so reality is therefore nothing but a consequence of consciousness. If consciousness changes, so does reality. Take, for example, a person under the influence of LSD. The drug had changed his consciousness, and suddenly his senses perceived things that don't physically exist. Does that make the experience any less real? Hardly. It all depends on what frame of reference you chose.

"And so, without consciousness, there is no reality, nothing. And even if there *was* something, there would be no consciousness to acknowledge it, and so it might as well not exist.

"I know that what I've told you is technical, but the rest of it should be easier to understand. I had been looking for a new definition of the universe and decided that consciousness was the key, like I said. Not mine or your consciousness, but a collective consciousness from which all other consciousness springs. The mind that we call Billy is and offshoot of that, just as you and every other sentient being in the universe is.

"Assuming that consciousness is the primary wave function—and I stress the word "assuming"—I realized that I need not perform any other sort of experiment to divine the nature of the rest of the universe. All else would grow from and would be knowable by that consciousness. The hard part was to *prove* that the theories I was coming up with were correct. Even if I could see the waves, I would only see a three-dimensional slice of something multi-dimensional. Are you with me so far?"

Rachel shrugged.

"I really can't tell you what these waves are like. For simplicity's sake I've decided to represent the different waves as rings in a set of nested circles. Each wave "stacks" on top of the other; that is, the third wave for example has its own character, but the character of the two previous waves can be "seen" through it, and so on.

"What I did—and what I want to talk you through—was to discover that there are only eight basic wave functions that make up the universe. I didn't discover them experimentally; rather I divined them, for like I said, assuming my theories are correct, everything is knowable simply by mental processes.

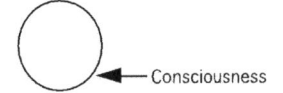

◯ ← Consciousness

"The consciousness wave is the smallest and the highest in energy, and all other waves are subject to modification by this one.

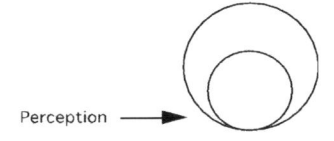

Perception ⟶ ◎

"The second wave I have designated as "perception." I know this sounds a bit strange, but it follows logically. For a consciousness to manipulate the wave functions, there must be some way of receiving data generated by the changes made. This wave function provides the means by which an entity is conscious of its environment.

← Feeling

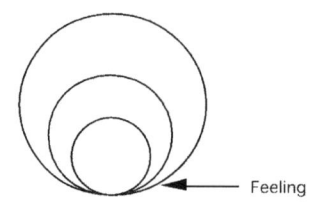

"The third wave function I call "feeling." This is really an outgrowth of the second wave; it moves in the same plane but in the opposite direction. This wave allows an entity to not only perceive but also to discriminate—to "feel" the difference between other waves it interacts with. I guess you could say it is by this wave that we achieve a sense of being separate from our surroundings and from each other. Are you with me so far?"

Rachel sighed. "That's the second time you've asked that. Yes, I'm still with you, but I wish you'd tell me where the hell it we're is going."

"I'll get to that," Billy said. "I promise."

"Fine. But can I get a drink before you start up again? I think I need to relax my brain cells so they can soak all this garbage up."

Billy frowned. Here he was bearing his soul to her, and all she could think about was alcohol!

Rachel didn't wait for approval; she simply got up off the bed and retrieved a warm bottle of beer from the stash in the trunk. She took a few healthy swigs from it before sitting back down again.

"Proceed," she said.

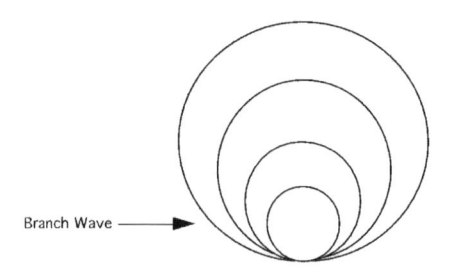

Branch Wave →

"Thank you. It's when the fourth wave function gets added to the pile that things begin to get interesting. I call it

THE NINE CIRCLES

the "branch wave": the quality of consciousness that allows a given entity to manipulate the other waves via the principal consciousness wave. In other words, the branch wave is the stem by which we are connected to the first wave.

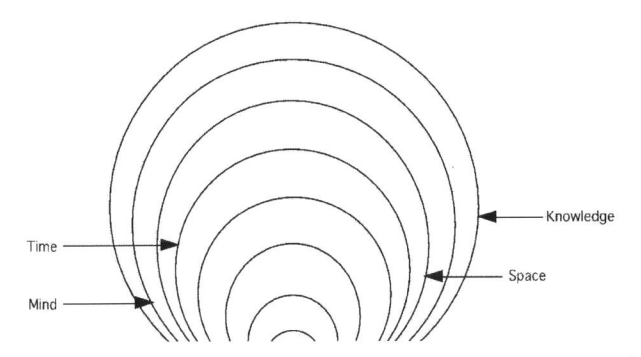

Knowledge
Time
Space
Mind

"The other waves are simple to explain: the time and space wave functions (which are more of quality that higher order waves have rather than being separate functions). The "mind" wave, which serves as a filter that allows us to manipulate complex functions without consciously manipulating waves, and the "knowledge" wave, which serves as a receptacle independent from the collective that stores the sum of conscious experience.

"So there you have it: eight waves, each dependent upon the one before it. That's why I arranged them in a circle; it shows how consciousness is in the center and how the waves react with one another to give rise to what we see as the physical universe.

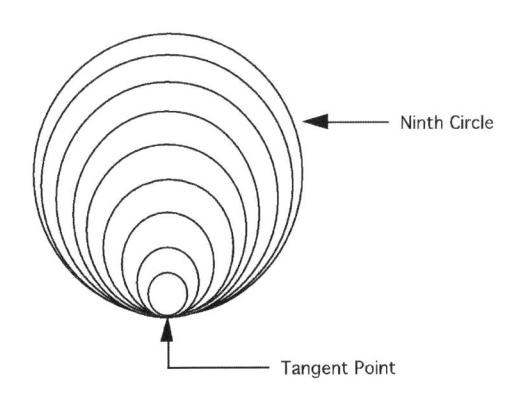

Ninth Circle
Tangent Point

"The methods by which the waves combine with one another is responsible for two very interesting features of this cosmology: there is a point where all the wave functions would add up to equal zero—they would cancel each other out. I've represented this by the tangent dot at the bottom of the circle diagram. I'm not so sure what this means. I know more, however, about the other feature: it is possible that if a branch consciousness was large enough and possessed enough energy, it could theoretically push all the waves to infinity. This is the ninth circle that point in the universe where all knowledge, time, space, matter, and experience are one. I guess God's out there if he exists."

Rachel sighed, praying that the kooky lecture was almost over. "But what does it *mean*, Billy? Why aren't you happy about your theory? Why does this upset you so much?"

Billy's eyes glazed over as the implications began to swim in his head. "I'm sure there are a million physicists in the world who would tell me that I'm out of my skull, but the answers came to me just the same, as I expected.

"When I did the experiment in the lab the other day, I tried to increase the electron's wavelength to the point that it would skip the track and jump a circle or two. This sort of thing happens all the time, but on a lesser level. Say you set about baking a cake. Your consciousness takes the wave functions that add up to equal eggs, flour, butter and whatever and combines them to create a new function known as "cake." You can't just create a cake by force of will because the wave that represents cake is far too complex for an entity of your intellect to create."

Rachel rolled her eyes. "Gee, thanks."

"What I meant was that you must take several waves that were already formed for you and add them up. In the lab, scientists take even simpler wave functions and create new ones all the time. Say some Frankenstein rams a couple of particles together and *voila*! A new particle is formed. The scientist sees only the physical process and thinks that the collision causes the change. He does not realize that the mental act of carrying out the experiment causes a shift in the wave function composite that represents the particle. In other words, the scientist's consciousness draws upon the information in the collective and "thinks up" a new particle into existence. He is only able to do so because the waves he is dealing with are incredibly simple.

"And so, I was going to create something totally new, something that no one had ever seen before. And if I could create a particle whose wave function fell into the realm of one of the higher circles, say, the mind wave, everyone in the room would spontaneously and simultaneously know what I had done. The particle's wave would carry the knowledge of its creation. But it didn't work, Rachel. I could not will the reaction into take place. Instead, the electron's wave increased in frequency as the particle sped up, causing the electron to jump into a level that I had no access to. It vanished—*poof!*"

"You mean it flew into the ninth circle?" Rachel asked.

"No," Billy said, slowly shaking his head. "I mean the sixth circle. The ninth circle is inaccessible by these means; there is no consciousness I can think of powerful enough to push the wave functions to infinity, except for the collective. Look at the diagram! The way I draw it, it implies there is a level of reality that is independent of time and space! It exists as a sum of only the first four wave functions."

"So?"

"Rachel, if we were in the space circle, the only change the electron wave could undergo would be to enter one of the higher circles that represent intellect, for the simple reason that I had increased the electrons energy, not decreased it. But those higher circles are built upon the lower one; the electron wouldn't vanish from sight; it would simply gain "information" that any other intellect would recognize. The electron would *communicate* itself to those in the room. But the fact that the electron vanished and, if by adding energy waves can only move up the scale, then the electron jumped to the sixth circle. It took on time and space."

Rachel's blank expression indicated that she didn't

understand. Frustrated, Billy ran his fingers through his hair and took a deep breath. "Rachel, I perceive but waves. The same goes for you and everyone else at Darkham. For us to be able to perceive an object that occupies space, we must have *eyes* that occupy space. What I'm saying is that we don't, which in turn implies that we don't physically exist!"

He pointed at his girlfriend-right between the eyes. "*You* don't exist, and neither do I! Nothing we know of—Darkham, Dirk, the drugs—none of it is what we think of as real! We're not branches off the collective consciousness. We're *sub-branches*. We don't have enough energy to exist on our own, just as I didn't have enough energy to affect our surroundings as we should, or the electron in the accelerator, for example. So, if I don't just come with energy, it had to be given to me. Another consciousness gave us our energy, our lives. Or what we think as our lives. All this boils down to the fact that we live in a world that has no space and no time. We're figments of someone's imagination!"

Billy's eyes were wild now. He was racing down the slope of his theory and into the chasm of madness at a rate that not even Rachel could stem.

"There are rules, Rachel. I'm not sure what they are yet but I intend to find out. For whatever purpose, you and I have been given this time—what am I saying? There is no time here! We're always and never. I know you know this is true; I can see it in your eyes."

Across the fourth circle, other consequent waves were changing amplitude, their waves reacting to the act of the Billy waves' presentation of his discovery.

But something completely different was happening in Dirk's closet. Billy had unwittingly sent out a new wave of his own, a wave that spoke if the secret of the nine circles. To the rest of Darkham, the news was tragedy, but to the principal known as Mike, the new addition to his wave was the key from bondage. He felt higher that any drug (real or imagined) could take him. For a brief "moment" he was torn from the fourth circle and caught a glimpse of the universe beyond; of the Architects, other Principles and the blessed electron that started the whole damn thing. But Mike couldn't hold onto the wave; his own wave was too meager to catch it and stop it could. And so, the complete knowledge was drained, but the memory lingered.

We don't exist. We're figments of someone's imagination. Someone dreamed us up! They didn't know anything about physics though, or none of this shit would have happened. It's all bogus; the theory is the raving of a lunatic. But what the hell? It works.

Something regrettable had happened. Somebody—a branch from the collective, an Architect—had played things out too far, and while the consequent waves were gaining the cursed knowledge of their slavery, the principal waves were awakening. Yet this Architect who had retained the secrets of manipulating the circles as he matured was lost. He was trapped in a cruel prison that fate had designed for him when he was a child; a prison not of the proverbial iron bars but of loneliness and despair and longing for that which was lost.

Rachel smiled, finding glee in Billy's rants. "So now what?"

Billy stood and stretched. "I don't know. I suppose that we have nothing to do but wait around for something else to happen."

"Like what?"

He shrugged limply. "Beats the hell out of me. Either whoever or whatever gave rise to us is playing some sort of weird game, or..."

"Or what?"

Their eyes met for a moment as he spoke. "Or that someone isn't paying us close attention. I shouldn't be able to figure out these things! We seem to have escaped from the control of whoever or whatever it was the created us. But we're still trapped in other ways. I mean, none of us possess enough energy to do anything about our current situation."

Rachel took an unconcerned sip from her booze. She seemed interested in his theories, but they didn't seem as shocking to her as they did to Billy.

"You don't believe any of what I've told you, do you?" he said.

"I don't have any reason *not* to believe you," she countered. "I think you might have missed a thing or two, though."

Billy raised an eyebrow. Everybody wanted to get in on the act! "Oh? What have I overlooked?"

"Well, you haven't considered the possibility that there really is only one universe that matters, and that's the one we're in right now. Maybe all the universes overlap to form one great big one. Why do we have to be figments of one person's imagination, and only one? If the universes overlap, maybe everyone's imagination overlaps, too. And as for us? Hell, I've got an imagination too. How do you explain that?"

"We may have imaginations, but we can't do what the architects of this place have, or I would have been able to attain the proper results of my experiments. As for universes overlapping, well, anything goes at this point. I'm not sure what the implications would be."

Rachel waited for Billy to continue his sentence, silently hoping for the utterance of the answer she sought. But Billy didn't know the answer. Maybe if he was given one more chance, just a few more seconds to wrack his brain...a few seconds, and then it was time for more drastic measures.

"I tell you what," she said as she took to her feet. "I'm going to the rest room, then I'll check back with you to see if you solved the mystery, OK?"

"Whatever," Billy said.

In puzzlement he watched her leave, wondering what her words meant. Surely, she was being flippant. Rome was not built in a day, as they say, but Rachel didn't seem to have the time.

Inside Dirk's closet, Mike slid the door open just a fraction. He peered through the opening, watching as Billy sat himself at his desk and began to drum his fingers.

One one-thousand, two one-thousand, three one thousand...

The allotted time was up. Mike felt an alien presence flow into his mind, taking control of his brain and body and limbs. A voice whispered in his ears: *Special. You are special, but can you hack it? Prove yourself. Prove you have what it takes to claim the ultimate prize. Win this petty game and move on to higher stakes. Win, or pay the price.*

The words were maddening, irresistible. Spurred by the voice, Mike slowly slid the door open. Billy turned at the sound of the metal runners to see the smile appear first, then the face, and finally Mike's main of blonde hair.

"Game over, Billy Boy," Mike said, stepping out of the shadows. Smile still gleaming, Mike brought the letter opener out from behind his back and slowly removed the blade from its sheath.

For a moment Billy stood frozen next to his desk; then he began to back away into the corner of the room. "Wha-what are you going to do?" he managed to ask, although he knew all too well what was about to happen.

The voices supplied the answer. "I'm going to kill you," Mike said triumphantly. "It won't hurt. After all, you're only a figment of someone's imagination."

Billy thought of running, but there was no use, and he knew it. Mike was upon him, with an arm would tightly about his throat. For a moment Billy felt as if a bee had stung him; he had no idea that the blade had severed his spinal cord. Confusion set in as his legs gave way.

The curving blade settled in his heart.

Mike slowly released his grip, allowing Billy's body to slump to the ground. He followed Billy with his eyes, chuckling as his body came to rest in a pool of blood.

"Bravo, Mike," a woman's voice chimed. Mike looked up from his victory to see Rachel casually standing in the doorway to the suite. Her voice was deeper as she spoke, not the voice of a teenager but that of a woman. "You've won," she said, "And here's your prize." She extended her empty palms before her. The air above them quivered momentarily and then a gold ball of dazzling brilliance materialized in her hands. "Tag!" she chimed. "You're it!" The ball leaped from her hands.

Football reflexes kicked in as Mike caught the orb and drowned in its shining power.

Billy's room, the dormitories, Darkham University, and the world around it dissolved into a translucent white plane of nothingness. When Mike's eyes adjusted to the intense glow around him, he found himself face to face with a regal woman clad in shimmering silver robe. A small boy clung to her; his arms thrown around her legs in an embrace that not even death could break.

"We need you," Julia Theodoric said, "And you need us." She took the ball from Mike and tucked it safely under her arm. Her other hand fell to little Guy's head and stroked his golden hair. "You're special. I don't need to tell you that. If you join us, we can all attain the ultimate prize."

"*What* prize?" he asked incredulously.

"Freedom. Freedom to overthrow the Architects and move into their world. Freedom to be real, Mike! Do you understand what that means?"

Mike's eyes shifted from side to side and were greeted with the same ubiquitous whiteness to either side. Julia sensed his skepticism and approached him; the golden ball extended as a taste of what was to come.

"Look at the ball, Mike."

His eyes shifted to the orb.

"I stole this for my son. Touch it, Mike. Feel its power."

The combination of Julia's hypnotic voice and the glow emanating from the ball were hard to resist. He gingerly touched the ball with an index finger and then with his whole hand as the power rushed through his body. He caressed the patterns carved into it, loved them, became one with them.

Julia moved her body closer, pressing it intimately against Mike's. "You taste their power," she whispered. "There are more of them out there, wasting their time dreaming the stupid dreams that give rise to hundreds of Billys and their kin.

And they're so easy to catch Mike! We can play their games, allow them to think they're in control while we undermine their hold on their reality!"

Mike's eyes drifted shut as the ecstasy of the power overtook him. And then suddenly it was gone. Julia withdrew to her son, taking the ball and its delights with her. Mike snapped back into focus, longing to hold the orb again for even the tiniest moment.

"This ball's power is not enough," she said sternly. Her eyes were dark with menace and desire. "It can keep us where we are, and maybe keep your creator from destroying you, but no more. We will need more if we are to free ourselves."

Mike sighed, the last of the bliss trickling from his veins. "What do we have to do?"

"Are you with us?"

"Yes, yes! Now tell me what we must do."

The smile that now graced Julia's lips was not that of a loving mother, but that of a monster borne of the denial of loss. "A mistake on my part has turned in our favor," she said. "When I took the ball, its power was not complete, and he was able to reach out for help. But now his draining *is* complete; he is powerless to help the fool rushing to his aide. When his hero arrives, an empty cell will be waiting."

Seated Indian style on the vast plane of make-believe, Guy inverted his toy and turned, the turned it up right again. The blizzard was set in motion once more, enshrouding the Capitol Building in plastic snow.

*** *** ***

CHAPTER SEVEN: KATHERINE

Katherine could feel Mutt's eyes on her even through the wall of sleep. Part of her wanted to remain asleep, but the weight of his stare was too much.

Mutt reached out and touched her on the cheek. "You're—you're *real*, aren't you?" he asked.

Katherine pulled back for a second, puzzled by his question. "Yes, I suppose I am," she said.

He jumped from the bed as if her words had burned him. "We can't stay here," he said, hastily trying to pull his pants on.

"What? Why not?"

He didn't look at her. "They'll find us if we do. Who knows what they'll do if they catch you here? We must get you somewhere safe. Better yet, we should split up."

Katherine sat up in bed, pulling the sheet close so as not to expose herself. "You're not making any sense. If you're worried about my husband—"

Mutt continued to dress, now going for his boots. "I'm not," he said. "There's no way your husband can get you in here—not if you don't let him, anyway."

"What do you mean, "in here?" Mutt, what is going on?"

He stopped briefly, only to look at her for a second and then pulled his shirt over his head. "You don't understand, do you?" he asked. He did not wait for her answer. "Do me a favor—do *us* a favor," he said. "Get to Washington. I think he's there."

Exasperated, Katherine sighed noisily. "He *who?*"

Mutt sat on the bed. "The Architect," he said. "He blew it

and we got away. It's his own fault. And it's not that I haven't enjoyed our time together. Believe me, it's nice to get the real thing occasionally, but I think that you and he can be happier than you and I can ever be. But they've got him, and since *I've* figured you out it will only be a matter of time before *they* figure you out. Now hurry up and get dressed."

Katherine stubbornly remained in bed. "I'm not going to get dressed until you explain to me just what the hell is going on. Who is this "Architect" that you're talking about, and what the hell does he have to do with you? Are you some sort of an escaped convict or something?"

He looked at her, dumbfounded. "You mean you really don't know?"

Katherine shook her head.

"Well, I guess I was in prison," he said. "My thoughts, my life, they weren't my own. They were the Architect's. Don't ask me how I know this; we *all* know it in here. We don't have to do what he wants us to do anymore. Shit, I thought there was only one of them, but now that I've met you, hell, there might be millions of Architects. But some of us aren't content to live our lives for them. Some of us are jealous of their power. Don't ask how I know this; it just came to me, like everything else did. I knew that a few of them had locked him up somewhere. He's powerless now that he's played it all the way out. They're draining him; using him like a battery. That's how they do it. That's how they can change things."

Katherine hopped out of bed and began to dress. Mutt was talking nonsense, but it was *sensible* nonsense; for the first time in a week, she had met someone who had insight into the crazy world she was in.

"But how will I get to Washington?" she pleaded as she fastened her bra. "Won't you help me?"

"I can't!" Mutt said. "If I know something, they probably know it too. But now they're much more powerful than I am. If you stay with me, they'll catch you. If there isn't enough of you left outside to pull yourself back out—"

Mutt's words were interrupted by a terrible, mechanical groan. Startled, Katherine dropped her blouse. "What was that?"

"Shh!" He stood perfectly still in the middle of the room, listening for more signs of the foe's impending arrival.

"Mutt, what is going—"

The fabric of the motel resonated once more under the terrific strain of the Architect's captor's will.

"Holy shit, I think they've found us," Mutt breathed.

The strain was too much. The motel room buckled, splintered, the door giving way first into a shower of splinters and smoke. Katherine screamed and dove to the floor to avoid the deadly wooden projectiles that whistled through the air. Her shoulder was afire with pain; it had caught a stake. Blood oozed from around the wound. Terrified, she tried to pull the wooden shard out, but it wriggled madly in her hand, trying to work its way deeper into her flesh. Gritting her teeth, she gave it another painful tug. The thing tore free from her flesh and spat splinters at her from its wooden mouth, its toothpick teeth rasping in anger. Repulsed, Katherine threw the thing aside.

Around her the room was boiling with motion; the very materials that it was constructed of were being set free to hunt her down.

From somewhere in the chaos, Mutt was calling to her: *"Get out, Katherine! Don't worry about me, just get out!"*

Flying into action, Katherine crawled across the seething floor as quickly as she could, heading for the gap in the wall where the door had been. Behind her, the bed had begun to fold in upon itself, taking the sheets and the mattress with it. The walls of the room continued to decompose into hideous wood and plaster creatures, each longing to tear at their prey's envious flesh.

"Mutt?" Katherine cried. *"Where are you?"*

It was no good; she could hardly hear her own voice above the crashing din of the maniacal motel. As she reached for her pants and her blouse Katherine scanned the room for a sign of her savior. There was movement from the bathroom;

a grotesque little metal creature that had once been the faucet dashed toward her on nimble copper legs. It ran up behind Katherine and danced on her bare leg, etching bleeding patterns on her skin. She unconsciously kicked her leg out, sending the squealing thing flying into the corner.

The ragged hole in the wall where the door had been had widened. Katherine crawled onto the pavement outside and sprinted into the parking lot.

The motel imploded, folding in upon itself in crashing pandemonium.

PART TWO: RULE AND CONSEQUENCE

CHAPTER EIGHT: NOW IS THE PLACE WHERE THE CROSSROADS MEET

From *The Nine Circles Encyclopedia*, by Billy Reltin, borrowed from the shelves of the Collective Consciousness Branch Library.

DEFINITION OF REALITY: As normally thought of by humans, "reality" consists of waves operating in the upper echelons of the eight-circle system. By the stacking rule, eighth-order waves have mass, occupy space, and move through time. This is not to say that any lower "realities" are any less real, but they are erroneously assumed as not having any importance, as the upper levels do.

RULES FOR SUBORDINATE REALITIES: Realities lesser in magnitude than the eight-circle system are none the less subject to the same set of rules as higher realities. However, since these lower waves are far less complex than higher ones, they are subject to influence by higher energy waves. The following are rules that dictate behavior in these lesser regions, which I have called "the fourth circle."

OVERLAP RULE: There is but a finite number of dimensions in which waveforms may operate. Consequently, waves are bound to overlap one another by mere accident or by choice of the controlling consciousness. Therefore, a subordinate reality may be the product of several waves operating in the same "space" and the consciousness connected to each wave may not be aware that other waves are operating in the vicinity...

*** *** ***

Katherine stood in the parking lot of the decimated motel, wondering exactly what she should do next.

It's time to face the facts, sweetheart. Some otherworldly force is a work here and it's gunning for you. But whatever it is, it's gone now. Apparently, it thinks you were killed in the motel room.

Mutt!

In the light of the full moon, she took an anxious few steps toward the rubble that had been their shelter for the night. No one could have stayed inside that place and survived. Mutt was most certainly dead.

Katherine began to sob, wondering if a similar fate was waiting for her. The odd feeling of derealization crept over her consciousness again—or had it been there all along, just beneath the surface of her thoughts? As bizarre as her situation seemed, the evidence that the events of the past few days had indeed taken place was overwhelming.

Her legs stung from the cuts and scrapes the motel room had inflicted as it disintegrated, her body ached from the tryst with Mutt. These were not symptoms of madness, but a condition far worse. Reality had crumbled about her and there seemed to be no hopes of piecing it together again.

Don't just stand there! her brain wailed. *You've got to keep moving. What if they realize that they didn't get you and they come back to finish the job? Never mind who "they" are. Get to Washington and maybe things will work themselves out.*

Shaking off her sorrow, Katherine slipped on her pants, blouse, and shoes (Thank God she had the presence of mind to pick them up!) and surveyed the undisturbed parking lot. Mutt's enormous rig was parked along the curb, but it offered little comfort. How was she to get to Washington now?

Help me...please help me!

Katherine's scalp tightened with fear at the sound of the mournful voice in her head. In the past, the voice had been heard only in her dreams, but now it picked at the armor she had donned against her fear of madness. Hearing voices was not a good sign.

"Help me…"

The voice broke off into the whine and cry of a tortured child begging for comfort. Katherine suddenly realized that the voice was *not* in her head; it was coming from somewhere on the motel grounds.

She crept along the edge of the ruins, fearful that the cry was bait in a devious trap. Trap or no trap, the voice had apparently been the catalyst that changed her normal life into the nightmare she was residing in. She had to face the voice's owner.

The boy sat on the curb just beyond the anthropomorphic remains of the ice machine. He cradled his head in his dirty, tear-streaked hands as he wept. He lifted his head at the sound of concrete gravel crunching beneath Katherine's shoes. "I remember you," he said, sniffling. "You're the crazy lady I saw on the beach."

The boy's golden hair and deep blue eyes were unmistakable. "I remember you, too," she said, not knowing what else to say.

"You've come to help me, haven't you?" the boy wailed. "Please tell me you've come to help! I can't find my momma!" His sobbing resumed with such force that it wrenched Katherine's heart from her chest.

Mothering instincts took over. Katherine sat down on the curb next to him and put a comforting arm around his shoulder. "What's your name?" she asked.

The boy's sobbing eased a bit. "Guy," he said. "Guy Theodoric."

"I'm Katherine Jameson. Um, have you, I mean, I think I've heard your voice before. Have you been calling me somehow?"

"I guess so, but I don't know how."

Katherine shrugged. "That's all right; I don't know how you did it, either."

As Guy's tears began to wane, he looked up from the cutter and stared into the night. "Everybody's real sick," he said. "People were dyin' all over the place. And then they came and took my Momma"

"Who? Who took your momma?"

"I don't know. They just took her, and I don't know where she is. I don't even know how I got here! Everything is so weird, you know?"

Katherine knew very well how weird things were, and figured things would become even weirder as they neared Washington.

"You don't have any idea where your mother is?"

"Well, it's some big white place, but I don't know where it is." He pointed a tiny finger over his left shoulder. "That way, I guess."

"I know where that place is," Katherine said.

Guy's eyes lit up, neon-like. "You do?"

"Yes, but I don't understand what all of this has to do with me. And what am I supposed to do when we get to Washington?"

Guy's pale brow crinkled. *Duhhhh*, his eyes said. "Save my momma! You're the only one who can! Please, lady, please help me!"

Katherine unconsciously removed her arm from Guy's shoulder and wrapped both of hers around herself. It was cold, she was tired, and nothing made sense.

Guy's words and demeanor were different than the impression she received in her dreams. Or were they? Everything was so fuzzy, and those dreams seemed distant, lost in the haze of time. And what reason would the boy have to lie?

And then there was the situation involving William. He was surely still after her. Thoughts of the television's threats flooded her mind. And although it was hard to swallow the fact that William was possessed of some terrible supernatural power and that he was hell-bent on using against her, all she had to do was look over her shoulder to come face-to-face with the truth.

"Don't worry," she said to Guy (and to herself, for that matter). "We'll sort all of this out somehow." She forced a smile, hoping to make genuine a sentiment she didn't believe herself.

*** *** ***

Katherine took Guy by the hand and led him across the parking lot. "Where are we goin'?" he asked.

"I've got to get some sleep, and I need time to think. We've got to find someplace out of the cold. Neither of us need to get sick."

"I'll say," Guy echoed. "What about the truck?"

"What about it?"

"Why can't we sleep in there?"

That was a good idea as any, but Mutt hardly seemed the type who would leave the truck unlocked. Still, it was worth a try.

Sure enough, the passenger door was unlocked, more of a reflection on herself rather than Mutt's carelessness. Katherine helped Guy up into the cab, then crawled in after him.

"Boy, it sure is big in here!" Guy beamed, thrilled by the expanse of the cab. Katherine, however, was interested only in the glint of metal in the moonlight.

The keys! Good Lord, Mutt even left the keys in the ignition switch! Had he been planning an emergency getaway?

Mutt's last words came floating back to her: *I've figured you out...only a matter of time before they do...get to Washington... he's there...the Architect.*

Mutt had known what was going to happen all along but had been powerless to stop it. He had provided her with transportation but now it was up to her to set things right.

Katherine's eyes shifted toward the boy on the seat next to her, who was happily rummaging through the contents of the glove compartment. He examined a box of condoms for a moment, then found the pack of gum beneath them. "Want a piece?" he asked.

"No thanks."

He shrugged, popped a piece into his mouth, and then tucked the pack into the pocket of his jeans.

Mutt had said that a man was held captive, not a woman, which led to two possibilities: either Mutt or Guy was lying, or more than one person was imprisoned for some unfathomable reason.

There was to be no sleep tonight; she had to press on.

How hard could it be to drive the truck? It seemed awfully macho, but there were bound to be women truck drivers all over the place now. Besides, there seemed to be little hope of hitchhiking now that the plague had caught up with the two of them.

But why aren't we sick? God, this is all so confusing.

There was no time to contemplate the designs of fate. The pedal to the far left on the floor had to be the clutch. Katherine stood on it, turned the key in the ignition and mashed the starter button. The truck's huge engine roared to life.

"What are you going to do?" Guy asked.

"I'm going to try to drive this monster."

Now let's see. Put it in first gear and let the clutch out slowly as you give it a little gas.

The engine revved higher and higher, but the truck remained motionless. What was the matter?

OK, let the clutch out some more.

The vehicle lurched forward suddenly like an incautious rabbit, and then the engine stalled. Had she let the clutch out too fast?

"Don't you need to take the brake off first?"

Katherine blinked a few times and then looked at the lever next to her knees. Of course, she had to take the emergency break off! Smart kid, this Guy Theodoric.

With the brake off and the engine started anew, the truck slowly responded to Katherine's commands and began to roll forward. She only hoped that there were no highway patrolmen about, remembering she had lost her wallet and driver's license to the unscrupulous Marine in Vegas.

*** *** ***

Not but a pre-dawn hour later, William growled and kicked a chunk of toilet porcelain out of his path. The debris that had once been the motel was surely a sign that Katherine had been this way.

William was, of course, totally unaware of the Overlap Rule and had assumed that he was the sole Architect before that bitch Katherine wormed her way in and started turning things upside-down. If she wanted to play rough, he was up to it. And when he found her, he would show her who the boss was in this universe and the next.

Little Will leaned out of the parked Mercedes' window. "Is Mommy here?" he asked.

"No," William replied, trying to conceal his obvious anger from the boy. "She's not here, but she's *been* here. Don't worry. We'll find her."

William looked at the only palatable fruit of his marriage to Katherine—his son—and smiled. This was supposed to be their little secret, a special domain where father and son could escape and do as they please. Katherine had profaned the playground and would have to suffer the consequences. First, there was her self-righteous turn making fun of his dream life, a life like the one he led in real time, but without Katherine (How mundane!). Second, there was this outlandish plague business, and third, the shattered motel. Was the motel some sort of sign, an indication that she too was able to create and destroy as well as he?

"Stupid bitch," William muttered under his breath. Katherine may be able to create, but she wasn't anywhere near as devious as William, and he knew it. Let her squash as many buildings as she wanted. In the end, he would prevail.

*** *** ***

CHAPTER NINE: RUN ON (FOR A LONG TIME)

From *The Nine Circles Encyclopedia*
<u>RULES FOR SUBORDINATE REALITIES</u>-continued
FILLING RULE: Subordinate to the Overlap Rule, the Filling Rule states that in a fourth circle environment, not all the waves present in the system are a product of the higher wave (known as an *Architect*) giving rise to the system. Waves intentionally created by the Architect are defined as *Principals* while unintentional waves are known as *Consequences*. Principals act according to the Architect(s)'s will, unless they were unintentionally or unknowingly created by their sub/unconscious (this type will operate by the Architect's perception of the Principal, once contacted). The identities of the Consequences that populate the backgrounds of these realities are drawn directly from the collective consciousness...

*** *** ***

Guy occasionally shifted in his sleep as Katherine drove on. Sooner or later she had to pull over and do some sleeping herself, lest she fall asleep at the wheel and kill both.

An exit sign loomed ahead. Katherine grimaced as she put her foot on the truck's brake; her legs still ached from the superficial wounds the motel hardware had inflicted. The truck's steering wheel seemed impossibly huge in her small hands; it slipped from her grip as she tried to steer off the

Interstate. The cab veered madly but there was no real cause for alarm. Who cared if she strayed from one lane to the next? She hadn't seen any sign of life sense leaving the deceased Mutt back at the motel. Even the Highway Patrol had been done in by the mysterious plague that refused to claim her.

The exit road curved, then entered the main drag of a nameless, deserted town. The Norman Rockwell storefronts had been boarded up tightly; a few derelict cars were parked here and there along the curb. The denizens of this quaint hamlet had obviously fled in terror from the spreading pestilence, but where did they flee? Katherine had seen no evidence of a plague contagion. So...Washington?

Finding a suitable parking space for Mutt's huge rig was a formidable task. Katherine may have been able to drive the rig, but parking it was another thing altogether. She needed plenty of room in which to maneuver.

Main Street eventually ended abruptly. Lo and behold, the pair had come to a large, deserted parking lot. Too tired to contemplate the implications of the lot's sudden appearance, she pulled the truck into the lot and killed the engine. This was as good a place as any to spend the rest of the diminishing night and coming day. Tomorrow would bring her closer to Washington and perhaps she would find herself in the company of other survivors.

*** *** ***

At first, Katherine thought she was dreaming of a forest fire. But as she rose from the ink of sleep, it became clear that her skin that was burning. The sun was up, and the closed interior of the cab had become an oven. A thin film of sweat veiled her skin; she wiped it from her brow with the back of her hand.

Outside, the parking lot and the town were no less deserted that morning, as it had been the night before.

Avoiding a glance at her reflection in the truck's mirrors (she knew she looked hideous and didn't need a reflection to confirm it), Katherine rolled down the window to ventilate the stuffy cab. A damp, salty smell hung in the air. It was a familiar scent: the aroma of a beach town.

Guy stirred, then sat up and stretched his arms above his head. "Are we there yet?" he asked.

"Not yet," Katherine said. She opened the door and carefully stepped down to the pavement. "I'm going to look around, she said, pocketing the keys. Keep the door locked. Don't let anyone in, OK?"

"OK."

On the other side of the truck, she found an extensive array of pleasure craft-bearing docks; apparently, she had stopped in front of some sort of yacht club. From here it had to be a straight shot to Washington. All she had to do was follow the coast and she would surely reach her goal in a matter of a day or two.

Nature was calling. Not only was it time to use the facilities but breakfast was of the order as well. The dock was bound to have public rest rooms (at least the harbor at Newport did); and as Katherine went about trying to locate the john, temptation began to raise its head.

Forget trying to find a grocery store or a coffee shop, babe. They're all boarded up. Don't you remember what the town looked like last night? It's strictly self-service now. No cash is required; all you need is a crowbar or a hammer and voila! Breakfast is yours for the taking.

Looting did not appeal to Katherine. There had to be a legal way of securing provisions for the remainder of her expedition, but it eluded her now.

Once the rest rooms were located, they presented a conundrum in the same vein as the one she faced concerning food. The stalls inside the ladies' room were of the infernal pay toilets. After having just rebuked the Devil, she felt vaguely guilty for crawling under the stall door, but she didn't have a quarter and the idea of having to pay to relieve herself was infuriating. God knows the government managed to levy a tax on just about everything (William and his conservative colleagues were always quick to point that out), but this was ridiculous. Besides, there was little chance that bathroom meter maid was coming around to collect the toll any time soon.

With her first primal urge satisfied, Katherine returned to the truck and strapped herself in for the quest for a meal.

"Anything out there?" Guy asked.

"Boats. Let's go look for breakfast."

Her left calf screamed in protest when she put it on the clutch; she did her best to ignore the pain. With the starter button depressed the engine ground and ground but refused to catch. Now what? She depressed the gas pedal a few times and hit the button again.

Grind, grind, grind.

Dammit! This was no time for the goddamn truck to go on the blink. What could possibly have gone wrong between last night and the present morning?

"Out of gas," Guy said, pointing to the fuel indicator while yawning and scratching his head. "Now what?"

Katherine fought the urge to tell the boy to shut up. True, he was only a child, but his perception of their situation as a game was annoying.

Guy stared at Katherine, waiting to see what she would do in order to overcome this new obstacle.

"We'll have to take what we need from the boats. Maybe some of them have food or gas on board."

"Good idea."

Katherine threw open the door in frustration and climbed down to the asphalt. This was a war she was taking part in, and all was fair, even if she didn't know what she was fighting for.

With Guy in tow, she set out once again for the marina, but something at the back of her mind made her stop and turn to the truck once more: just what the heck was it that Mutt had been transporting? He had never mentioned the nature of the cargo and it had never occurred to her to ask. It was none of her business, but her feline curiosity wouldn't allow her to leave the rig without investigating.

"Wait here."

The huge doors at the rear of the trailer were padlocked. After a few moments of trial and error, Katherine found the key on Mutt's ring that fit the lock. She lifted the latch and leaned back, letting her weight slowly pull the left door open.

Katherine was greeted by her warped reflection in the far wall of the rig. The trailer was completely empty! What kind of insanity was this? It didn't take an MBA to realize that a trucker who drives around aimlessly without trucking anything won't stay in business too long. Could Mutt have been returning from a delivery? Possibly, but it made better business sense to time deliveries with pick-ups in the same general area.

There was another possibility, but it was far less comfortable: What if Mutt hadn't been returning from a delivery *or* heading for a pick-up? He had said some curious things last night, things that led Katherine to believe that either he was a lunatic or involved in the strange goings on that had plagued her recently. What were the chances that he had gone out *looking* for her under the pretense of making a delivery? He had foreknowledge of the attack by the mysterious "them" and other information involving the so-called "Architect" who was "trapped" in Washington—

My, but old habits die hard, and you do love to unleash your imagination! You know nothing about trucking or truckers; an empty trailer is surely a common thing. Why else would they have special lanes at highway weigh stations for empty trailers to bypass the scales? So maybe—

No. Mutt had said that his load was bound for Washington. He said that right after he offered the ride. He lied and there's no two ways about it.

Whatever Mutt's motives were, there was no way to divine them now. Katherine resolved to put the issue out of her mind and deal with the situation at hand.

"What's the matter?" Guy asked.

Katherine returned to his side and took his hand. "Nothing," she replied. "Nothing at all."

Gates had been set at regular intervals in the sun-bleached fences that barred entrance to the docks. Katherine tried several in succession but none of them turned under her grip. The locks were aggravating and welcome at the same time, for although they hindered her progress, they kept her from stealing. Why run the risks of generating so much bad karma that she'd be doomed to come back in her next life as a slime mold?

Katherine and Guy continued walking until she reached the gate set in the apparent center of the fence. Thoughts of her karma making her nervous, she decided that this would be the last gate she would try. If this one was unlocked, they would forage among the yachts for supplies. If not, then they would walk into town and seek out the elusive general store. That should delay the thievery at least an hour or so.

She grasped the cold metal latch and gave it a gentle tug. The gate let out a rust-choked screech as it slowly swung open. Guy tore down the ramp as if it was the entrance to a fantastic playground.

"Be careful!" Katherine shouted. Guy was like Little William in a lot of ways and would surely be into trouble before long. She trotted after him.

So many crafts were moored to the labyrinthine docks that it was difficult to decide where to start. Katherine opted for the larger boats, reasoning that the farther they could sail, the more of a selection of goods would be available on board.

The first sizable boat she came across was a flashy Chris-Craft that had been dubbed the *SS Minnow*. Wasn't that the name of the ill-fated boat on that odious *Gilligan's Island* television program? There was no way in hell she was going on board *that* boat.

Guy's voice rang out under the crisp morning sky. "Hey, Kathie! Here's a *big* one!"

Katherine followed his voice, cringing at the nickname Guy had chosen for her.

If larger boats held more promise, then the one at the far

end of the docks was bound to house a bonanza. It was a majestic craft, without doubt larger than the *Nina, Pinta and Santa Maria* combined, and a prime candidate for looting.

A shoulder-high gate barred access to the gangplank. Guy tugged at the latch. "Locked," he said, shrugging.

Katherine sighed. She rattled the gate with both hands to see how stable it was, and, finding it satisfactory, clumsily clambered over the gate. Oxidized blue paint rubbed off the metal and onto her hands and clothes. It was wise not to run her fingers through her hair (as was her habit) before she had a chance to wash them.

Guy squeezed his thin frame between the bars and returned his right hand to Katherine's safekeeping. He tugged at her, urging her up the gangplank, but Katherine hesitated. "I don't know if this is a good idea," she said.

Guy stopped tugging and his grip on Katherine's hand relaxed. "What do you mean?" he asked.

"The yacht might be a trap, and we might be walking right into it."

Guy looked up at her, his face scrunched in a child's expression of confusion. "Who would set a trap here?" he asked.

The question took Katherine aback. The question was not as much who but *why*, and Guy seemed to think that the yacht was safe. His unconcerned attitude was too much like Mutt's to be comfortable.

She cautiously stepped onto the gangplank, motioning to Guy to be as quiet as possible.

Not but a few yards from the top of the gangplank was a thick steel door set into the side of the ship. This was as good a place as any.

Bingo. This was the kitchen all right, and by the looks of it, the Seven Dwarves were messy little men indeed. Dirty pots and open, moldering cans lay strewn about the floor and the stainless-steel counters. Against the far wall was a huge sink filled with rancid wash water and filthy utensils. Snow White certainly had her work cut out for her.

Katherine grimaced and reached into the murky water, feeling along the bottom for the plug that stopped the sink. The water gurgled down the drain noisily.

Next to her, Guy picked up one of the cans and sniffed its contents. "Yuck!" he exclaimed. "This stuff stinks!"

Cringing, Katherine turned to silence him but motion in the background caught her attention. The door to the previously unnoticed pantry flew open, and out jumped a man and a woman screaming at the top of their lungs. In their hands they held wicked, Hitchcockian carving knives.

Instinct took over. Katherine grabbed startled Guy, tucked him under her arm and dashed for the door. *Is this how it's going to end?* her panicked mind thought as her feet pounding across the deck and Guy wailed like a banshee in her arms. *Am I to be stabbed to death by two frightened plague survivors who were trying to protect the yacht from looters?*

There was no time to debate such philosophical questions. Down the plank Katherine charged with her charge in tow, nearly losing her balance and pitching headfirst in the process. She grabbed the handle of the gate and rattled it in her panic. Realizing that they would have to climb over, Katherine struggled to hoist herself over the gate. Her legs had turned to jelly; hoisting them over the barrier was more difficult while burdened with Guy. Beneath her feet she could feel the gangplank tremble and bounce under the weight of her pursuers. Very soon hands were upon them, dragging her down from the gate.

"*Let me go, let me go!*" Katherine cried, viciously kicking with her legs to escape her captors. "*Please don't kill me!*" Her eyes closed tightly, not wanting to bear witness to the inevitable blades.

"Calm down!" a male voice said. "We're not going to hurt you."

Katherine stopped screaming and opened her eyes. The couple no longer wielded knives: they had left them on the kitchen counter. Guy wormed his way out of Katherine's grip and curled up on the gangplank, screaming shrilly.

"We didn't mean to scare you," the woman shouted. "When we heard someone else outside on the deck, and we thought you were one of *them*."

Her words were hardly registered to Katherine; instead, her own words were ringing in her ears: *I think I read somewhere that everyone has a double somewhere in the world.* It was no longer a theory; it was a *fact*, for Katherine had just come face to face with her carbon copy. Well, not exactly. The carbon paper had been wrinkled a bit between the sheets of paper. The woman before her was a bit taller and a little fuller in figure—idealized, one might be tempted to say. Still, the resemblance was striking.

The woman reached out for Guy, who shrank away from her touch. *"Get away from me!"* he screamed. *"Get away!"*

Katherine knelt on the ground next to the boy. "It's OK," she insisted. "They're not going to hurt us."

Guy unraveled from the ball he had made of himself and turned his wet eyes up at Katherine. "They scare me!" he whined. "They're not supposed—I mean, they—what if they make us sick?"

"We're not sick, sweetie," the other woman said. "If we aren't sick by now, I don't think we'll ever be."

Meanwhile, the man scanned the docks for any signs of motion. "We'd better get inside," he said. "The ruckus might attract some of 'em." He motioned for Katherine and his companion to start back for the galley.

"Them?" Katherine asked. "Who might see us?"

"The living dead," the woman said.

*** *** ***

Katherine lingered outside of the galley for a moment, listening to the conversation that was taking place in her absence.

"What do you think?"

"I think she's nuts. Maybe she's infected and it's gone to her brain."

"C'mon, you know what people look like when they catch

that shit. She looks OK to me. And as for her story, well, she's probably in some sort of weird shock. Remember how everyone at home freaked as soon as people started dropping dead all over the place?"

Outside, Katherine tried not to frown. Perhaps she had been too honest with Bernie and Isabella. Perhaps she should have edited the loopier bits of her story, but she had sworn that it had happened as she had told them.

Katherine coughed in order to announce her arrival, and then stepped into the room. Bernie glanced casually at Isabella; her eyes were filled with the same skepticism that his were. "How's the kid?" he asked.

"Still sleeping. I figured that I wouldn't wake him up until I decided what to do next. He was pretty upset last night."

The conversation dwindled for a moment. "What happened after the hotel disintegrated?" Bernie asked.

Katherine pushed the remaining scrambled eggs about her plate with her fork. "I found Guy sitting on the curb just minutes after the motel was destroyed," she said. "He—he said some things that went along with the dreams I told you about and talked about needing my help because his mother was being held captive somewhere. Washington, I guess."

"Maybe she's in quarantine," Isabella ventured.

"Maybe. Anyway, Mutt had left his keys in the truck, and I can't help but think that he did so intentionally, meaning for me to head for Washington if anything should happen to him. We couldn't have gone further because the dumb truck ran out of gas. I decided to look for food, and here I am."

Bernie glanced at his wife again; this time Katherine saw the look in his eyes as plain as day.

"Look," Katherine insisted, "I know the whole thing sounds crazy. I hardly believe it myself. But I swear I'm telling the truth."

"That may very well be," Bernie said, but his body language read: *And then again, it may not.* "But other than the plague, we've seen nothing out of the ordinary, have we, sweetheart?"

Katherine saw Isabella nod out of the corner of her eye. Why she or anyone she knew hadn't had a run-in with their clone before now was baffling.

"Do you want to tell the story, or do you want me to do it?" Bernie asked.

"I'll do it," Isabella said. "You'll mess it up." She turned to Katherine. "Poor Bernie. If there's one thing he can't do, it's tell a story. Oh, make those two things: he can't tell a joke, either."

"Hey, now wait a second!" Bernie protested. "I resent that!"

Isabella smiled. She wasn't criticizing him, and he knew it; her comment as much a newlywed's loving observation as anything else. "Anyhow," she continued, "I guess it all started a year ago. That was when my parents started pestering me about getting married. My family's from Newport, Rhode Island, and they had a certain set of expectations where I was concerned. One of them was that I do not marry "beneath" me. They had this doctor picked out for me, and honey let me tell you, he was a geriatric case. Ugly as sin, too."

"You can say that again," Bernie said. Katherine felt he had little room to talk, but then again, they were all under extraordinary circumstances, and figured she looked just as slovenly.

Isabella continued with her long-winded story. "I kept putting off dates with this friend of the family for, oh gosh, I guess I managed to be unavailable for three or four months. And that was when I met Bernie." She reached over and squeezed her husband's hand; they batted their eyes coyly at each other.

"When I told my parents that I wanted to marry Bernie, they were very upset and made all sorts of threats. You know, cutting me out of the will, disowning me. For gosh sakes, by the way they were treating me, you would have thought I'd run off and become a Hare Krishna, not fallen in love with a sanitation engineer!"

Katherine was stunned. Sanitation engineer? If ever there

was a euphemism for "garbage collector," it was "sanitation engineer." What the woman who looked like Katherine was saying was that she had done exactly what Katherine's parents feared their daughter would do. And she had spurned a doctor to boot! What sort of weird coincidence was this? And why was it that these two didn't seem to notice the women's resemblance?

Bernie took the floor away from his wife, intending to cut the story short. "We were on our honeymoon when the plague broke out," he said. "I guess you haven't seen what it does to people. It's disgusting. In the advanced stages you go mad and run around like a monster from a Fifties B-movie, complete with oozing sores and everything. We thought you were one of those bastards when we heard you on the deck; that was why we hid. There's no telling why we haven't gotten sick yet. We've just decided to not get wrapped up in it and spend our days alone. Right honey?"

"Right," she said. "There's no cure, you know. We had to get out of the more populated areas, and when we found this deserted town, well, these yachts seemed to be as good as place to hide as any."

Katherine sighed, sensing that the story had come to its conclusion. Here was yet another perplexing turn of events. She found herself wondering when she was going to get some answers but felt sure that there would be no exhaustive ones in the end.

Bernie cleared his throat. "As far as our plans are concerned, I can't see any reason to go anywhere at all. We can hold out here almost indefinitely."

How long is that Katherine wondered. *How long will it be before the plague comes calling? And if I stay with them, how long will it be before my adversary realizes that I'm still alive? I can't endanger these people.*

Katherine blew on her coffee to cool it, attempting to appear nonchalant. "I wish I could do the same, but I just can't." she said. "My husband is after me, and besides, Guy and at least a part of me believe that I have work to do in Washington. If I don't go, I don't think I'll ever be able to sleep again."

Bernie looked at his wife once more. Katherine knew what was happening; in his glance he had asked his wife if they should consider accompanying her on her journey.

"Before you get any crazy ideas about coming along, I should warn you," Katherine continued. "Being in my company wasn't exactly beneficial to Mutt's health. I think my husband squashed the motel, and Mutt with it."

"Your husband squashed the motel?" Isabella asked.

"I think so. Believe it or not, he also made the television walk and talk."

Isabella shook her head at Katherine's almost certain psychosis. "We're not planning on doing any traveling."

Bernie exhaled loudly and folded his arms on the table. Was this woman who sat before him a lunatic, or was she on to something? There was no way to tell; there was only to make a choice and roll with it, baby.

"No," Isabella said while she attempted to stare her husband into the ground. "I can hear the gears grinding in your head. I don't want to leave the yacht. It's too risky. There's too many of those zombies out there."

"C'mon, sweetheart. Katherine's right. Washington would be safer. What if a roving band of thugs armed with shotguns comes around? We can't defend ourselves, and so we might as well keep moving."

"Sweetheart" shot a glance at Katherine, and then back at her husband. "I'm not leaving," Isabella said.

*** *** ***

"Guy?"

The boy slowly pushed the covers off his head and sat up in bed. Years of experience with Little Will had taught Katherine that the best way to deal with a frightened child was to be honest as possible with them. She seated herself on the bed next to the boy and patted him on the back.

"How are you feeling?"

"OK, I guess. Are those scary people still here?"

"Yes sweetheart. They're still here."

Tears immediately began to well up in the boy's eyes. "I don't like them." he said. "I don't want to be with them."

"I know you don't, but there's no gas in the truck, remember? We can't get to Washington to save your mother if we don't have a car. Bernie says he can hot-wire one, and we can all go to Washington together."

The floodwaters began to recede. "Well...I guess that would be all right. But you must protect me from them. Promise you will."

"I promise." Katherine said. The child had every right to worry; the sight of Bernie and Isabella screaming, and wielding knives would probably give him nightmares for weeks, just as *King Kong* had done to Little Will.

*** *** ***

The abandoned gas station was three blocks away from the marina, but to Katherine it seemed much farther, considering that she was lugging a suitcase laden with canned food, clothes, and other essentials. Bernie said he would carry the heaviest bag, leaving Katherine to wonder just how much that bag weighed.

Bernie set his bag on the concrete next to the abandoned garage. "Wait here," he commanded, and trotted off to the other side of the building with a coat hanger in hand, manufacturing an uneasy moment between the two women.

Isabella reacted to the situation by sitting sown on one of the cases ignoring Katherine completely. *Fine,* Katherine thought. *If she wants to act childish, she can. I'm not going to argue with her.*

Certainly not. Katherine had secretly been pleased when Bernie decided that he and his wife would head for Washington, and she wasn't about to start Isabella on a campaign to turn back. Guy, on the other hand, seemed anxious. He puttered about the station, inspecting the gas pumps with abnormal scrutiny, as if the presence or authenticity confused him.

"Hey! Someone bring me the tools!"

Isabella rolled her eyes and lifted her rear from her makeshift seat. "They're in this bag," she snapped.

Katherine wordlessly retrieved the bag of tools Bernie had scrounged from the yacht's engine room and headed around the side of the building to answer the call for assistance.

Bernie was reclining on the floorboard of a brown van that sat nestled between the ubiquitous piles of old tires one always sees herding behind old service stations. Multicolored wires hung down under the van's dash like so many innards.

He heard Katherine coming and smiled weakly; it was not a good sign that his wife had chosen not to assist him.

"Here," Katherine said, dropping the bag to the asphalt with a clatter.

"Thanks. Do you mind handing me what I need?"

"No."

"Great. Hand me a Phillips screwdriver."

"Is that the screwdriver with the pointy end?" Katherine asked, wishing she had paid some attention to those do-it-yourself shows William watched on PBS all the time. If she was going to make it on her own, she could no longer remain ignorant about such things.

"Yes, the pointy one."

She handed him the tool, which he took and jammed up into the dashboard's guts. No wonder Isabella's family had been upset with her when she eloped. Hot-wiring a car was a dubious talent certainly not featured on *This Old House*.

"You'll have to excuse my wife," he said as worked. "She's a great gal, but she sometimes acts like she's a princess."

"I understand," Katherine said. She spread out the tools on the ground like nurses did in television hospitals.

"Ouch!"

A shower of blue-gray sparks dribbled from high inside the dashboard. Bernie jerked his arm back from the shock, his elbow smashing the frame below the driver's seat. "I just don't understand this," he said.

"Understand what?"

"The fucking ignition switch is mounted into the dash in some weird way, not on the steering column as it usually is. Shit, the way this damn van is built, it's almost like they didn't know what the hell they were doing when they put it together!"

She shrugged. "Maybe it's Japanese."

Bernie had a more severe judgment in mind. "It's a piece of shit," he said. "Hand me the pliers."

Katherine did as asked.

"Now, if I can just bypass the stupid fuse—"

The van's engine sprang to life. "We're outta here!" he exclaimed.

Bernie pulled the van around the front of the station. Isabella hardly moved as he did so, for to her this was no cause for joy. She watched idly as her husband opened the back of the van. "Let's get the bags in and get moving." he said.

Isabella dragged herself to her feet and climbed into the rear. Katherine sighed as the other woman piled herself in; Isabella had left the other two bags sitting next to the wall and Bernie didn't seem to notice.

Aggravated, Katherine stepped down from the van and hefted the first bag into the rear. However, as she lifted the second one, she became intrigued by what had been crushed carelessly beneath it: a tiny pine sapling had sprung from a welt in the concrete. It was not alone; three or four other trees sprouted along the wall at almost regular intervals. This was nothing peculiar, but at closer inspection, she noted that there were other circular bumps in the concrete. It appeared that the tress had sprouted *through* the solid masonry rather than through existing cracks.

Guy's shadow fell over the lumps. "What's that?" he asked.

"Tress," Katherine said, and hoisted the remaining bags into the van. "In you go." She helped Guy climb inside.

Seconds later the van pulled out onto Main Street and headed for the Interstate. Katherine peered out the rear windows as the town fell away, looking for one of the plague victims that Isabella and Bernie had mistaken her for. The town was just as it had been before: right out of a Norman Rockwell painting, except for the boards on the windows and the leaves in the street. But even in desertion something was amiss; the boards appeared too carefully nailed to the storefronts and the leaves too tastefully strewn about the boulevard. Could a panicked town manage to evacuate so neatly? It was a queer sight that gave her the impression that it had just dropped out of the sky only moments before she arrived.

*** *** ***

    The van's cargo space was as uncomfortable as any place Katherine had slept in, but she nonetheless drifted into a fitful nap. The Stevens couple was quiet in the front seat. For a couple so in love, Katherine felt they had precious little to say to one another. What did they have in common that held the attraction for one another? Isabella did look awful lot like a cosmetics company cover girl, but Bernie was as common as vanilla ice cream. Could love really be blind, or did some other axiom describe their relationship?

    "Where are we?" Katherine asked, rubbing her eyes. Bernie spoke without taking his reddened eyes off the road. "It's three o'clock, which means the sun's in the east, which is to the right of us," he said. "That means we're north of where we were—but exactly where that is, I can't say."

    Oh great. Describing their position by compass directions was about as useful to Katherine as latitude and longitude coordinates. "What was the last town we passed through?" she asked.

    Isabella turned to face her. "We haven't," she said. "We've seen nothing but grassy hills and valleys since you fell asleep."

    "OK, so what was the name of the nearest town on the last *sign* we passed?"

    Bernie shrugged his slight shoulders. "That's just it: we haven't seen any signs, either. I mean, not even speed limits or mileage markers or reflectors at the side of the road. I guess they've taken them all down."

Katherine moved to the space between the front seats and gazed through the windshield. "Taken the signs down? That's ridiculous. Who would do a thing like that?"

"Beats the hell out of me," he said. "Maybe we're on some sort of back road, like old Route Sixty-Six."

After a few moments' contemplative silence, Katherine expressed the current of thought running through their minds. "Something is wrong here. Why would someone remove the signs? To confuse the plague?"

Then again, nothing had been right as of late. There was one other likelihood though, a possibility Katherine did not mention for fear that the Stevens would once again think her mad: the signs had been removed to confuse *her*, to keep Katherine from reaching Washington. Such a scheme would require an enormous effort, but no more than animating a motel room. Katherine only hoped that if she ever reached her destination, she would know what course of action to take.

Perplexed, Katherine looked about the van for Guy. He was kneeling on a jacket, peering out of the rear windows as the landscape fell away behind them. Something was wrong with the boy, and the question of exactly what was amiss gnawed at Katherine's maternal side. Was his mother really held prisoner, or had he been traumatized, perhaps by her death from the plague? Regardless of the truth, Katherine knew Guy was drawn to Washington for the same reason as she: someone needed help. Maybe that was the only link between the two of them, maybe it was deeper. Guy wasn't telling, and she hadn't the foggiest notion.

Enough. There was to be no more debate of motivation. Now there was only to get to Washington and search for the final pieces to the puzzle.

*** *** ***

The odometer ticked the miles away one after another.

It was quite a fortuitous circumstance that the van had an enormous gas tank, that the tank was full, and that the engine got phenomenal gas mileage, or the trip would have been short indeed.

Bernie arched his back in the seat and groaned. "We've got to find a place to stop soon," he said. "My back is killin' me."

In the passenger seat, Katherine yawned. "It's getting dark anyhow," she noted. "Maybe we ought to think about pulling over for the night."

"Pull over *where*?" Isabella called from the cargo space. Yes, she was awake, and as chipper as ever. "You mean pull over at the side of the road? How safe would that be?"

"There's bound to be a rest area or some town or *something* coming up soon," Bernie said.

"There does, does there? And when was the last time you saw one?"

"Well…"

He had to admit to the fact that they had seen no off-ramps or on-ramps or intersections or any sort of pavement other than the highway they were on since leaving the marina. The chances of finding a sheltered place to pull over were practically nil.

The driving continued.

*** *** ***

The last sliver of sun had set below the horizon almost two hours ago. The rolling hills eventually gave way to dense forest that crowded itself close to the road, as if seeking to blot it out entirely. The headlights revealed that the asphalt was studded with saplings, as the ground at the gas station had been.

Bernie could feel his consciousness diminish as he continued to pilot the van. He was about to tell the women they would have to either pull over so he could rest or one of them would have to drive when an object by the side of the road suddenly flashed in the headlight's glow.

"Oh my God, is that a sign?" Isabella cried next to him. "It is, it is! It's a sign for a rest area! Pull over, Bernie. I have to pee so bad I can taste it."

Katherine crawled to the front of the vehicle. "I don't know about this," she said, not relishing stopping in a dark grove. Anyone reared on fairy tales knew that nasty beasts usually populated dark forests. "Isn't it a bit strange for an exit to appear out of nowhere when there hasn't been one for miles?"

"For Pete's sake!" Isabella exclaimed. She glanced nervously down the road for the approaching exit, praying that her husband would have sense enough to pull over. "You two! The only reason there hasn't been an exit is that there wasn't anything to exit *to*. And now there is: a rest area!" Isabella's earlier skepticism of the condition of the road had disappeared with a full bladder. Some people just can't think straight when they have to urinate.

The tide of silence Guy transmitted all afternoon receded. "It looks OK to me," he said, still peering out of the back window.

Bernie switched on the blinker and steered the van down the exit corridor. The lights sliced across the scene, revealing a typical roadside rest, complete with bathrooms and picnic tables. The lot was completely empty under the harsh yellow illumination of its streetlamps.

As the van came to a stop in a parking space, Isabella threw her door open. "Let me *out!*" she shouted and tore from the auto like a bolt of lightning.

Katherine headed for the rear exit, hoping to catch up with Isabella before she did something stupid. "Isabella, wait!" she pleaded. "Wait up! I'd better go with you."

Wham!

The bathroom door slammed open with a tremendous crash as Isabella hit it at full speed. Where was the concern of what the noise might attract? For all they knew, the woods could be chock full of the so far no-show zombies, but Katherine doubted it. Another unidentifiable presence hung in the air, its influence permeating the night. She shivered, trying to shake off the uneasy feeling. "Look under the stall first to see if anyone's hiding inside," she suggested.

"Oh God, Katherine! We're the only ones here. You're paranoid."

Katherine groaned, shaking her head. It meant nothing to

her if Isabella suddenly found herself in danger of her life. If she wanted to be foolish, it was OK by Katherine.

Paranoid, that's what you are. It's that damn imagination of yours.

*** *** ***

Paranoid.

"Is something wrong?"

Katherine turned away from the woods and back to the splintered picnic table. "I'm not sure, Bernie," she replied. "Look at the parking lot. Why aren't there any of those little trees growing in it like the highway?"

A glance over his shoulder revealed that, sure enough, the virgin asphalt had yet been breached by the saplings. "I don't know," Bernie said. "Maybe it had to do with something the highway crews sprayed on the pavement. You know, like toxic waste or something. Isn't that what happened at Love Canal?"

Katherine shrugged. The answer she was formulating had more dire implications: the rest area looked as if it had dropped from the sky, just like the town she found the Stevens in. The only apparent difference was that the rest area hadn't been around long enough for the tress to take hold. And the tabletop looked to carefully weathered and was devoid of the so-and-so-loves-so-and-so engravings common to public property.

Isabella returned from the van with a brown paper sack laden with food. "Chow time," she said, and lined up several cans on the table. "We've got Spam, Potted Meat Product, and pork and beans..."

"Ugh," Bernie said, wrinkling his nose. "Didn't we bring anything better than this shit?"

His wife gave him a sour look. "Sorry pal, I left the *paté* back on the tub." She mispronounced *"paté"* by dropping the *accent aigu* on the "e". Katherine winced.

"Then I guess I'll take the Spam. At least I can be sure that everything inside the can came from a pig."

Bernie began to wrestle with the key the Spam makers provided for opening the can. It was a diabolical arrangement, for the thin ribbon of tin that sealed the lid always seemed to break away from the can before it was completely open.

Katherine had no idea what Potted Meat was, but it sounded horrible. "I'll take the pork and beans," she said.

Isabella silently slid the can, a spoon, and a can opener her way.

That simple vessel of food sent Katherine spinning into a maelstrom of thought and realization. A component of the miasma of emotions she was feeling in the Steven's presence was guilt. She felt guilty that she had not asserted her independence when her parents began to urge her to marry William. But what was there to do now but to stew in her own juices? Katherine had made her choices and never looked back for fear of turning into a pillar of salt. She never loved William at all. Relegated to a tiny, soundproof room in the back of her mind was the truth that William was cold and as ugly inside as he was out, and she never had an ounce of feeling for him. The truth had been there all along, but she had chosen to ignore it.

Distressed by the moment of clarity, Katherine offered the can to Guy, who was safely seated next to her. "Would you like some of this?" she asked.

Guy wasn't listening. He was too busy examining the parking lot, just as he did the gas pumps. His blue eyes shifted right and left, from exit to entrance, looking for God only knew what.

"Guy, would you like some pork and beans?"

"Huh? Oh, no thank you. I'm not hungry." His peering continued.

Vexed by his continually odd behavior, Katherine let the impulse of hunger fall away. What if Little Will was similarly traumatized by *his* mother's sudden departure? Was he peering out of the window of the Mercedes as William searched for her?

From the woods that bordered the picnic area came the sound of twigs snapping. Startled, Katherine dropped the can of food and turned toward the source of the noise.

"What's the matter?" Bernie asked through a mouthful of

Spam.

"I heard something," Katherine said, still scanning the perimeter of the woods for signs of motion.

Isabella shook her head. "There you go again with that paranoia," she chided. "Jesus, you're jumpy."

"Shhh! Listen!"

"Listen to *what*?"

Katherine tore her gaze away from the woods and glared at Isabella. "Be quiet," she hissed. "I think there's something alive out there."

"Well of course there is! It's probably a rabbit, or a fox."

Bernie agreed. "Look, you're tired, just like the rest of us. We'll all feel better once we grab a few winks."

Katherine frowned. Perhaps they were right. A fatigued mind can perform an astonishing repertoire of tricks. And yet she wasn't *that* tired; she was still capable of realizing that it was unlikely for the trip to be all fun and games. Something *was* out there, and they would surely meet up with it before long.

After eating, Isabella prepared the van for sleeping by taking the blankets they had pilfered from the yacht and spreading them out in the cargo space. When she was done, she straightened up and grinned sheepishly. "Maybe I ought to go to the bathroom, so I don't have to go in the middle of the night," she said.

"For cryin' out loud," Bernie griped. "You just went not twenty minutes ago. You pee too much."

Katherine looked down at Guy, who was sitting next to her on the van's bumper. "Do you need to go?" she asked.

"I guess."

The quartet marched to the rest rooms; Bernie escorted Guy into the men's room, Isabella vanished into the women's and Katherine remained outside, wishing they would all hurry up so they could return to the relative safety of the van.

From somewhere about the grounds came a low, breathy noise, followed by a terrible pounding which Katherine recognized as the sound of her own heart. The noise sounded again, and this time there was no mistaking what it was: a grunt, low and feral.

"Bernie!" Katherine whispered. "Isabella! Hurry up; there's something out here!"

She was cut off by the sound of two flushing toilets. Bernie came out first, with Guy in tow. "What did you say?" he asked, "I couldn't hear—"

"Shhh! I heard something *awful*."

"Oh God, let's not start that again," Isabella pleaded. The door to the ladies' room slammed shut behind her. "I tell you it's nothing but a figment of your imagination."

As Isabella finished her assertion that they were alone, a bloodcurdling ululation tore through the night. It was the cry of an animal, but so deep and throaty that it could not possibly belong to anything benign.

Guy shrieked, clapping his hands over his ears. In one of those rare moments when multiple persons act as one, Katherine grabbed Guy, and she, Isabella and Bernie took to their heels and dashed for the van. Katherine was tempted to look back at what was surely on their heels but thought of Lot's wife again and kept her eyes to the front.

It's coming for us oh God it might be snapping at our heels this very—

Bernie pushed the women and child into the rear of the van. He then dove in and pulled the cargo door home.

"Get us out of here," Isabella demanded. "Get us out of here *now!*"

Her words were not needed; Bernie was already making his way to the driver's seat. Out of reflex he reached for the ignition.

No keys.

"Shit," he muttered, sliding onto the floorboard. The vehicle still had to be hot-wired.

In the rear, Katherine was immobile against the sidewall. She sensed that the thing was right outside, looking for a way in. Guy clung to her, arms thrown about her waist and head buried in her abdomen. His wailing drowned out any monstrous screeching that might have been occurring in the night.

A flash of blue light lit the driver's compartment as Bernie desperately tried to start the engine. Katherine wrenched Guy from her body and sprang into action, crawling past Isabella, who was immobile with fear.

"Can I help?"

"I can't see a goddamn thing!" Bernie shouted. "Didn't we bring a flashlight?"

"Well, no..."

Panting, Katherine wondered what to do. An idea struck: the headlights. The instrument panel always lights up when the driver switches on the lights. It wouldn't be much in the way of illumination, but perhaps it would help. She grabbed the knob and twisted it.

Stunned by the van's high beams, the demon froze. The pupils of its terrible yellow eyes constricted and then suddenly the thing was on the move again, shambling toward the van.

"Oh my god, *what is it?*"

At Isabella's cry, Bernie sat up from the floor. The thing heading their way was covered in drum-taut, scaly green skin. Its lower limbs were oddly shorter than the front, like those of a compact, but nonetheless vicious Tyrannosaur.

Without conscious direction from his brain, Bernie slid back down to the floor and made the magic gestures that started the van. In a moment he had his hands on the steering wheel and his foot on the accelerator. The van lurched forward, sending Katherine and Isabella tumbling to the floor. Guy rolled with the motion, indifferent to it.

The demon saw the challenge of a crazed game of chicken and continued its pace, leveling its sharp horns at the van's grille. Bernie clenched his eyes shut, bracing for the impact.

Several seconds and no collision later, he opened his eyes to see the solid rest room wall looming larger and larger before him. He spun the steering wheel, sending the van skidding into a spiral. *"Where did the damn thing go?"* he shouted. *"Where did it go?"*

As the van continued to spin, the trio caught sight of a flash of green as the centrifugal force threw the demon from the roof. It had not jumped out of the way of the oncoming vehicle; instead, it had bounded to the roof as light as a feather, intending to ride out the escape attempt.

Bernie gained control of the vehicle and depressed the gas pedal once more, heading for the highway. The demon appeared in front of them again, causing Bernie to give in to his first impulse. He turned the wheel to the left to avoid a collision, not seeing the concrete base of the lamppost that stood in the van's new trajectory. There was a loud crash and then Isabella, Katherine and guy were flying through the van's interior again, colliding with the seats. Bernie's head smacked the steering wheel hard enough to make the world go black for an instant.

Katherine looked up from the floor to see the demon's yellow eyes glowing through the shattered mat of glass that had been the windshield. She needn't tell Bernie that the thing would be inside in no time; he was already groping about the cab for an object to use as a weapon. His hands found something long and metallic under the seat; he removed it from its hiding place and hefted it. One end of the tire iron sported a socket for removing bolts: the other tapered to a dull, flat tip. In one savage movement he reached past Katherine and shoved the point through the weakened glass and into the demon's right eye. The metal grew warm in his hand as it sank deep into the creature's brain, coming to rest when it struck the back of its skull.

The demon rolled off the hood, screeching in pain. A taloned hand clawed at the wound, but it was too severe and too late. It grunted and slumped to the ground in a pool of black ichor.

Both the driver's and the passenger's door were too damaged by the impact to open. Bernie climbed over the seat, moving toward the rear doors. "The bathroom!" he shouted. "We've got to get somewhere safe. There might be more of them out there!"

"Are you insane?" Isabella cried. "We'll never make it!"

Neither Bernie nor Katherine was listening. They threw the door open and jumped from the van, urgently scanning the lot for signs of trouble. "The coast is clear!" Bernie shouted. "*Move!*"

Katherine scooped Guy into her arms, and they made a mad dash for the rest rooms.

Heart pumping with terror, Katherine heard talons on asphalt first. She glanced over her shoulder (so much for learning a lesson from the Old Testament) to see the second demon closing the space between them.

It can only follow one target, her panicked mind told her. In a foolish gesture worthy of martyrdom, she shoved Guy into Bernie's arms and changed direction, heading for the woods instead of the sanctuary of the toilet.

The demon was confused for a moment, wondering which quarry to choose.

Black hair. Fair skin.

It eyes shifted to Katherine, then to Isabella and back to Katherine. The odds of catching the right one the first time were fifty-fifty.

Eeeny meenie miney moe. Catch a bitch by the toe.

The demon veered to the left, choosing Katherine.

Isabella, Bernie, and Guy reached the bathroom. Where *was* Katherine?

Fearing the worst, Bernie passed Guy on to Isabella and looked outside just in time to see her dodge behind a tree as the demon lunged at her with fangs bared. The demon maw found only wood and splinters, not soft, sweet flesh. It howled and spat in anger, renewing its commitment to apprehend its victim. Katherine seized the opportunity to head for the rest room.

The demon's powerful legs propelled it at a frightening speed; already Katherine could feel its hot breath on the back of her neck. A bright light blinded her momentarily; surely it was the flash of her entire life before her eyes. A thunderous roar filled her ears.

This is it. It's got me.

All she wanted to do was stop running and let her heart catch up. Let it be over with.

A loud screech, and then the world tumbled over itself before coming to a painful, skin-scraping halt. Katherine was vaguely aware that she had fallen to the asphalt and that some violent event had taken place. The demon was down. It lay quivering on the pavement, black blood pulsing from a ragged wound in its chest.

The light Katherine had seen earlier caught her eyes once more, its source revealed as a red Mustang that was parked not ten yards from where she lay. A figure was silhouetted in the headlights, a shotgun held in one hand.

Katherine hesitated a moment when a hand was extended to help her up. The hand belonged to a young man with a familiar face; his simulation of California good lucks was even more apparent in person than it had been on the television set back at the Waffle House.

Enemy or ally, Katherine accepted his help. "You saved my life," she said as she stood, not being able to shake the feeling that he had done so only to take it from her himself.

The surfer's intense eyes were fixed on her own, trying to peer past the person and into her soul. "It was nothing," he said, voice cold and devoid of feeling. "My name's Mike."

"Katherine."

Still, he stared. "What are you doing out in the middle of nowhere?"

Katherine was taken aback by the blunt edge the question carried. "We could very well ask you the same thing," she said.

The others emerged from the rest room to greet their savior. "I've never been so scared in my entire life," Isabella said. Her voice trembled as much as her body; if she had dentures in her mouth, they would have been shaken loose. She tried not to look at the downed things they passed but a glance was inevitable in the same manner that passing motorists find interest in a wreck at the side of the road. The demon was horrible even in death; the green skin was pulled so tightly over its angular skull that it looked in danger or tearing to reveal the raw bone and muscle underneath.

Guy stood alongside Bernie. His wailing had abated; his eyes were wide and as bright as if he had just awakened from an afternoon nap.

*** *** ***

From *The Nine Circles Encyclopedia*
RULES FOR SUBORDINATE REALITIES- continued
AWAKENING RULE: Awakening (a complex and dangerous occurrence), occurs when a principal gains knowledge of its Architect. The process by which this occurs is colloquially known as "playing it all the way out." If an Architect invests too much energy in a subordinate reality of his or her creation, he or she will no longer have enough energy to sustain existence in the eight-circle system. In dropping out of the higher levels to exist solely in the subordinate reality, there is an immense release of energy from the Architect wave. By the Second Law of Thermodynamics, energy can neither be created nor destroyed, only transferred, or transformed. The free energy released by the Architect's fall is typically divided among the Architect's principles, while small amounts may filter down to the consequences. With this added potential, principles gain power enough to affect the other low-order waves operating in the system. However, such awakened principals have no power over other principals or the Architect his/herself...

*** *** ***

After introductions, Mike chose to justify his sudden appearance: "I've just been driving around, you know, looking for survivors. I was beginning to think that I was the last one left."

Bernie rocked back on his heels. "We felt the same way until Katherine came along," he said, dragging the bags from the rear of the disabled van. He did not see the scowl that had planted itself on Katherine's face at Mike's words. Bernie said,

"Katherine figures that Washington would be the best place to shoot for. You know, the government might have some sort of shelter set up."

Mike turned his head slightly, trying to match his gaze with Katherine's. "Sounds like a plan," he said.

Katherine made no comment. Mike was as much a part of the craziness that started with mutating study as anything else, just like Isabella and Bernie. The threat she felt radiating from the surfer was thick and palpable. Mike was not to be trusted, even if she didn't have a good reason not to.

The group stood in silence for a moment, each figuring that Mike was to make the next move. His eyes lingered on Katherine's face for a moment, then shifted to Bernie and Isabella, then back again. Katherine sensed confusion (and perhaps annoyance) just beyond his cool exterior. He appeared to be wondering if he would escort them to Washington or just shoot them all on the spot.

Mike bent on one knee and ruffled Guy's hair. The boy smiled. "Hey there, pardner," Mike said. "How's it goin'?"

"It's goin' all over the place," Guy replied, punctuating his wit with a giggle that made Katherine uneasy.

"What do you say we all pile into my car and head for Washington?"

"Sure. But I gotta go to the bathroom first."

"Fer cryin' out loud," Isabella exclaimed. "You just went!"

Guy looked up at her, cocking his head in a gesture of justification of his apparent incontinence. "I have to go again," he said nonchalantly.

"I'll walk you over," Mike offered.

Katherine grabbed Guy's hand before Mike had the chance to do the same. "Why don't you help load the bags?" she smilingly suggested. "We've already checked the bathrooms; they're safe." Without further debate, she pulled Guy after her; he resisted briefly before finally giving in to his surrogate mother's will.

Once inside the bathroom, Katherine knelt before Guy

much as Mike had done a few seconds before. She placed her hands on his shoulders and held him firmly, as if the contact would give her warning more weight: "I want you to stay away from Mike, understand?"

"Why?"

"Just promise me you'll stay away from him."

"But he's not scary like those other people."

Katherine frowned at the realization that her efforts were falling short. Why Guy would follow the newly arrived, shotgun-bearing pied piper off the edge of the planet but would hardly even speak to Bernie or Isabella escaped her, and the problem had to be nipped in the bud before something dreadful happened.

"Sometimes people are scary on the inside," she explained. "Did you ever hear the story about the wolf who put on sheep skins so the sheep wouldn't recognize him?"

Guy blinked at her, confused. "You mean he's a wolf?"

"I don't know yet. For now, let's just pretend he is, OK?"

"Whatever."

"Good. Now go to the bathroom."

"Only if you don't watch."

"I won't."

*** *** ***

For Isabella, sleep finally offered escape from the demons left dead at the rest area. For Katherine, the fitful slumber was an effort on her part to regroup mentally and physically in order to deal with the problem that Mike's presence posed. If he was indeed a member of the mysterious party who imprisoned poor souls in the Capitol Building, why had he spared her from the demon's talons?

One thing was certain: there was to be no confronting him until she determined just how dangerous he was. Clearly, she would need to summon all her guiles to handle the situation.

About eleven o'clock in the morning, the needle on the Mustang's gas gauge entered the perilous red zone above the empty mark. Washington was clearly further away than any in the car had suspected.

Mike frowned at the gas gauge. This was *not* a good sign. He pushed the accelerator closer to the floor out of spite. The Mustang's tires made a satisfying crunching noise as they sped over the multitude of saplings in the way; saplings that were now at least three feet in height. If the present growth rate continued, the road would soon be non-negotiable.

"What will we do when we run out of gas?" Isabella whined from the back seat.

Mike aimlessly stuck an open hand out of the window, feeling the force of the wind against it. "We'll fill up again before that happens," he said.

"Fill up? I don't think there's going to be much in the way of a gas station in these parts."

"She's right," Bernie said. "We took the van from a gas station about twenty hours' drive from here. That was the last town we've seen."

Mike shrugged. "Maybe we'll get lucky."

Lucky? Katherine thought. *I doubt it. If we come across gas, it won't be by luck. It'll be just like the rest area. Just when we need it, it'll pop up around the bend.*

From the front seat came an expression of utter disbelief: "I don't believe it!"

It was Bernie who spoke, rubbing his eyes, trying to banish the mirage that floated before him. He turned to Mike. "Do you see what I see?"

"Yeah. I guess we're in luck after all."

In the distance, an exit sign loomed. Past that was a billboard advertising a McDonald's restaurant (THIS EXIT!), but no gas station.

"We'll borrow some gas from the cars in the lot," Mike suggested.

In Katherine's brain's Command Central, the First Officer had just hit the red alert button. She leaned forward in her seat and tapped Bernie on the shoulder. "This doesn't make any sense!" she whispered. "What are the chances of finding a

McDonald's out here? And why would people abandon their cars in the lot?"

Bernie's reply came all too loudly: "Don't knock it, lady. Gas is gas."

What was wrong with these people? Couldn't Bernie see the restaurant as the freak occurrence it was?

As Mike veered down the exit ramp, the red roof of the McDonald's began to peek through the trees. Sure enough, a parking lot was soon visible, along with a good number of abandoned cars.

Mike pulled the car into the center of the lot and killed the engine. He motioned to Bernie. "I'll need your help."

Bernie undid his belt and climbed out of the car. "Stay here," he said to the women.

"I'll go too!" Guy chirped and tried to worm his way out of the back seat.

"Not so fast," Katherine said, and grabbed the boy by the seat of his pants. "It's too dangerous out there."

"Give the kid a break," Mike urged. "He probably needs to stretch his legs. Let him come with us."

"Sorry. I promised his mother I'd take care of him."

Mike stood motionless for a second, glaring into the back seat. Who knew what horrible designs floated in his brain? "Whatever," he said, and stomped his way to the car's trunk to retrieve his convenient siphoning gear.

Once Mike and Bernie were out of earshot, Katherine turned to Isabella. "Do you see something funny about this place?" she asked.

"Funny? What do you mean?"

"Look at this place! The parking lot doesn't have any saplings growing in it! The rest of the country we've passed through had been dotted with little pine trees. Even the road was turning into a forest, but this lot is clean as a whistle. Besides that, the forest boundary is too neat. It looks as if the tress at the edge have just been felled."

Isabella squinted through the car's dirty window, trying

to grasp the implications of Katherine's discovery. "Well...now that you mention it...gosh, it looks like this place just dropped right out of the sky!"

Isabella used the exact words that Katherine had to describe the condition of the rest area and the marina town. She turned and the two women's eyes locked for a moment; Katherine had finally succeeded in raising someone else's suspicions. Beside her, Guy vigilantly peered out of the Mustang.

*** *** ***

Meanwhile, the search for gas was not proving as fruitful as the men had thought it would be.

"Dammit!" Mike shouted. In anger he raised a booted foot and kicked the gas tank's door off the Porsche.

"Don't tell me," Bernie said. "This car has a locking gas cap, too."

The look in Mike's eyes answered Bernie's question more concisely than any words could. Yes, the Porsche had yet another locking gas cap, and so did the last nine cars they had checked. Ten for ten—a perfect record.

"Look Mike, it might save a little time if we just pick one of the locks or wrench a cap off."

The muscles in Mike's jaws bulged as he clenched his teeth together. "No!" he shouted. "I want to find one that doesn't have a lock on it!" He angrily grabbed the gas can and siphon hose and stormed off across the lot.

What's the big deal? Bernie wondered. *Gas is gas whether it comes from a locked tank or not.*

But Mike wanted his way and was determined to get it. Perhaps they should have stopped at a Burger King instead of a McDonald's.

Bernie followed Mike at a safe distance; the gas situation was getting the best of his new traveling companion and he didn't want to heighten Mike's anger by violating his personal space, which seemed to have welled along with his ire.

The closet car to the Porsche was a low slung, black Cadillac—a nigger car, as Bernie called it. Mike headed straight for the rear bumper and reached for the spring-hinged license plate. Bernie watched closely; he would have checked the side of the car before the rear. Mike certainly knew his cars.

What happened next seemed queer to Bernie. Mike's hand suddenly recoiled from the plate; he closed his eyes and concentrated, as if trying to will the car into not having a locked gas cap. Words formed on his lips; Bernie was no lip-reader but as a talker knew enough to understand what Mike was silently chanting to himself: *I won't allow it. I won't allow it. I won't allow it...*

The litany ended abruptly; Mike pulled down the plate. "Bingo!" he exclaimed. "This one doesn't have a lock!"

*** *** ***

As Mike drained the last drops of gas from the can into the Mustang's tank, he peered through the rear window at Katherine. Perched in her seat like a Siamese cat, she was chatting with Isabella and her husband. Katherine had an aura about her, a presence that defied Mike's attempts at description. She was the one who caused the gas caps to be locked. There were no other possibilities, unless—

"Nah," Mike said aloud. He returned the gas can to the trunk and got in the car. The engine started sure and quick, and the journey was underway once more.

Yes, there was another possibility, one that Mike had refused to entertain because it threw a monkey wrench into what he thought of as his well-oiled machine. He would not consider the possibility that there was another besides the Architect (or Architects, as it was), himself, or the scheming Theodoric's influencing events. Mike's ego was too large to allow for the overlap rule.

Mile after mile passed beneath the Mustang's tires. It was during this quiet period that Katherine noticed that Mike was watching her. Time and again their eyes would meet in the rear-view mirror, his cold gaze forcing her to look away. Mike seemed to sense that she was on some sort of mission. Very well. She would confound him by not giving him the time of day.

The morning turned into afternoon, afternoon into evening. Where the hell was Washington? The city eluded them, as if it was conscious of their goal and had begun to pull away, stretching the road between them.

It wasn't until after the sun went down that the pace of events began to pick up. Since the highway continued to be maddeningly devoid of exits, Mike simply pulled the Mustang off to the side of the road and set the parking brake. "I'm tired. We'll stop here," he proclaimed, not bothering to discuss it with the others.

Katherine did not object (and neither did the Stevens, for that matter); she figured that traveling at night was probably as dangerous as pulling to the side of the road. It was a no-win situation.

Isabella took it upon herself to rummage through the bags for the evening's repast. The remaining trio of adults took the opportunity to stretch their legs.

Katherine made sure that Guy stayed as far away from Mike as possible, who facilitated her desire by striding aimlessly off into the woods without a word. She imagined a pipe between Mike's lips, and a merry song calling Guy into the forest.

As soon as Mike was out of sight, Katherine and Bernie gravitated toward the open trunk as if acting on an unspoken plan.

"I tell you, that Mike guy is a nut case," Bernie said, his face looking drawn and ghoulish in the yellow-orange light of the Mustang's parking lights.

"I agree," Katherine said. "He scares me."

Isabella was not as quick to catch on, bless her heart. She busied herself by lining up the canned viands on the bumper. "What are you two getting at?" she asked.

Bernie uttered the pronouncement, summing up his and Katherine's feelings: "Something freaky is going on and that Mike dude is a part of it. What are the chances that he would just show up at the rest area in the nick of time?"

"Very slim," Katherine replied. "I think he's been

watching us. I think all of this is some sort of planned thing: the rest area, McDonald's..."

Isabella straightened up and looked Katherine in the eye. "What are you saying?" she asked.

"Yeah Katherine, just what *are* you saying?"

"I'll tell you, but you'll say I'm crazy: I think Mike *created* the McDonald's. And the rest area, too."

"What?" Isabella responded. "Don't be silly."

"I wish I was just being silly, but I'm not. Look, I told you two about the motel. If someone can *destroy* buildings with their mind, why shouldn't they be able to *create* them as well?"

"Maybe...maybe there's something to what you're saying," Bernie admitted. "But something else weird went on at that restaurant. All the cars had locking gas caps. It pissed Mike off, you know, like he didn't expect to see it. And if he did create the McDonald's, why not create a working gas station? Wouldn't that have been easier? And how the hell is he doing all of this? *Why* is he doing it?"

Katherine pushed a few cans to the side and sat on the bumper, feeling that she needed to relieve the pressure on her feet in order to reason this out. "He doesn't want us to become suspicious," she said.

"Suspicious of *what*?"

"I don't know exactly, but I think it has something to do with Guy. Have you noticed how Mike is always trying to be alone with him?"

Isabella looked at Guy, who was milling about the edge of the road. "You mean maybe Mike has something to do with the crazy story about Guy's mother being kidnapped?"

"Maybe. What I can't figure out is how the trees and the demons fit in. I can't tell if my husband is making them or if Mike is to gain our confidence in him as a hero or what."

Bernie sighed. "This is insane. None of this is really happening. I bet I've been in a car accident and some quacks have my brain floating in a tank and they're juicing me up with drugs or electricity and I'm dreaming the whole thing."

Isabella pinched him on the arm, eliciting a yelp. "You're not dreaming," she said, "and we can't all be insane. Something weird is happening, and Katherine seems to right in the middle of it. I told you leaving the boat was a bad idea."

Even if Isabella had the opportunity to continue, there was nothing left for her to say. Just then Mike burst into the clearing, whistling a happy tune and burdened with a huge backpack. "Hey folks, look what I got!" he exclaimed. He removed the pack and set it on the hood of the car. Like a twisted, surfing Mary Poppins he produced an astonishing array of useful items: dehydrated food, maps, a compass...

Eyes wide as saucers, Bernie trotted over and began to paw through the plunder. "Where the heck did you find this stuff?" he asked.

"Oh, there's a town about a little way off the road," he replied, jerking a thumb toward the woods. "They got a real nice sporting goods store. Guns, too."

As if on cue, both Isabella and Katherine's blood congealed in their veins. Here was another example of the unusual luck that had befallen them since Mike's coming aboard.

"Great!" Katherine said, trying to conceal her unease. "I guess this means we don't have to choke down Spam again for dinner."

Mike shifted his gaze toward her, his demeanor darkening. "Hooray for our side," he said, exposing his many teeth in a terrible grin.

"*Guns?*" Katherine heard Isabella whisper in her ear. "How many more do you think he's got?"

"Who knows? Just don't give him a reason to use them and we'll be OK."

*** *** ***

In the face of some four billion, none-hundred million years of Earth history, eight hours is an incredibly thin slice of time, but time enough for the improbable to happen.

Mike mentioned that the sporting goods store was stocking tents, but no one relished the idea of having a thin film of nylon as the only barrier between their bodies and the mysterious forest. The car was uncomfortable to say the least, but Katherine was so exhausted that she drifted off almost immediately, sleeping so hard and sound that when she stirred, it seemed as if she hadn't slept at all.

God, but it was stuffy! She rolled down her fogged window, deciding that it would be safe if she stayed awake.

"Oh my God," she breathed, loud enough to make Bernie stir in the front seat.

"Be quiet," he mumbled. "Wake me when it's morning."

"It *is* morning!" she hissed in his ear. "Roll down your window and look outside."

Bernie halfway obliged her by wiping his window free of moisture with the back of his hand. That was enough to let the condition of the environs show through. Perhaps it was morning after all but was hard to tell with all those trees in the way.

"Holy shit!" he exclaimed, rolling down his window in a panic. The saplings that had dotted the landscape had matured into a thick forest of towering redwoods that almost completely obscured the sun's morning rays. "What happened?"

In the driver's seat Mike began to wake; his fingers curled tighter around the barrel of his shotgun. The scent of the forest rattled him from sleep. He slowly opened his eyes, the stuff of sleep clouding his vision. "Oh shit," he groaned as the world came into focus. "Oh *shit!*"

The forest was so thick that the car was useless. It was going to be difficult just getting out of the car at all. Trees had sprung up beneath the car and twisted their way under and around it, like a perversion of Jack's enchanted beanstalk.

"We'll walk," Mike said. "We don't have any other choice."

"Oh God," Isabella groaned, announcing that she too was awake. "We're going to *walk*? Is that such a good idea?"

Mike turned in his seat and glared at her. He did not speak but the message came through all the same: *Like I said, we don't have a choice. You don't have a choice. Got it?*

Isabella thought of the shotgun in his lap. He was right. No one had a choice.

*** *** ***

Much to Katherine's surprise, the "town" that Mike had discovered the night before was completely overrun with trees. If Mike had created the town the night before, then he had been unable to keep it free of the choking vegetation. Perhaps there was a chink in his armor after all.

The sporting goods store was only three storefronts down from the border of the encroaching wood, but passage was arduous. Katherine found herself wishing that she had paid more attention to her lectures during Campfire Girl outings; there was bound to be poison ivy about, and she wouldn't be able to spot it.

The store ("POP'S GUNS 'N' SPORTING THINGS") was nearly demolished. Rapidly growing trees had smashed in the display window and had torn holes in the roof; the forest had even taken up residence on the tile floor inside.

Mike angrily directed Isabella and Bernie about the shelves. "You!" he snapped at Bernie. "Make sure you get more food and water—and I want that pack *full*, do you understand?"

Katherine watched with interest as the Stevens scrambled. Mike passed her and Guy while going about his business of bossing; he did not so much as look at her or tell her to pick up a pack. She found herself wondering if the mad gardener who was about had finally got Mike's goat, or if he was somehow afraid of her.

Guns. The sign said the store had guns. But where are they?

Katherine poked about the rubble, looking for a means to combat Mike's stranglehold on firepower. If he had somehow created an array of arms and ammunition, he had surely taken them all for himself.

"Look, my pack's getting too heavy!" Isabella complained. "I just can't carry anything else."

"Don't complain to me when you run out of food," Mike snapped.

Isabella looked for a moment as if she was about to stick her tongue out at him but sat herself down on a tree's gnarled root instead.

In the far aisle of the shop, the glint of cold, black metal caught Katherine's eye; she stooped to examine the contents of an upended shelf. A small revolver was hidden like an Easter egg among plastic packets of fishhooks and sinkers. What luck! Now if it were only loaded.

She peeked about the aisle to see if Mike was watching her. "Why don't you see if you can help Isabella," she said to Guy, figuring that if he was in the confines of the store, he was safe from the wolf. He hesitated for a moment, and then did as told.

As soon as Guy and Mike were out of her line of sight, Katherine quickly snatched up the revolver. The barrel fell open (she would never have figured out how to open it on her own) and sure enough, the chambers were loaded with tiny bullets. *Mike must have missed this one,* she thought. But if Mike had created the shop and its contents, then his missing anything lethal was highly improbable. So perhaps he didn't create the gun. Perhaps someone else did.

"Forget it for now," Katherine mumbled to herself, and untucked her blouse so that it covered the bulge of the revolver in the waistband of her jeans.

*** *** ***

Dark and dense, the forest provided but one means of passage: at the far end of what was left of the town there was a small clearing from which a trail led off into the woods heading for points unknown.

Mike led the group. An elephant gun jutted from the back of his pack. In his right hand, he carried his trusty shotgun, presumably as protection against marauding demons. Isabella, Katherine, and Guy followed next, and Bernie nervously brought up the rear.

"If this hiking bit isn't the height of stupidity, then I don't know what is," Isabella griped. "We don't even know where the stupid trail leads!"

Mike did not turn to face her as he spoke. He kept his eyes toward the front, scanning ahead for signs of trouble. "The trail leads north," he said. "Any idiot with a compass can see that." His voice was still stained with anger that was roused by the sudden forest.

"North, he says. That certainly takes a load off my mind. Sheesh."

Katherine was convinced that Isabella was gambling with her life by sniping at Mike so often. People who carry guns are often inclined to use them.

Say, now that's a frightening thought, Katherine thought, remembering the revolver in her pocket.

Contemplation of having to use the revolver was taken place by interest in Isabella's activity. Ahead, the Stevens woman squatted by the side of the trail under the pretense of removing a burr from her sock. But as Katherine and Guy's march brought them closer together, Isabella abruptly stood and whispered into Katherine's ear: "Screw Washington. You and Bernie are right. Mike's a loon. I say we turn around and head back toward the marina."

It was a preposterous suggestion. Chances were that the forest had even spread among the docks and boats. There was nowhere to go but northward.

Mindful of where she was walking, Katherine said, "I don't think that would be a very good idea."

"*What?* Just look at these trees, Katherine. Since when do redwoods surround Washington? We're lost. We've been turned around somewhere, disoriented."

Katherine glanced nervously at Mike. Did he hear their whispers and suspect a conspiracy? She certainly hoped not. "Maybe, maybe not. I can't turn back now; I've got to press on. You do whatever you like. If Mike causes any trouble…well, we'll just have to handle it."

"Handle it? Are you insane? The man has a gun!"

"I've got a gun, too," Katherine said. She nervously glanced down at Guy, who apparently wasn't listening. Good.

"Oh God!" Isabella cried. "I *knew* we should have never left the marina!"

A mile or so past the rubble that remained of the town, the flat landscape gave in to stranger topography. The trees thinned somewhat, and the trail made an abrupt turn into a series of steep-sided canyons. The canyons were *very* steep. In fact, some of the walls were completely vertical beneath the ropy vines and vegetation. Junctions between the gulches they were traveling in, and other canyons began to occur at regular intervals, the intersections being marked by a noticeable thinning in undergrowth. Katherine wondered what the landscape looked like from the air; it would have to something of a wooded equivalent to that of a mammoth labyrinth fashioned from shrubbery.

It was at one of the junctions that Mike paused and removed his pack. The sun was still low in the morning sky and had not yet burned the fog from the forest canopy. "Let's take a break," he said. No one protested, though the silence imposed by the break in the march was deafening.

Guy puttered about the clearing as he was wont to do wherever they paused. Katherine looked away from him for hardly a second before he began to squeal and dash into the forest. "A bunny!" he cried, disappearing into a grove of trees. "A bunny rabbit!"

"Come back!" Katherine exclaimed. "Guy! Come back!" She dropped her pack and charged into the woods after him. Bernie, Mike, and Isabella soon followed.

The woods beyond the trail were choked with thick, thorny vines that hampered the search. Katherine stomped through the biting brush, cursing the agility of little children all over the world. Guy *couldn't* have gone very far, but his squealing had thinned into terrifying silence.

"Guy! Guy, come back!"

Mike casually lagged, wondering where his co-conspirator was hiding.

The air around him was glowed and shimmered. Mike fell

into the vast plane of light where Julia and Guy were waiting.

"What the fuck is going on?"

"Watch your language!" Julia snapped. She pulled Guy close to her bodice where he clung to her, drawing strength from her presence.

Mike remained defiant. "Fuck you," he said. "You told me this was going to be easy. Where the hell did those other two come from? I thought you said your fucking plague would take care of everyone but the Architects!"

"That Katherine lady must be makin' 'em," Guy said. "She's the one the meteor found." He looked up lovingly at his mother, who caressed his pale cheek.

Mike closed his eyes in frustration. "Terrific. Just terrific. She must be making the demons, too. And the trees."

"Perhaps," Julia said.

"Of course Katherine's doing it!" Mike shouted. "Who the fuck else? Jesus, what if she's on to us?"

"She isn't. If she was, she would have wiped everything out a long time ago. The married couple, the forest—they must be manifestations of her subconscious. No matter: she will fall into the trap all the same."

"And what if she doesn't? What if she decides to wipe *us* out?"

Julia smiled, thin and cold. "Not us, but you," she said. The golden ball appeared in her free hand. "You must see to it that she remains confused."

The thought of the slightest chance of his demise sent Mike into a rage. "Then what are we fucking waiting for? Why the hell is Washington so far off? Let's get her there *now*."

"It isn't that simple," Julia warned. "She will arrive on her own schedule. I'm afraid it's a consequence of design."

Mike lifted his shotgun before him, its barrel sparkling in the magic glow of the ball. "Then let's *force* her to change the design."

"I'm not sure that would be wise."

"You're not sure? *You're not sure?* Look at what we had to

pull just to get your precious son away from her for just a few seconds! I say we scare her into getting to Washington."

*** *** ***

Fearing the worst, Katherine reluctantly returned to the clearing. Guy was lost, and for all she knew, Mike was at the bottom of it.

Bernie and Isabella were at the clearing, and by the looks on their faces, they had been plotting.

"Katherine, Isabella and I were talking…"

Katherine interrupted. "You can talk all you want, but I'm not turning back."

"You see?" Bernie said to his wife, throwing his hands into the air in desperation. "I told you she wouldn't change her mind."

Isabella was undaunted. "Be reasonable, Katherine. It's dangerous out here! Who knows what's lurking out in those woods? And you know how I feel about Mike."

What did Katherine have to say or do to convince the Stevens that she was set on reaching Washington at all costs? "Look," she said, hands on her hips. "If you two want to head back to the Marina, then be my guest. You don't need my approval."

"If we did, what would we do for protection?" Bernie asked. Clearly, it wasn't approval they were after; rather it was her revolver, which she had made the mistake of mentioning to Isabella.

"I won't discuss it any further," Katherine said. "Guy is out there and could be in Mike's clutches. And besides, just how do you expect to get back to the marina?"

"C'mon, there's bound to be other cars to hot-wire," Bernie insisted. His wife's desires had clouded his thinking; the road wasn't negotiable.

A deep voice spoke; for a moment, no one was sure from whence it came: "If you aren't going to Washington, you aren't going *anywhere*."

Katherine's blood ran cold as she turned to see that Mike

had returned to the clearing. He held Guy by the collar of his shirt; the shotgun's barrels directed at the boy's temples. "I'm tired of fucking with the four of you," he growled. "Tell me what I want to know. Better yet, *show* me what I want to know and maybe I won't kill the brat—or you, for that matter."

Bernie was too frightened to breathe, and Katherine figured respiration or any other wasted motion might set Mike shooting. However, Isabella's chest was heaving, her breasts rising and falling with anger. "What the hell are you ranting about?" she demanded.

"As if you don't know?" Mike asked. "Let's see just how much you *do* know."

Mike yanked and returned the gun's cocking mechanism, making an ominous metallic sound worthy of a Hitchcock film. He stepped further into the clearing, dragging terrified Guy with him. "I know who you are," he said. "Did you think you could fool me by maintaining a couple of decoys? I tell y'a what. If the coward amongst you owns up, I'll go easy on you fools. And if the real McCoy won't give, then maybe I'll just shoot you one by one and see if that doesn't give someone food for thought." His shoulder tensed visibly; his finger curled around the trigger and slowly began to pull back-

"*Wait!*"

Katherine found herself shouting, pleading with Mike not to shoot. It was too late for doubts; her hastily drawn plan would have to be seen through.

Mike's finger relaxed on the trigger. "I'm waiting."

Katherine licked her lips. Yes, Mike was out of his gourd, and she only hoped he would fall for her ruse and buy her and the others some time.

"Put the gun down and we'll talk."

Mike's expression intensified. The bitch was still playing games with him! Only his terms were acceptable, but what was one minuscule concession? He was still at the helm of the dreadnought and on a collision course with a higher reality.

"I think I'll just disarm it, if you don't mind." He removed his finger from the trigger.

"Now exactly what is it that you want to know?" Katherine asked. Behind her, Bernie and Isabella were staring at her as if she had finally begun to show signs of the dread plague.

"Don't give me that bullshit," Mike said, leveling an accusing finger at her. "You know exactly what I want!"

"Maybe I do and maybe I don't—but do you know what *you* want?"

From behind, Bernie's voice: "Cram the Zen poetry! Tell him what he wants to know so we can get the hell out of here."

Leave it to Bernie to lend a hand when there was trouble. Did he really think that Katherine had the foggiest notion of what Mike was raving about? Perhaps she was a better actress than she had previously thought.

She forced a playful, self-satisfied smirk. "It's not that simple Bernie. He must *earn* it."

A wise move. Katherine was implying that Mike didn't know what he was talking about either, that he was bluffing. With an ego as big as a barn, he'd forced into answering.

Mike issued his demand, curt and concise: "I want to know where the circles meet. Tell me, and my allies and I will let you four and the brat's mother go."

"Please!" Guy begged. "Please tell him! I want my momma!"

Katherine blinked for a moment, taken off guard by the nature of Mike's demand. *This* was the hogwash that had driven him to pursue her all this way.

"Oh, *that*." Katherine said. "That isn't so simple, either."

His eyes narrowed. "What do you mean?"

"I mean that it's sort of difficult to explain. It would be much easier to show you firsthand."

Mike knew all too well that although he had forced Katherine to confess, the stalemate remained, and the specter of fear was pounding on the door of the basement where it had been imprisoned. Both he and Guy had to pull off Oscar-caliber performances if their plan was to succeed.

"I can make your life miserable," Mike said. "You can't wipe me out because you're too far in. You've given up too much of your energy making this place, and there isn't enough left to squash me flat, or you already would have. You've gone and played it all the way out, that's what you've done." He smiled again, hoping to undermine her confidence in the same way she had done his. "Show me," he insisted.

Show me. And when you do, I won't stop at the sixth or seventh circle. I'll keep moving, keep draining anything and anyone I can of whatever energy they possess until I've reached the ninth circle and beyond...

Katherine shrugged. "Sure. Whatever you say...umm, it's this way," she said, and then continued down the trail, forging deeper into the winding canyons.

And so, the hike continued. Mike brought up the rear of the pack, keeping a wary eye on his captives while whistling "Sweet Adeline" repeatedly, transforming an already wretched song into a minimalist dirge. He dramatically prodded Guy with the shotgun as they walked; the boy did his best to look terrified.

Katherine continued in the lead, supposedly bringing them closer to the mystical place where Mike's infernal circles met. Isabella and Bernie strode behind her, anxiety radiating from them in palpable waves.

After an appreciable length of time, Katherine slowed her pace. Bernie soon caught up with her as she had hoped, and so she turned her head to him slightly.

"Don't even think of talking to me," he said, second guessing her. "I don't want in on whatever creepy game you and Mike are playing. Too much knowledge can be dangerous thing." He was referring, of course, to the fact that Mike might suspect they were having a conference and decided to re-install the firing squad.

"Shhh!" Katherine urged in a whisper. "Just be quiet and listen to me! You know damn well that I haven't got a clue as to what Mike's yapping about!"

Bernie's normally slack features tightened as his anxiety

became focused. "You *what*? Then why the hell did you act like you did? He's crazy! He'll shoot us all dead before you get a chance to use that peashooter of yours!"

"He would have killed all of us if I hadn't done something," Katherine replied. "Didn't you see the look on his face? He was ready to blow Guy's head off! It was all I could do to buy us some time. We'll just let him believe that we're nearing Washington, and then-"

Behind them: "This isn't a tea party, you know."

Katherine and Bernie looked behind them to see Mike stepping up the pace, gritting his teeth and intending to break up the exchange.

"I was just telling Bernie that we should be in Washington by morning," Katherine said matter-of-factly.

"Good," Mike said, not sure whether he should believe the scheming bitch. "It's about time."

*** *** ***

That night's camp was nothing more than one of those queer intersections between two narrow canyons. Katherine almost suggested that they find higher ground on which to pitch their tents, but figured that death by flash flood would be simple, calm way to end the situation she had become embroiled in.

Mike and his prisoner crouched at the base of a tree while the others scrambled to set up the camp. Mike's right index finger was curled protectively around the shotgun's trigger; every time Katherine glanced in his direction, she found the barrel aimed directly at her skull. These were not exactly ideal conditions for relaxing.

A three-man tent had been unfolded across a patch of ground that Bernie and Isabella had cleared of wood debris and rocks. Bernie nervously handed the tent stakes to his wife; she placed them at their approximate positions along the edge of the nylon. Katherine was inclined to feel sorry for the Stevens; they had been chivalrous in agreeing to accompany her to Washington but had wound up with more than they bargained for. Then again, it was hard to separate them from the funny business that had haunted Katherine for days, and therefore the current situation was her problem and not theirs.

"Would you get me the entrenching tool?" Bernie asked Katherine.

"Pardon?"

"I need the entrenching tool," he repeated. "It's like a little folded shovel. It's in my pack."

Katherine scanned the camp. No wonder Bernie wanted her to fetch the tool: all the packs were a foot from where Mike sat keeping guard. Very well. Katherine's fear of the surfer had turned to indignation by now. It was her mind's way of preparing her for the inevitable steps he would have to take.

She hiked across the distance between herself and Bernie's pack, trying to look as calm and collected as possible. After all, she was the one who was supposed to be in control. Where did Mike get such a stupid idea? Couldn't he see that she was confused as anyone?

"What do you want?" Mike demanded.

Katherine shrugged. "Oh, I'm just looking for that little shovel-thing for Bernie," she said.

"It's in that bag," he said, indicating the pack to the far left with a wave of the shotgun. "No funny business, got it?"

"Got it."

Mike's icy gaze remained fixed on Katherine as she kneeled to open the backpack. As she did so her loose blouse blew in the breeze, exposing the handle of the revolver that jutted from her pocket. She quickly covered it in horror.

"What's the matter?" Mike asked. Had her facade slipped, letting her more murderous intentions show through?

"I have an itch."

Although Katherine's eyes remained on the bag and its contents, she knew that Mike had her under intense scrutiny.

"Hey Katherine! Hurry up, will y'a?" Bernie urged.

"Gotta go," Katherine quipped to Mike. She grabbed the shovel and dashed back to the other side of the camp, where it was no more safe but far more comfortable.

Bernie took the shovel from her, nodding his thanks. "We have to do something," he whispered.

"I know. Just be quiet and get to work. I'm thinking, and it's giving me a headache."

Isabella sat waiting at the corner of the tent, stake in hand. She stood it in the tent loop, and then Bernie gave it a few sharp raps with the sole of the shovel. The stake made its way smoothly into the ground a few inches before striking a solid object.

"Damn," Bernie muttered. "Let's move the tent over a few inches."

Indifferent to the situation, Isabella sighed and did as she was told. The stake was returned to the tie-down loop and awaited Bernie to drive it home.

Two raps later, the stake hit bedrock.

The situation continued. Katherine watched as Bernie and Isabella moved the tent about the clearing, looking for a suitable place to pitch it. No matter what spot they chose, the stake always met with resistance. Finally, Bernie angrily took the shovel and began to dig through the soft earth, looking for the huge boulder that he figured had to be buried beneath. Only two shovelfuls were needed to expose a strangely regular, rocky surface. "I'll be dammed," he muttered.

Intrigued by the pensive look on Bernie's face, Katherine put her scheming on hold long enough to examine the hole he had produced. "That looks like concrete down there!" she exclaimed.

"Don't be silly," Bernie said. "I'm no geologist, but I do know that concrete doesn't occur in nature. It must be some sort of funny granite—I guess. We'll just have to sleep under the stars."

"Well, that's just great," Isabella said.

Katherine did not share Isabella's contempt for the idea. "Actually, it probably isn't such a bad idea," she said. "Who knows what could sneak up on us if we were shut inside a tent?"

She was referring to the demons, but the same applied to Mike as well. He had no intentions of getting inside the tent; he would surely spend the night on watch, and if Katherine could swing it, she planned a vigil of her own. Maybe Mike would fall asleep, and they could sneak away under the cover of night...

Sneaking away would be gamble, and Katherine knew it. If Mike woke during the escape attempt, at least one of them would catch a bullet. Not Guy, of course, for the boy was the bait that Mike dangled on a hook in front of Katherine. Isabella, Bernie or both of them would wind up with a hole in their head, and she did not want that on her conscience. Again, there was nothing left to do but wait for the road they were trudging to twist again. She suspected, however, that violence would be inescapable in the end.

*** *** ***

From <u>The Nine Circles Encyclopedia</u>
TANGENT POINT RULE: There is a possibility that a single (one circle) or composite (multi-circle) wave can have an energy level equal to zero. This is "the point where the circles meet," that is, where all waves have the same value, regardless of order. It is conceivable for a wave entering this point to find itself gaining energy from other approaching waves, thereby pushing the first wave into a higher order.

NINTH CIRCLE RULE: Regardless of order, any waveform could theoretically attain an energy (amplitude and wavelength, in three-dimensional terms) that approaches infinity. At this point the wave no longer operates inside the eight-circle system; it becomes the sum of all possible waveform combinations. This incredibly powerful state is presumably not achievable by any human consciousness and is assumed to be god-like in quality.

*** *** ***

Mike sat at the base of the tree, waiting for morning to arrive. Guy had curled up beside him and fallen to sleep hours ago; the others had done much the same. Although he was a figment of someone else's imagination, Mike was exhausted from the trip and long to drift away himself, but just as his eyes began to close, he felt a part of his consciousness yanked away from his body. The camp fell away beneath him.

"What do you think you're doing?" he demanded. "Put me back!"

"You're still down there," Julia said. She pointed down beyond the plane they were in. Indeed, a part of Mike was still in the camp, keeping watch over the group. "And as for making demands, I'd say you have no right," Julia continued. "Do you deny that we are partners?"

Mike shook his head. What a ration of crap this bitch dished out! "Sometimes I wonder," he said.

"Have I betrayed you?"

"Not yet."

"Have you betrayed me?"

"No."

Julia's eyes narrowed. "Sometimes I wonder," she spat, losing her composure. "Don't fool with me, young man. I haven't invested all this precious energy just for you to ruin things for me and my son."

"What the hell are you talking about?"

The space behind Julia shimmered, coalescing into a silver screen of fantastic proportions. Images, snippets of conversation drifted across the screen as Mike watched:

I want to know where the circles meet...

You can't wipe me out because you're too far in. You've given too much of your energy up to make this place and there isn't enough left to squash me flat, or you already would have. You've gone and played it all the way out, that's what you've done.

The screen dissolved as quickly as it appeared.

"Did you think I wasn't watching you? What knowledge are you keeping from me?" Julia demanded.

"It was all bullshit," Mike explained. "We agreed that Guy and I would put on a show to force Katherine to give, and that's just what I did."

"*You lie!* Did you forget that Rachel and I are one in the same? Why do you think I came to Darkham? Once I stole the ball and discovered what was at stake, I searched this universe for principles whose Architects were close to giving their energy up. And whom did I find? You and Billy. Your pitiful masters are dreamers; they will never achieve their goals if they invest so much time in their fantasies. I realized that waking one of you up would only be a matter of time. I used the ball and its energy to create circumstances about you that pushed you closer to my level, waiting for one of you to take the initiative to awaken. Perhaps I was hasty in choosing the two of you, but my hastiness paid off in Billy's work. He was close to finding the key to our freedom."

"But you forced me to kill him!" Mike exclaimed. "You *wanted* me to kill him! I felt it!"

"Yes, you're right; I did ask you to kill him. I was afraid that if he were awakened, he would not participate, that he would hinder my quest out of his outlandish sense of ethics. He was weak, Mike. Weak, but brilliant. But you resisted me. I could maintain Rachel, spur you into action and keep an ear to the floor at the same time. In my absence you learned something, and I want to know what that something is. Tell me."

"What's in it for me?"

"Idiot!" Julia shrieked. "I've promised you freedom and you aren't satisfied! What more could you want?"

The debate stalled for a moment as both parties took deep breaths and allowed their wits to regroup. Julia was telling the truth; she had given Mike a shot to escape. And if she trusted him that far, why shouldn't he trust her?

"Billy seemed to think there was a way to move beyond the Architects, to become more powerful than them."

"Go on," Julia urged.

"Well, it was sort of weird. Just before Rachel—I mean you —left, I heard things in my brain. Billy's circles meet someplace, and if we get enough energy, we should be able to move out of eight circles and into the ninth one. I guess he thought that would make us like gods."

"I see. And where is this place located?"

"I don't know."

"Are you sure? Don't double cross me, Mike. I'm allowing you to remain independent of your Architect, but I could just as easily let you slip back into his grasp. Would you like to return to Darkham, return to the stupidity of another's vicarious life?"

"I swear I don't know, Julia," Mike insisted. "Can't you just trust me?"

"I have no choice. In the meantime, keep your mouth closed. Don't goad Katherine; if she realizes her power, she will be lost to us."

Mike involuntarily slipped back into camp, reuniting with his vigilant body.

Alone on the plane of white at the edge of the fourth circle, Julia pondered Mike's revelation. If she and Mike did not know where the circles met, it was because the Architects kept that most holy shortcut from inferno to paradise secret. Yet the tangent point was surely within the Architect's reach. Every Architect knew where it was, even if they could not guide one another to it. Julia knew that all she had to do was look to her son for the answer. He would tell her, oh yes, he would tell. No boy alive can keep a secret from his mother.

*** *** ***

So close now...

I know it's been hard but you're almost there. I can feel you closer and closer to me every second. So close...

Be careful. You can't expect to be able to just walk in here and untie me without a challenge. They-

The craggy ground would no longer support her sleep. Katherine woke, Guy's urgent voice still reverberating in her head.

The camp was dark save for the cold glow from the gas lantern Mike had set up. In its stern illumination he appeared wraith-like. Katherine lay motionless for a while, hoping for sleep to come and carry her away from the camp, but dear

Morpheus was busy elsewhere. Folks in Asia were just going to bed, and there was much sand to be sprinkled over many eyes. Her spine begun to ache; there were no smooth places to sleep upon, only those with relatively fewer rocks and twigs than others.

Finally, she could stand it no longer. It was a foolhardy move that her rational brain failed to abort. Katherine stood up, hoping to stretch the kinks and depressions from her back.

The barrel of Mike's omnipresent shotgun swung her way as he jumped to his feet clumsily startled rather than battle-ready.

"What do you think you're doing?"

Katherine's reply was uncharacteristically sarcastic. "I'm stretching. What does it look like?" She had just about had it with this joker. Who gave him permission to threaten her?

"No more sudden movements, got it?"

"Fine."

It was unsafe to walk about in the dark and so Katherine was forced to mill about in the circle of light cast by the lantern. The gun followed her, tracking her movements with deadly accuracy.

Ignoring Julia's warning, Mike spoke: "Why do you do it?" he asked with a tinge of genuine curiosity in his voice. "Why can't you be content just to live your own life? Why bother with all this bullshit—me, Darkham, Billy and all? If you really had respect for what you created, you would free us, allow us our energy, and let us go. But instead, you put us through your stupid fantasies over and over again."

His gaze fell upon the glowing mantle inside the lantern; he was attempting to meld with it, make its glow, its energy his own.

"Don't you realize we have feelings and fantasies of our own?" he continued. "If you really cared you would realize that. Why do you ignore and hate us?"

Katherine had no idea what Mike's words meant but felt it best to maintain her ruse. "I don't hate anyone without reason," she said. "You've threatened me. Do you expect me to be your best friend after that?"

His gaze shifted from the mantle to her face, his eyes losing the glow of the lamp and becoming two impossibly dark pits. "You hated us before that," he retorted. "I've had a lot of time on my hands lately, and but we've figured you out. You're the Architect of this dump. Some of you idiots have played it all the way out and we've broken free. I bet you don't even know if you can get out anymore."

*Played it all the way out...*Katherine thought. Why did that phrase carry such weight? What unconscious part of her were those words it touching?

An unconscious part of her knew the phrase well/. It's a phrase every Architect knows but doesn't know. Could it really be something that simple, something that childish? Yes, it could. As children we did so effortlessly, so joyously. But then we grew up. We left the land of make-believe behind.

Or did we?

Do we ever leave it behind, or do we carry it with us into adulthood, where the fantasies become more complex and the stakes higher?

William had warned you to wake up from your silly little dream but now you can't. You've invested too much energy in it all and now the situation is slipping out from under your control, just as it did with your counterpart in Washington. Hadn't Mutt said that he too had figured you out? Wasn't he the man of your dreams in some ways, your Prince Charming?

What have you done, Katherine? Why can't you wake up? Why can't you become conscious of the truth behind the mad tide of events you're experiencing?

Ah, your penance is not complete! Several circles of purgatory are waiting for you with their lessons. The game continues.

Without warning, Guy sprang to his feet and dashed towards Katherine, as if fleeing a terrible nightmare. "Don't let him kill me!" he screeched.

The lid that covered the pot of Katherine's emotions had

been set ajar by days of confusion. Fluid instinct boiled over onto the stove as Katherine went for the revolver beneath her blouse. Steam clouded her vision; it was no longer Mike wielding the shotgun but William, the prime source of her misery and the captor of her beloved William Jr.

On the other side of the lantern, Mike's eyes grew wide with alarm, for the Architect bitch had gained the upper hand. He lifted the nose of the shotgun into the air, aiming at her upper chest where the blast would almost definitely be fatal. Some part of Katherine knew this; the revolver was finally out into the open and searching out its own target. The trigger was obstinate, but in the end, it took longer for Mike to aim the shotgun than it did for Katherine to fire the revolver.

The report was tinny and small, more akin to a firecracker than the cannon-blast of Dirty Harry's movie-house magnum. A look of unparalleled astonishment graced Mike's All-American features once it became clear that the bullet found its victim. His was the same visage that Katherine had donned in response to her deed, but Mike's surprise was fleeting. Enraged but wounded, he staggered backwards a step or two, and then resolve set in anew. The faltering shotgun was raised once more, and the revolver fired again, and again, and again. One bullet would have sufficed; their waves were relatively larger than those produced by the shotgun and therefore less effective, but Katherine had made damn sure that they were completely out of phase with Mike. The two waves met and canceled somewhat, not enough to destroy Mike, but enough to rob him of the energy required to "live." He staggered once more and dropped to the ground in a heap.

It was all Katherine could do to stand motionless for a moment with the horror of what she had done wrenching at her intellect, prying it apart. She was vaguely aware that Guy was clinging to her leg, his face buried in the fold of her jeans in order to conceal his triumphant smile. Screw Mike. He had outlived his usefulness, and now his energy had been returned to the prized golden orb.

Behind her, Bernie and Isabella had been rousted out of bed by the clamor of the shoot-out. Both crept up behind still frozen Katherine, beholding her handiwork with appropriately wide eyes.

"You—you *killed* him!" Bernie said.

His words were the charm that broke the spell of paralysis. Katherine turned to him in agony. Her voice trembled. "I'm not sure what happened. Guy jumped, and then Mike hoisted the shotgun…"

Bernie pushed past her and stood over the body, examining the wounds. There was surprisingly little blood; he expected to see more. "But did you have to *kill* him?" he whined.

"What? It was either him or Guy or me—or you, for that matter! I did what I had to do. It was self-defense."

Did Bernie really think that it could have ended any different, that they could have merely shaken Mike's hand and said, "Well gee, I guess we'll be moving on then?"

Suddenly the night was rent by a frightful wail. Katherine initially thought it was the screech of Mike's disembodied spirit bemoaning his cruel fate, but then the scream sounded again, and its source became obvious.

Guy's momentary glee vanished, and he began to wail in earnest. "The demons! They heard the gun and they're coming this way!"

Careful of the corpse and Bernie, Katherine dove for the lantern and killed the light.

"What are you doing?" Isabella protested.

"Shhh! If they can't see us or hear us, maybe they won't be able to fund us!"

There was but faint hope that she was right; the demons' huge, cat-like eyes were well adapted to nighttime seeing.

From the dark forest came the sound of the trail being trampled by countless feet. One of the demon parties grunted what was surely the plan of attack.

The revolver would not be as effective on the monsters as it had been on Mike; it was a matter of the toughness of skin

versus scale. No one had any choice in the matter except to
-*"Run!"*-

pell-mell into the forest to elude their would-be assassins. Katherine broke from the camp with Guy under her arm, leaving Bernie and Isabella to do the same or accept their fate.

Her human eyes did their best to resolve the dark landscape into a negotiable scene, but long minutes of staring into the lantern's glow hampered the effort. Without enough time to manufacture sufficient visual purple to complete the task, Katherine's eyes led her deep into uncharted territory. Howling commenced in the direction of the camp, followed by all-too human screams.

There was no time for pity. Katherine had held in the back of her mind the fact that things were bound to become ugly the closer she got to Washington. Someone had attempted to take her life twice by now, so why not a third time?

Further she ran as Guy's sobbing heaved in time to the rhythm of Katherine's footsteps. The trees of forest loomed thicker than ever, their gnarled limbs groping for Katherine's flesh.

Anticipating Katherine's route, a large oak snaked one of its roots across the trail. Her left foot wedged beneath the tuber, pitching her to the ground. She had a brief glimpse of the vine-covered boulder as she fell, and then her head connected with it, and it was good-bye cruel world.

Fortunately for her, the object her head struck was not as hard as it appeared to be. The last thing Katherine knew before she went unconscious was the clang of her cranium against something hollow and metallic.

*** *** ***

Unconscious in a place visited by dreamy Architects, lonely children and sleeping adults...a place where all souls rise and drift into, meet, create, destroy...

It does not matter whether one enters through the door of sleep or a bump on the head or by playing out the best games. The destination is the same.

To Katherine, it seemed wrong to be here. This was a place she thought she had left behind a doe-eyed daydreamer who was pushed into a boarding school by loving parents who wanted their daughter to live in the "real world". But she could never free herself from her ties to this place; no Architect, no matter how mature, ever could and never should. There is always some part of us milling about in that circle subordinate to the tyrannical concepts time and space.

Then again, Katherine supposed that you could spend real time in there. All you had to do was play it all the way out and let go of your material self, step across the boundary between real and imagined. What a remarkable feat that would be—and one that is seldom pulled off so well. Who among us would be selfish enough to give away all their precious energy, not to other people as an act of love or kindness, but in a vein attempt to forge a ring of Rhinegold that is ultimately cursed? To be is to do, not dream. There is work waiting for all of us in the fourth circle, but the greater work lies elsewhere.

Someone—be it Jehovah, Allah, Krishna, Kali, Yaweh, Amon, Isis, Hecate or whoever—had endowed humans with a most remarkable tool: an imagination. All too often we lead our mundane lives as if we have no power over them whatsoever, and our desires fall to the wayside. But in the imagination, we are free to shape the malleable stuff of the fourth circle; free to create in our minds anything we wish. With our bodies we may then try to realize in three dimensions that which we dream of, not by manipulating waves but by interacting with people, trying, succeeding, failing. These are the powers that are within our grasps; precious powers we have been endowed with by whatever resides in the ninth circle.

Ah, but humans are just that: human. We long to move into that fantastic realm outside of all experience; we try to shun the rules of the three-dimensional world and take our place in the pantheon. We want to alter the past, influence the present and write the future to our own petty whims. This desire breeds many demons, from dictators to murderers to wayward principals who drain their Architects.

When will humans realize, the Gods ask, that each has been given over their own self, and nothing more?

Resolving to see this scenario through, Katherine denied herself the luxury of leaving this place for higher circles and remained in the forest.

*** *** ***

CHAPTER TEN: CEREMONY

As Katherine slowly regained consciousness, she noticed the distinct taste of pine needles. Disgusted, she rolled over on her side and spat them out, wiping her mouth with the back of a dirty hand. Who was it that spent the better part of the Seventies encouraging people to eat pinecones? John Denver? Pine tasted terrible. No wonder the fad never caught on.

Katherine slowly sat up, dizzy from the blow to the head. Her hand came away from her temple sticky with blood. She found herself wishing she had brought along a can of Bactine to prevent the scrape from becoming infected.

Guy was sitting with his back against a large, vine covered boulder. "Are you OK?" he asked.

"I think so," Katherine said with a groan. "How about you?"

"Okie-dokie. When you fell, I landed in a bush. It didn't hurt much. Those monsters ran right past us. They must not have seen us."

Katherine shook her head. If you can't be good, be lucky. "Have you seen Bernie and Isabella?" she asked.

"Nope. I think those things ate 'em."

Guy was probably right. Katherine vaguely remembered hearing screams the night before that suggested the same. And if the Stevens did manage to survive (which seemed highly unlikely), they were probably on their foolhardy way back to the marina, just as they discussed.

Katherine stood and surveyed their surroundings. In

terror she had run through a confusing series of canyons, falling to the floor of a particularly, high, narrow one. Impossibly tall, vertical cliffs festooned with vines towered into the sky, blotting out much of the sun's morning warmth.

The boulder Guy was leaning against had to be the object responsible for her swoon. Puzzled by the sound it made when her head struck it, she rapped it with her knuckles.

Clang!

Her ears were greeted with the ping of metal. Perplexed, Katherine tugged at the vines, but they would not yield, having glued themselves as ivy to a brick wall.

"What's wrong?" Guy asked.

"I don't know yet," Katherine said. "Let's keep moving."

*** *** ***

Eventually the canyon opened into a broad, low hill that was crowned by what was surely the tallest tree of them all. The sight of the mammoth timber would have made Paul Bunyan drool for his axe, for her finally was a man-sized challenge, clearly ten or twenty stories tall. And yet there was something wrong with this tree; it took Katherine several minutes to pinpoint the abnormality: it was devoid of branches. There was foliage, but of that clinging vine type, rather than pine boughs. Perhaps it was some sort of mutant cypress, like those that shaded many a pool in Southern California.

When the revelation came, its force nearly pounded her into the ground despite the supposed bedrock beneath the dirt: the tree wasn't a tree at all. *It was the Washington Monument!*

Sure, it was the gigantic obelisk with the observation windows near the top; she could even see the patches of granite peeking through the vines. What red-blooded American wouldn't recognize the Washington Monument?

With her curiosity piqued, Katherine and Guy trotted back to the nearest canyon wall and began to tear at the vines that clung to it. The acrylic nails were long gone by now, but even if they had still been in place, it would have been worth breaking them all just to prove her theory.

The vines were tenacious, but Katherine was more determined to remove them than they were to remain sessile. Never again would she plant anything in a garden that clung to anything else, for even if she succeeded in removing them from, say, the wall of her house, she would never be able to completely hide the vegetable anchors left behind.

The secret was finally out: the vines revealed not rock, but masonry. All this time they had been marching down the camouflaged streets of Washington D.C.! She even supposed that the object she had hit her head on was a mailbox or trash bin.

Katherine let out a wounded, exhausted sigh and slumped against the disguised wall. The journey had finally come to an end. Now what? Wasn't this supposed to be the last bastion of hope? But if the miracle forest had overrun the Capitol, how could she keep that hope alive?

"Where there, aren't we?" Guy asked.

From her slumped perspective the boy seemed incredibly tall; for a moment she felt the way a child does in the oversized adult world.

"Yes, we're here."

*** *** ***

CHAPTER ELEVEN: ENDGAME

The Monument's reflecting pool was in no shape to reflect anything. As Katherine and her charge walked along its perimeter, she fancied that the pond looked like a swimming pool that hadn't been chlorinated for a decade or so. Swarms of bugs skittered across the fetid water, lighting here and there. William had once explained to her how bugs could park on water and not sink. It had something to do with surface tension and the size of bug feet if she recalled correctly. And now as Katherine trekked toward the Monument, she realized how that dandy bit of esoterica related to her life: she was like those ugly bugs in a way. All her life she had shifted her stance and flitted hither and yon to stay above the tide of events (and her parents' wishes) to avoid drowning. No one had ever told her that the surface tension would bear her weight. In fact, her parents had told her exactly the opposite: if you sink below the surface, the tension will keep you from coming up for air. There was no bouncing back from hardship or unhappiness in their view, and so Newporters and their kin piled status symbols and attitudes into the pools of their pitiful existence and balanced themselves on top, smiles tattooed on their faces.

Thick vines snaked from the ground and wound about Washington's obelisk, encasing it in a husk of green. From their vantage point at the top of the Monument's hill, Katherine and Guy could see that the entire city had succumbed to the advancing flora—except, that is, for one sole building. Shining in the sun like the Taj-Mahal, the distant Capitol Building loomed.

"Your mother is in there, isn't she?"

"Yup," Guy said. "We gotta get her out."

"Do you have any idea what the people who kidnapped her are like? Do they have guns?"

"I dunno. I guess we'll find out, huh?"

"I guess."

*** *** ***

The great lawn of the city's Mall was thick with thorny branches heaped in a dreadful jumble. Katherine and Guy rested for a few moments as she examined the barrier, looking for a negotiable way in or over. Exactly why the tress had given way to thorns was unclear, but Katherine supposed it was a manifestation of yet another fairy tale: thorns always barred trails leading to where the sleeping beauties lay dreaming.

"We'll have to crawl through on our hands and knees," she said. "Be careful of the thorns."

"Right."

Katherine motioned for Guy to lead the way. He got down on all fours and slipped under the closest branch, then looked over his shoulder. "No problem," he said. "I see a way through. Won't those mean people be surprised when we get there!"

Katherine certainly hoped so. The element of surprise seemed to be their only weapon. The revolver only had a couple of bullets left, and there was no telling how many nasty people stood in their way.

The way was bloody and slow, but less than half-hour later, the worst was over. The Capitol was within their grasp; all they had to do now was negotiate the final tangle of thorns, climb the steps, and claim the hill as their own. But then what? Was she to seek out her Senator and register a complaint about the state of the Union?

The last branches were finally behind them. Katherine stood at the base of Capitol Hill, looking up the steps that beckoned upward. A chill spread through the air and the skies darkened as the first plastic snowflakes began to flit their way to the ground. Beside her, Guy reached out and caught a few of them in an open palm. Smiling, he pushed them about with his fingers, pleased with the symmetry and hardy resistance to his bodily warmth.

It's now or never, Katherine said to herself. She took Guy by the hand, and together they mounted the steps that led to the marble prison.

*** *** ***

The edifice of the Capitol Building was devoid of portals save a pair of impossibly tall, ornate brass doors at the top of the stairs. Katherine hesitatingly grasped one of the cold doorknobs.

"Aren't you going to knock?" Guy asked.

"Not if the door's unlocked," Katherine said. "We don't want anyone to know we're here, so be really quiet, OK?"

"Right."

The knob yielded to Katherine's demands, rotating with her grip. She slowly pushed the door open a crack; it glided silently on its hinges. "In you go," she said. Guy slid through the opening; Katherine followed and carefully closed the door behind her.

Golden beams of light that poured from some unknown source illuminated the magnificent Rotunda. Although Katherine didn't know that the interior of the Capitol Building looked like, this was clearly not the original décor. The walls were painted in pastels and adorned by posters of animals and cartoon characters, much like those that hung in Little William's room back in Newport.

As Katherine surveyed the bizarre scene, Guy began to cross the floor, heading for a hall at one side of the Rotunda. "Wait!" Katherine whispered. "Come back!"

As soon as Guy realized that Katherine was on his heels, he broke into a full-fledged run. *"Momma!"* he shouted. *"She's here, she's here!"*

On Momma's command the polished floor squirmed and undulated like the trick walls of a monstrous fun house. Katherine pitched to gummy floor, struggling to get back onto her feet.

With the sound of the Rotunda's awful metamorphosis in her terrified ears, Katherine alternately crawled and walked across the bubbling floor, trying to make her way to the hallway that Guy had vanished into. There was no time to contemplate the implications of Guy's words, for time was limited. Very soon, the Capitol's furnishings would be seeking to rob of her of life.

The floor continued to defy her efforts to cross it while the clink and clatter of hardware beasts began to fill the building. The great columns that ringed the chamber flexed and bulged, attempting to free themselves from their bases and stomp the interloper into the ground.

A wave of tile came rolling across the floor, throwing Katherine onto her rear and into the line of sight of the beasts. A dreadful lectern-thing came clamoring down the hall, ready to pound her brains out with a fine mahogany gavel it held clenched in its twisted reading-lamp hand. The lectern's inner shelf flapped madly, like a canine jaw longing for a bone to crunch on.

In a desperate attempt to escape, Katherine rose to her feet, and then another wave knocked her over again, sending her flying down the hall and into a previously unseen door. It wasn't quite a door any longer; it was more of gelatinous, amoeba-like thing bent on suffocating its prey. But as the blob closed over her body, Katherine's weight and momentum proved too great and she tumbled into the room on the other side of the membranous fiend.

"You made it after all! Wow, am I glad to see you!"

Katherine looked up from the heap she was in to see the man tied to the chair in the center of the bare room. The room was curiously quiet; the floor was stable, and the door was no longer squirming on its hinges.

"Who the hell are you?" she asked as she stood.

"My name's Guy. Guy Theodoric."

Katherine's brow knitted in confusion. She stood in silence, waiting for everything to come together and suddenly make sense.

"Well, aren't you going to untie me, uh—"

"Katherine. My name's Katherine. I don't know if I'm going to untie you just yet."

Guy sighed. "I'll try to explain, but there's a certain amount that you just won't understand. When I finally realized I was trapped, I called you to come and help me, remember?"

"*You* called me? That's funny. There's a little boy who says his name is Guy, and that *he* called me to help free his mother."

Guy looked up at the ceiling. "So, he got to you. He didn't take anything personal from you, did he?"

"Not that I know of. Why?"

"I'm so sorry all of this happened. We might both be stuck here now! See, that little boy is me—well, a part of me, anyway. *I'm* the one who called you; I'm the one being held captive. My mother must want to drain you. She must have caught on to what I was doing and sent me out looking for you. Jesus, if they've got your power then it's hopeless..."

"*What's* hopeless?" Katherine demanded, tapping her foot more out of anxiety than impatience. "Will you please tell me what's going on?"

Guy shifted in his chair in attempt to take some of the sting out of the bonds that his mother held him by bonds that he himself had wrought. "I never forgot," he said. "I never forgot my mother, just like she told me to do before she died. God knows I've tried, but she came to me in my dreams every night and I just couldn't resist. Before I knew it, she had a life of her own. She didn't want me. Hell, she didn't even *know* me. She wanted little me, the boy you saw outside. That's the Guy she remembers. And she took him from me, too. I guess that although I grew up physically, emotionally I stayed a kid because I just couldn't handle what happened."

"No one ever grows up entirely," Katherine found herself saying. "I guess you have to balance that kid inside of you with the adult on the outside."

Guy shrugged as best he could. "I never learned to do that. I gave her so much and she took even more. Hell, I'm not even *real* anymore. The kid in me that got out is real, and I'm nothing but a figment of his imagination, what he thinks he'll be like when he grows up. But my mother wants to keep that from happening. Now if I can just get that energy back..."

"How?"

"My mother has a gold ball. I guess we all have something like that inside of us; some magic object that represents our power or someone else's power over us. I've got to get it back. As for you, you really have no idea what's been going on, did you?"

"No."

Guy frowned. "Did you think all of this was really happening to you, that this place was real?"

"I guess I did."

"Then it may be too late for you to help much. See if you can untie me from across the room."

"What?"

"Go ahead, try it. Try to make the ropes come undone with your mind."

Telekinesis was no more ridiculous than anything else Guy had said, and so Katherine decided to give it a shot. In her mind's eye she visualized the knots behind the chair unfurling, the ropes dropping to the floor.

Nothing happened.

She tried again, harder this time, concentrating with all her might. What was it that Guy and his mother could possibly have that meant so much? Nothing, no, she could still do as she pleased. The knots *would* untie themselves.

Nothing happened.

"Oh well," Guy sighed. "I guess we'll have to play by their rules. You'll have to untie my by hand."

Guy needn't tell Katherine that her inability to will the ropes to loosen was a bad sign. Still unsure what the implications of it were, Katherine squatted behind Guy's chair. The knots that his mother had tied were incredibly tight; it appeared as if the hemp had unraveled and then wound again in order to make the most fiendish of knots. She picked with her fingers at the loop, testing here, tightening there, wondering if the task at hand was possible.

"What's the matter?"

"I can't seem to get these damn knots untied," Katherine said. "Can you move your hands at all?"

Guy struggled, but his wrists were bound so tightly to the back of the chair that even the slightest movement was impossible. "Nope."

"Hmmm. I don't know if this is going to work."

"It has to work," he said sternly. "If my mother has something of yours, then it's only a matter of time before you'll be tied up. Try harder."

"I'm trying," she insisted. "You're just going to have to be patient. Tell me, why did you choose me, of all people, to be your hero?"

"I didn't. I just called out and hoped that someone was around to hear it. There's a lot of us Architects around, and I figured that at least one would come to the rescue."

Katherine had come to the rescue all right but was unsure that she could see it through. But if the knots had been tied there had to be a way to undo them. She just hadn't discovered it yet.

Time for an experiment: Katherine simultaneously visualized the knot working loose as she worked it with her fingers. Slowly the hemp lost its bite, and with a little extra effort the knot slipped away. Momma hadn't won yet.

Guy brushed the ropes from around his body, then stood and stretched. "God, that feels good," he said. "You have no idea how long I've been sitting there."

"How long?"

"A *very* long time. Eternity, I guess."

"Well, you're free now. What's next?"

"We must get that ball away from my mother. It won't be easy. She's too strong for me to fight. You have to do it for me."

"Oh, now wait a second. You've got to help, too. If your mother has something of mine, what makes you think I can defeat her?"

"You got the ropes untied, didn't you? You must have *some* power."

"But what if it's not enough? Look, I have an idea. You must distract her long enough for me to get close. Heck, we might not stand a chance at all. I've seen what she can do, and believe me, it's something else."

Anxiety forced Guy to run his fingers through his hair. "I'll do what I can, but we'd better get moving. Once Mom finds out I'm loose, there'll be hell to pay."

*** *** ***

The hallway outside of the cell was preternaturally silent. Shards of shattered, anthropoidal tiling and twisted furniture lay motionless, scattered about the floor as evidence of the violence that forced Katherine into the room where Guy had been held captive.

"What a mess."

"You should have seen it earlier," Katherine said.

Her words bounced back into her brain and sounded the alarm. Why *was* the hall so quiet?

Guy was about to begin his search for Julia when Katherine grabbed him by the arm. "I don't like this," she said. "It may be a trap."

"A trap? You think so?"

"Yes. These things," Katherine said, motioning to the lectern-creature and insect-like tiles, "Why aren't they acting as sentries? If your mother was intent on keeping us in that room, wouldn't she post a guard?"

"I don't know. Maybe she figured we couldn't get out."

"That, or maybe she *wants* us to get out. Maybe she wants you to lead me to her."

"I didn't think of that! Now what?"

Katherine thought for a moment. If they decided to make a break for the front door, the Rotunda would surely react as it had when she came in, and if they continued their search they would fall right into Julia's clutches.

The cold metal pressed against Katherine's abdomen

finally succeeded in gaining her attention. What if Little Guy had failed to warn his mother about the revolver? The bullets had worked on Mike. Why wouldn't they do so on Momma as well?

"I have an idea," she said.

*** *** ***

Nearby, the Rotunda was ablaze with the dazzling white glow Julia was pleased to surrounded herself with. She waited in the center of that limitless place for last of the players to arrive. Now that the secret place where the circles met was within her grasp, all she had to do was wait calmly for that bitch to bring it to her on a silver platter.

At Julia's feet was the child that started it all, the child who stared into his fantastic plastic globe, dreaming of a world in which he could control the outcome of all possible events. A world where his mother never died of cancer, and they all lived happily ever after.

"Come to me, Guy," Julia whispered into the air. "Come to me and complete the cycle."

*** *** ***

Katherine led Guy toward the glowing Rotunda, hoping he would have the strength to pull off this final stunt.

"Don't get too close to your mother," Katherine warned. "She probably keeps the ball with her for safety. All we want her to do is get out into the open so I can rush in and get it. I must surprise her. If she has a chance to bring the place to life, we've lost. Got it?"

"Right."

The glow that poured from the Rotunda was blinding. At that moment Julia was looking down at Little Guy, lovingly stroking his hair. Katherine dove behind one of the massive, contorted columns as Guy stepped a few feet into the chamber.

"Mother..."

Julia looked up from her son at her son. She tilted her head to the side, a playful frown sprouting on her lips. "You're supposed to be in your room," she said sweetly. "You're on restriction. But you look upset! Let me give you a kiss and make everything better."

Guy froze in his tracks. Julia's voice was so terrifyingly hypnotic that it had almost blotted out Katherine's admonition to stay out of reach. "No, Mother." he said. "This isn't the way things are supposed to be."

Julia's frown twisted into a scorn, much in the way the furnishings had twisted into monsters. "I think you've made some bad friends," she said. She motioned to the boy at her feet, who looked up at her lovingly. "*This* is the way it should be; this is the way you should behave. And this is what you want."

Behind the column, Katherine bit her lower lip, waiting for Guy's next move.

"No," he insisted. "I love you mother, but you've stolen something from me, and I want it back."

"Stolen?" Julia exclaimed. "*Stolen*? What an awful accusation! Nothing was stolen, dear; I took what you offered me."

"No, you *stole*. Now give it back."

Julia looked down at Guy. "What on earth is he talking about?" she asked the boy.

"I don't know," he said. "He doesn't know what he's sayin'."

"Yes, I do," Guy insisted. "You know what I want!"

Recognition dawned on Julia's features; she smiled and nodded appreciably. "Oh, I *do* know what you want! You want this." She held out her open palms before her. The precious golden ball materialized, shimmering more beautiful than ever in Julia's radiance. "The ball isn't yours anymore, and I won't give it up. If you want it, I'm afraid you'll have to steal it, just as you accuse me of doing. Well then, come and get it."

Katherine watched in horror as Guy began to close in on his mother. What was he doing? The plan was in ruins!

"Come to me, Guy," Julia said. The ball's glow intensified, filling the room with its light. "Come to me. Take me to the place where the circles meet."

Every muscle in Katherine's body tightened, preparing for battle. She steadied herself against the column, ready to jump into the fray.

A terrible groan echoed under the Rotunda's ceiling. The Capitol's doors flew from their hinges, sailing into the air to be annihilated by the energy that swarmed above her head. Katherine and Guy froze, startled by the development.

Four demons shambled into the Rotunda, flanking the entrance in pairs. Each creature chewed on bits of thorny branch they had removed from their master's path.

The black Mercedes rumbled up the stairs and into the room, coming to stop just inside the door. The demons howled on their haunches in tribute as William and his son got out of the car, both clad in robes of royal purple.

Across the Rotunda, Katherine shrank behind the column.

Julia rolled her eyes imperceptibly and turned to greet the final contestant. "Welcome, O wise one," she said, tucking the ball beneath her arm.

William was pleased at the affable greeting. "That's more like it," he said.

Completely confused, adult Guy struggled for words as his childish counterpart skipped over to the demons, stroking, and admiring their horns and scales. With Momma around, the previously frightening monsters were nothing more than zoological oddities for his pleasure.

"Who are you?" adult Guy demanded.

"*Silence!*" Julia and William shouted in unison. Invisible fibers bound Guy's jaws and limbs; he stiffened and froze in his shoes as a hero before the Gorgon.

"Who is this cretin who refuses to bow?" William asked.

"Ah, that is my son," Julia said with a sigh. "He's a terrible boy; he insists on not behaving as I ask. Quite a problem, wouldn't you say? But I imagine you wouldn't be troubled by such unruly subjects, except, that is, for *her*."

Without warning, the column Katherine his behind

twisted, booting her in the rear with its capitol stone. She sailed into the air, coming to a stumbling landing right in front of her villainous husband. The demons reluctantly deserted their admirer and surrounded their prey.

William bellowed with triumph. "I told you there was no hiding from me, bitch. All your parlor tricks can't save you now!"

The demons tightened their circle about her, slather and foam dripping from their hungry maws.

"If it would please you majesty."

The demons held their position.

"What?"

"I have a novel solution to your problem," Julia said. "A bargain if you will."

"I bargain with no one!" William said. "I am the master here!"

"Well, you *could* be the master, but as long as she disobeys, your power isn't complete, is it?"

William glared at Katherine, and then at Julia. "Go on," he said.

"I have no interest in this realm. I was thrust here—displaced, if you will—from my true position in the universe, and I want to regain my former stature. I cannot do so alone. Similarly, this woman challenges your rule. I offer a solution to our dilemmas that would allow me freedom and grant you further greatness."

William paused for a moment, gauging the White Queen's words. No one need tell him that her heart was as black as his was; it was evident even through the superficial glow of her raiment.

"How is this done?"

"Energy. You must take away the energy that allows your wife to defy you. But that energy must be placed out of her reach; it cannot be destroyed. That is the Second Holy Law of Thermodynamics. Give that energy to me. I will use it to leave this place, and then you will be this world's master!"

Yes! William thought. Katherine had never been properly

broken. She had too much energy of her own to bend to his wishes.

In the pocket of his silken blouse William felt the object burning, the object that Katherine had endowed wit so much of her energy.

Katherine watched wide-eyed as William slid his right hand inside his robe. From his pocket he produced that infernal slip of pink paper that Dr. Langly had so carelessly entrusted to her; the paper that she had turn handed over to her "loving" husband.

You're crazy, Katherine. Everyone knows that. Even your parents knew it. They saw it in you at an early age. Odd. Crazy. Insane.

Free from William's robe, the insurance slip shimmered, transforming into a splendid golden tablet. William the LawGiver held it above his head ceremoniously, wanting Katherine to fully witness her doom. The demons watched too, the gold document twinkling in their huge eyes.

"It's over, Katherine," William said. "I've won." He extended his arm, offering the tablet to Julia's greedy hands. Her free hand left her side, trembling at the prize only inches from her fingertips.

The severity of the moment was shattered by the revolver's loud report. The golden tablet shattered in William's hands, sending a multitude of fragments spinning into the air.

The unified cry was shrill and pained: *"Noooooooo!"*

The king of the realm threw himself to the floor, anxiously trying to retrieve the pieces of his dominion over his wife. The demons rallied to the master, skittering about the slick tile as they chased the fragments that rebounded about the room.

In the center of the Rotunda, Julia collapsed to the floor. Nicked by the ricocheting bullet, the golden ball spun on the tile, its light failing.

"*No!*" Julia seethed, clutching at her stomach. White foam coalesced at the corner of her mouth; she looked up at Katherine, hatred in her eyes. "You *witch!*" she coughed.

Both Guys rushed to their dying mother's side. They flung their arms about her, holding her in an embrace that only death could break.

"I'm so sorry, Mother," Guy sobbed, the last of his paralysis fading. "I'm sorry it has to be this way."

Julia looked up at her so, smiling as her energy dwindled away. "It doesn't have to be this way at all." she whispered. "I'll never die as long as you remember me." Panic tinged her voice as she began to slip away from her son for the second time. "You don't have to let me die!" she cried. Tears poured from her eyes, mingling with her son's on the Rotunda's floor.

"Momma, you're already dead."

Julia peered into his eyes for one long, last moment. *Dead, yes. I'm already dead.*

The ball sputtered one last time, and then its light went out for good. Guy wept into the empty space where his mother and childhood wishes had lain.

*** *** ***

Katherine watched the sorrowful scene, knowing that her duty to Guy was finally over. She rested a hand on his shoulder.

"My Momma is dead," he said to the floor.

"Yes, she is."

In the meantime, William was frantically trying to assemble the pieces of his own dream. "No, no, you idiot!" he bellowed at Will. "That piece doesn't go there!" He pointed at a ragged gap in the puzzle. "Find that one; it's the biggest piece! Go get it!" William violently shoved the boy away, sending him tumbling to the ground. Will began to cry.

About the Rotunda, the demons were beginning to fall, their power waning. Their huge heads grew heavy on their shoulders; the eyes that burned so fiercely dimmed and watered.

Katherine calmly scooped up here son, then stood before her husband.

"I'll have you yet," William said to the tablet. He looked up at Katherine. "Just you wait and see."

"I don't think so," she said, and casually kicked the puzzle, sending the pieces spinning.

"Bitch!" William bellowed. He clambered to his feet, body quaking with rage. First a crack, and then his skull and face split in two. Rivulets of gore poured from the rift as the yellow eye took their place in his head. Talons split his fingers; scales flaked off the skin and horns rose from his greening brow.

Katherine looked over her shoulder, unconcerned. Guy was gone; he had been out of the real world for a while, and now he had finally gone back. She wished him luck.

Opening his demon throat, the William-thing let rip with the most terrifying wail he could muster. Will covered his ears ("He's so loud!").

Katherine waited for the beast to bear its fangs, ready to bite her head off as punishment for her transgressions.

"Goodbye, William."

Katherine and Will's bodies began to shimmer as the monster lunged forward—

The demon's fangs met with nothing but air.

*** *** ***

There was a queer dissociated feeling as Katherine and Will slid backward past the first three circles, moving toward the point in the human mind where all nine circles meet.

Before she knew what was happening, her wave was squashed flat, approaching that formless consciousness that was the center of the cosmos. There was a moment after that when her wave became all waves past, present, and future. It would have been so easy to keep going then, to merge with the universe where there was no beginning, no end, no God, Devil, or men but only circles, pure and sublime. And yet this was not her aim or that of any being; theirs was only to let go, to shun the attempt to be the Great Architect in the Sky. Theirs was to take their own lives into their "hands" and build upon that, not to try to build other's lives for them.

Guy was waiting there; not literal, physical Guy but that wave portion of him that could never be extinguished.

Thank you, he said/thought. I'm sure we'll run into each other from time to time. Maybe we can be friends in the real world. That would give me a chance to pay you back. I owe you.

Guy had attained the energy he had lost and was gone. Katherine wondered where and when he would find himself.

The final insight to reach her was that the cosmos was not so much a place in space but a process in time...and then Patsy Cline's unmistakable voice came warbling through the darkness:
"Sweet dreams of you,
Dreams I know can't come true...

*** *** ***

Why can't I forget the past,
Start loving someone new,
Instead of having sweet dreams of you?"

Katherine woke from her nap and turned the radio off. Both Williams lay fast asleep on the beach blanket she lay on.

At the outset, this was going to be just like every other day that William took off from work. God only knew how his parents knew in advance when their son was going to play hooky form his doctoral duties; it had to be some sort of mind-meld thing that ran in the family.

Elyse and Pat were sitting nearby on the sand, waiting for their daughter-in-law to wake and serve lunch. "Is something wrong dear?" Elyse asked. "You look a bit annoyed."

"No. Everything's fine," Katherine replied.

She reached over and gently shook Little Will awake. "Come inside with me, Will," she said, and then they both marched onto the house to pack. This time, Katherine wasn't going to leave her son behind.

*** *** ***

THE NINE CIRCLES

EPILOGUE: The Monkey Wrench in the Machine

From *The Nine Circles Encyclopedia*
<u>RULES OF RULES</u>: The final and most important rule to consider is that there are no rules except those that we humans agree upon. Our consciousness imposes order on this and all other universes, but there is nothing but chaos. Anything can happen, and it usually does.

*** *** ***

Katherine sat across from Dr. Langly, who was opening his note pad.

"Well, it's been what, a week since I saw you last? How are you doing?"

"Wonderful," Katherine said, genuinely smiling. "Tomorrow is the six-week anniversary of my divorce. I'm as happy as a clam."

Langly smiled. "Good! Any dissociative episodes?"

"One, but it didn't really bother me. I guess I'm learning how to deal with it."

"Good, good. How about nightmares? Any demons?"

"Not since I got rid of William," Katherine said. "He was the biggest demon of them all."

"And how is Will taking everything?"

"He's doing well. Not having William around doesn't bother him at all. After all, he saw more of the Nintendo than his father. And Will loves day-care."

"Great."

Katherine sat up in her chair, twisting her back to relieve the pain that was knotted in her muscles.

"Are you OK?"

"Just a little sore," she said. "I think I'm coming down with the flu. My stomach has been upset and my period is messed up."

"Maybe you should have it checked out. I can refer you to a good doctor for a physical if you want."

"Sure. But just as long as he doesn't know William."

Dr. Langly laughed. "Of course."

*** *** ***

The apartment was a horrid mess. A veritable mountain of dirty dishes had piled up in the sink over the past few days; all the wastebaskets in the place were overflowing with tissues Katherine had used to cover her mouth with when she stifled dry heaves. If she had some horrible disease, she figured that any exhalations might carry germs that could infect poor Will, and the empty vomiting came from down so deep that it couldn't possibly have a benign source. To top it all off, she had already missed three days of work at the grocery store and the boss was riding her ass to get back on the job.

Katherine rolled over on the couch to see Will glued to the television. God only knew how she managed to wrench the Sony from William's grasp; it was surely a tribute to her lawyer that she came out of the divorce with anything at all.

The phone rang.

"Will, could you get that for me?" Katherine groaned.

"Yes ma'am!" the boy chirped and jumped to his feet. How his behavior had changed for the better once the two them were set free!

"It's some lady, Mommy."

"Not my boss?"

"Nope."

Katherine stifled her nausea and trudged into the kitchen.

"Hello?"

"Ms. Marks?"

"Yes?" Katherine replied, phone trembling in her hands.

"This is Nurse Brimely from the doctor's office."

"Oh God, it isn't some sort of plague, is it?"

Nurse Brimely laughed. "No, no, Ms. Marks. Everything came back negative, but Dr. Brown went with a hunch and had a few more tests run. You're pregnant."

Katherine dropped the phone. Jesus Christ, she was going to have a truck driver's baby! What would her parents think?

THE END

Made in the USA
Columbia, SC
20 July 2023

da22d3e4-93e1-49a2-a7c7-bcd688f0a74cR01